P9-DML-568

"Seamus Quinn is my father," Keely admitted, nestling closer to Rafe.

Rafe froze, afraid Keely might sense his reaction. He tried to keep his voice quiet, indifferent. "So...your name isn't Keely McClain. It's Keely Quinn."

"Umm. Keely Quinn," she murmured drowsily.

Rafe closed his eyes and cursed inwardly. This couldn't be happening to him. He'd been planning his revenge for months and everything had been set in motion just days ago. He couldn't stop now. Seamus Quinn had murdered his father and he'd have to pay!

But Keely was a Quinn. And with the exception of his mother, she was also the first woman he'd ever cared about. Rafe carefully slipped out of bed and walked to the windows. Streetlights still twinkled around Boston Harbor as the deep blue sky gave way to blazing orange and pink. He pressed his palms against the cold glass as he tried to bring order to the chaos raging in his head.

Rafe turned and looked back at Keely, curled up in his bed, the sheets twisted around her slender body. She looked so naive, so beguiling, her hand splayed over his pillow—such a stark contrast to the woman who'd driven him mad with lust the night before. He'd come to crave that contrast, the sexy siren trapped inside the innocent's body.

But how much longer would she want him? And how much time did he have to make her want him more than she wanted her family?

Dear Reader,

Over the past few months I've been overwhelmed by the amount of wonderful e-mails and letters I've received regarding my MIGHTY QUINNS series, published by Harlequin Temptation in September, October and November 2001. Many of you have already fallen in love with Conor, Dylan and Brendan, and are anxiously waiting to get your hands on the stories of the youngest three Quinn brothers. But for my first single-title release, I wanted to do something a little different. So I'm thrilled to introduce you to another member of this irresistible Irish family—Keely Quinn, a woman who finds not only her family, but a man she can't live without. And through it all, she finds herself.

It felt a little odd to leave the Quinn brothers behind and focus on figuring out what a female Quinn would be like. But as I wrote about Keely, I found she wasn't much different from her brothers—stubborn, impetuous, passionate. And in order to balance the scales, I had to give Keely a great hero. I think I found him in Rafe Kendrick—a guy who can stand up to any one of the Quinn brothers, and actually does just that to claim the woman he loves.

For those of you waiting to see the rest of this family happily married, I'm in the process of writing Sean's, Brian's and Liam's stories now. Look to see the last of these irresistible Irish heartbreakers take the plunge in the summer of 2003. In the meantime, be sure to check out my Web site, www.katehoffmann.com, for updates.

Enjoy,

Kate Hoffmann

KATE HOFFMANN

REUNITED

HARLEQUIN®

TORONTO • NEW YORK • LONDON
AMSTERDAM • PARIS • SYDNEY • HAMBURG
STOCKHOLM • ATHENS • TOKYO • MILAN • MADRID
PRAGUE • WARSAW • BUDAPEST • AUCKLAND

For my siblings,
Eileen, Lisa and Brad

ISBN 0-373-83515-9

REUNITED

Visit us at www.eHarlequin.com

Printed in U.S.A.

PROLOGUE

A COLD WIND RATTLED the windows of the tiny apartment above the brick storefront. Keely McClain pushed aside the lace curtains and stared out at the dark street in her quiet Brooklyn neighborhood. Snow gathered on the ground and she said a quick prayer that the storm would worsen and school tomorrow would be canceled. She had a math test and had frittered away her study time today at school passing notes to her friends and drawing cartoon pictures of the nuns.

"Please snow, please snow," she murmured. She pressed her palms together and said a quick prayer, then crossed herself.

Keely turned from the window and then hopped up on her bed, standing on the mattress só she could see herself in her dresser mirror. Carefully, she rolled up the waistband of her plaid skirt until the hem rose to midthigh, just to see what it looked like. Three rolls and a tug and the hem was perfectly even, as if her mother had made it that short. The nuns at Saint Alphonse required that school uniforms reach the floor when kneeling, a notion that every other girl in the all-girl school found positively prehistoric, especially in 1988.

"Have you finished your homework?"

Her mother's voice echoed through the tiny apartment. For as long as Keely could remember, it had been just them. She'd never known her father. He'd died when she was just a baby. But Keely carried a picture of him in her mind, an image of a strong, handsome man with a charming smile and a tender heart. His name was Seamus and he'd come to the United States from Ireland with her mother, Fiona. He'd worked on a fishing boat and that's how he'd died, in a terrible storm at sea.

Keely sighed. Maybe if she'd had a father around, she and her mother might have gotten along a little better. Fiona McClain had strong ideas about how her daughter should be raised and first and foremost was that Keely McClain would grow up a good Catholic girl. To Keely that meant no makeup, no parties, no boys—no fun. Instead of meeting her friends on Saturday morning to hang out at the mall, she was forced to help her mother at Anya's Cakes and Pastries, the shop right below their apartment.

When she was younger, she'd loved watching Anya and her mother decorate the many-tiered wedding cakes. Sitting on a high stool in the bakery's kitchen had been one of her first memories. And when she'd finally been given the responsibility of a real job, Keely had been too excited to speak. Every Wednesday afternoon, she'd dust the glass shelves that held the cake toppers and wedding favors and crystal goblets. She had passed the time by making up romantic stories about each of the little ceramic couples on the cake toppers, giving the grooms dashing names like Lance and Trevor and the brides pretty names like Amelia and Louisa.

She'd been just a kid then and her idea of true love had been more of a fairy tale than anything else. It wasn't the clean-cut, heroic guys that caught her attention now. Instead, Keely had found herself interested in the kinds of boys that her mother would call "bowsies" and "dossers." Boys who smoked cigarettes and boys who cursed. Boys who were bold enough to walk right up to a Catholic schoolgirl and start a conversation. Boys who made her heart beat a little bit faster just to look at them, and boys who weren't afraid to steal a kiss now and then.

Keely took one last look at her skirt, then jumped down from the bed. She grabbed her schoolbag. She'd always worked so hard to please her mother, but slowly she'd come to realize that she was not the kind of daughter her mother really wanted. She couldn't remain a little girl forever. She was twelve years old, nearly a teenager!

And she couldn't always be the dutiful daughter, couldn't always remember her manners and the proper way to sit in a skirt or eat soup with a spoon. There were times when she didn't care to think everything through and make the right decision. She reached into her schoolbag and pulled out a lipstick tube. A wave of nausea washed over her, and for a moment she was certain she'd throw up, just as she had after she'd walked out of the drugstore.

Her mother had always told her that her nervous

stomach was a sign from God. He was trying to drive the impurities out of her. Keely figured it was just punishment for allowing her impulses to control her behavior. But she had to admit that this time she'd probably gone too far.

It had been a dare and Keely had been too proud and stubborn not to accept it. Her friend, Tanya Rostkowski, had challenged her to walk into Eiler's Drugstore and steal a lipstick or else be banished from the cool girls' group. Keely had known it was a sin, but she never backed down from a dare, not even one that involved breaking the law. Besides, she wanted lipstick, and if she'd bought one with the money she made at Anya's, Mrs. Eiler would certainly have ratted on her to her mother.

"Keely Katherine McClain, I asked you a question! Have you finished your homework?"

"Yeah, Ma," Keely shouted. Yet another lie she'd have to confess to, though it paled in comparison to the lipstick.

"Then get ready for bed and don't forget to brush your teeth."

Keely groaned. "Bloody hell," she muttered, instantly regretting the curse the moment it left her lips. She already had enough on her curse list for Friday night confession. Lying and stealing would probably be worth at least five Our Fathers and ten Hail Marys. And Father Samuel was particularly harsh with foul language, although "bloody" couldn't possibly be a curse word, since her mother said it all the time—at least, when she thought Keely wasn't there to hear it.

"Bloody, bloody, bloody," Keely muttered as she undressed and hung up her school uniform precisely as her mother required. Then she slipped into a flannel nightgown and jumped into bed. When she realized that she hadn't brushed her teeth, she reached into the drawer of her bedside table and pulled out an old tube of toothpaste she'd hidden there. She put a dab on her tongue, then winced at the taste.

The trick always worked—unless her mother checked to see if her toothbrush was wet. It was just a tiny rebellion, but Keely felt that her teeth were her own and if she wanted them to turn black and fall out of her mouth when she was twenty, it was certainly her choice.

She leaned over the edge of the bed and reached beneath her mattress to pull out her journal. Sister Therese, her fifth grade teacher, had urged her students to start keeping a journal, hoping to perfect their penmanship and their grammar skills. And since that very first little clothbound book two years ago, Keely had written in her journal every night.

At first it had been a diary of sorts, but now that Keely had something truly interesting to write, she couldn't possibly write it, for fear that her mother might read it. So instead, she filled the book with drawings and stories, each one another tiny little rebellion. She drew wedding cakes, wild, crazy designs, decorated with colored pencils and markers. And designs for sleek, sexy dresses with high hemlines and daring necklines. And she wrote passionate, romantic stories and poems. And though she gave her heroines a different name, when Keely read them, they became stories of her own future.

And sometimes she wrote stories about her father. Her mother had always been tight-lipped about Seamus McClain, and Keely suspected that his death was still too much for her to bear. So Keely had been left to create a past for them both, a wonderful, romantic past. Fiona McClain became the most tragic of heroines, grieving so deeply that she couldn't keep a photo of Seamus around the apartment.

"Seamus," Keely murmured, scribbling his name on the corner of a page. It was an odd, but exotic name to her ears. In her imagination, he had dark hair, nearly black like her own. And pale eyes that were a mix of green and gold, the same eyes she saw in the mirror every morning. A vision of her father flitted through her mind. He was dressed in a fine uniform with shiny buttons and gold braid on the shoulders. And his fishing boat was really a huge sailing ship that crossed the ocean.

"One night, as Seamus's ship was nearing New York Harbor," Keely murmured as she wrote in a haphazard script, "a terrible storm blew in from the north. Being a fine sea captain, Seamus ordered his men to take down the sails to protect his ship from crashing on the cliffs near the harbor. He stood in the driving rain, his hands fixed to the wheel, his only thoughts of the important passengers sleeping below."

Keely reread what she had written and smiled. "But as lightning flashed, Seamus noticed debris floating around the bow of his ship. Another ship had crashed against the cliffs! Through the dark and rain, he could hear a soft and plaintive cry.'' Keely covered her mouth with her cupped hand to make the cry more realistic. ''Help. Help. Save me.''

Vivid images focused in her mind. ''Seamus turned the wheel over to his first mate and ran to the bow. There, in the water below, was a woman, struggling to hold on to a jagged piece of the broken ship. 'Do not fear,' he called. Seamus tore off his jacket and linen shirt, his broad shoulders and strong arms gleaming in the rain.'' Keely pressed her hand to her chest to feel her heart beating a bit faster. ''And then he dove into the icy water and swam toward the drowning girl.''

This would be the best part, Keely mused, when they spoke for the first time. '''What is your name?' Seamus asked as he brushed her long, flowing hair from her eyes. 'I am Princess Fiona,' the girl said. 'And if you save me, I promise to marry you and love you for—'''

''Are you in bed, Keely McClain?''

Keely jumped, startled from her dreaming. ''Yes, Ma,'' she called, glad that she didn't have to lie officially. That saved her at least one Hail Mary at confession.

''And then Seamus took Fiona's hand and swam for the ship,'' Keely continued in a whisper, scribbling as she went. ''Waves crashed around them, but Seamus would not let Fiona drown. For the moment he looked into her eyes, he knew he loved her. His crew dropped a rope ladder over the side, but the ship pitched and rolled and—''

"Did you brush your teeth, Keely?" her mother called.

Keely sighed dramatically. "Mary, mother of—" She stopped herself. Taking the Lord's name in vain was one of those things that might get her an entire rosary. "I'm going to do that right now," Keely shouted.

She tossed the quilt back, scrambled out of bed and hurried down the hall to the bathroom. She brushed up and down twenty-five times on each side and thirty in the front.

After she'd spit and wiped the paste off her mouth, Keely smiled. "And as Seamus carried his new lady-love up the ladder to the safety of his ship, the rain suddenly stopped and the moon broke through the clouds. And beneath the starry sky, Seamus leaned forward and kissed Fiona, sealing their love forever and forever."

"It's nearly ten and you should be in bed."

Keely looked in the mirror and saw the reflection of her mother standing at the bathroom doorway. She held a dish towel in her hands and slowly wiped her fingers. Even though her hair was pulled back in a tidy bun and she wore a plain housedress, she still looked like the princess in Keely's mind, with her bright green eyes and her mahogany tresses.

"Sorry, Ma."

Fiona McClain sighed, then stepped into the bathroom. She reached out and smoothed Keely's long, dark hair, staring at their reflection in the mirror over Keely's shoulder. "You're getting to be such a grown-up young lady. I almost don't recognize you." She flicked her hands through Keely's bangs. "We need to cut these. They're gettin' in your eyes and I won't have you goin' to school looking like some shaggy mutt."

Fiona's lilting accent was soothing to Keely's ears, like one of those pretty Irish love songs that her mother played over and over on the old stereo in the front room. Keely had tried so many times to imitate her, but her tongue just couldn't get the sound right. "Do I look like my da?" Keely asked. "Do I look like Seamus McClain?"

"What?"

She saw the flash of pain in her mother's eyes. But then it disappeared as quickly as it appeared. Over the past few days, her mother had been in one of her "moods." She'd grown silent and sad, her expression distant. She'd stare out the window for hours, her attention fixed on the front walk of their flat, as if she were watching for that someone, waiting for that person's arrival. And Keely's conversations about her day at school went unheeded and unquestioned. Today was one of those sad days, a day when Keely was certain that Fiona was remembering her long-lost husband.

"Have you said your prayers?" her mother asked.

"Yes," Keely lied. "Three Hail Marys and an Our Father." Forget the lie. She'd do penance later. "Tell me about him, Ma."

Her mother's eyebrow shot up. "Three Hail Marys? Did you do something bad at school today?"

"No. I was just getting a little ahead. In case."

"To bed with you," Fiona ordered, clapping her hands. Keely hurried into her bedroom and pulled the covers over her. Fiona sat down on the edge of the bed and kissed Keely on her forehead. For the first time in almost two whole days, she smiled. "It's time for you to sleep," her mother murmured. "I have an early day tomorrow. We have to make the cake for the Barczak wedding. Three tiers with a fountain in the middle. And if you're very good, you can come with me on Saturday when we deliver the cake."

It had been her favorite thing to do when she was younger. But now it was just a chore, time spent away from her friends and a free Saturday afternoon. But this time Keely didn't complain. Her mother had seemed so sad that she was willing to do anything to keep her mood bright. "Will we get to see the bride?" Keely asked, the same silly question she used to ask.

Fiona laughed softly. "Yes, we'll be stayin'. The bride wants us to cut the cake and help serve." She reached out and drew the covers up to Keely's chin. "Now, lay yourself down and go to sleep. And may you dream of angels."

"But what about my father?" Keely blurted out. "You always said you'd tell me when I was older and now I'm older. I'm almost thirteen and thirteen is a teenager. And a teenager is old enough to know about her father."

Fiona McClain stared down at her hands, twisted around the dish towel in her lap. "I've already told you. Your father died in a terrible accident at sea and he—"

"No," Keely interrupted. "Tell me about him. What was he like? Was he handsome? Or funny?"

"He was very handsome," Fiona said, a reluctant smile touching her lips. "He was the most handsome boy in all of County Cork. All the girls in Ballykirk were taken with him. But he was from a poor family and my family had a bit of money. My da didn't want me to marry him. They called him a 'culchie,' a country boy, although we lived in the country, too. But they thought he was lower class."

"But you married him anyway," Keely said, "because you loved him."

"He didn't have two pennies to rub together, but he had such grand dreams. Finally, I convinced my da that I couldn't live without him and he gave us his blessing."

"What else?" Keely asked.

"What else?"

"What did he like to do? What was he good at?"

"He liked to tell stories," Fiona said. "Your da could tell such stories. He had a silver tongue, he did. That's how he courted me, with his stories."

This was something new! Keely felt an instant connection to the man she'd never seen. *She* loved stories and all her friends told her she was good at telling them. "Do you remember any of the stories? Can you tell me one?"

Fiona shook her head. "Keely, I can't—"

"Yes, you can! You can remember. Tell me."

Her mother shook her head, her eyes filling with tears. "No, I can't. Your da was the one who could tell the stories. I never had the talent. The only talent I had was for believin' them."

Keely sat up and threw her arms around her mother's neck, giving her a fierce hug. "It's all right," she said. "Just knowing he told good stories makes me imagine him better."

Her mother kissed her on the cheek, then reached over and turned off the lamp. In the shadows, Keely saw her brush a tear from her cheek. "Go to sleep now."

She walked to the door and closed it behind her. A pale stream of light from the streetlamp filtered through the lace curtains, creating a pretty pattern on the ceiling. "He told stories," Keely murmured to herself. "My da told really good stories."

And though it was only a little bit of who Seamus McClain must have been, it was enough for now. For it gave her a small insight into the person she was. Maybe she wasn't meant to be the good girl that her mother wanted her to be. Maybe she was really more like her father—bold, adventurous, imaginative and daring.

Keely sighed softly. Still, she knew in her heart that her father, whoever he was, would never approve of her pinching a lipstick from Eiler's Drugstore. She made a silent vow to herself to return the lipstick first thing tomorrow.

CHAPTER ONE

A BRISK WIND buffeted the spot where Keely McClain stood. She turned into the breeze and inhaled the salt-tinged air. Far below her, the sea crashed against jagged rocks at the base of the cliff. Above her, clouds scudded across the sky, casting shadows on the hills around her. A memory from her childhood flashed in her mind as she recalled the fairy tale she once scribbled in her journal, the fanciful story of how her parents had met on a storm-tossed sea.

She tipped her face into the breeze, bathing in the mysterious spell that Ireland had cast. Time and time again, she'd felt this odd sense, a sense of belonging to this place she'd never seen before. This was land that had nurtured her mother and father, green and lush, colored by an unearthly light that made everyday scenery look magical. She could almost believe in leprechauns and gnomes and trolls, and all the other fairy creatures that populated this island.

Keely turned away from the sea and stared at the stone circle she'd come to find. It had been clearly marked on the road map, and though she'd been anxious to arrive in the small town that had once been her mother's home, she had decided to take a short detour.

She'd followed a narrow country lane off the highway, steering the rental car beneath arching fuchsia bushes and between drystone fences. And then, when the sky had reappeared, she found herself in yet another breathtaking spot, a wide field above the sea where cows lazily grazed. Closer to the cliff's edge, a stone circle sat silently in the dappled sunlight, a monument to Ireland's pagan past.

Back home in New York City, she had barely given a second thought to her surroundings, the scraggly trees or patches of trampled grass, the brick buildings that lined her street in the East Village. But here, the world was so incredibly beautiful that it begged to be noticed. She took one last long look, committing the sights and sounds and smells to memory, then hiked back to her car.

She hadn't intended to come to Ireland. She'd been in London, presenting a seminar with a famous French pastry chef and teaching new techniques for marzipan modeling. Since she'd taken over the bakery from Anya and her mother, she'd become known as one of the most talented cake designers on the East Coast, creating bold and original confections for a wide variety of special events.

She'd been so busy with work that she'd never been able to justify a vacation, so she'd decided on a working vacation. Between seminars, she'd seen a few musicals in the West End, searched antique stalls at the Portobello market for the old pastry molds she collected, and visited all the popular tourist sights.

But impulse drew her away from the bustle of the

city, compelled her to hop a train that wound across England and Wales to the Irish Channel and to board a ferry that crossed choppy water to a town with the quaint name of Rosslare. Yesterday, from the deck of the ferry, she'd caught her first glimpse of Ireland and, at that moment, felt something deep inside her soul shift, as if she had suddenly discovered a facet of herself that had been hidden until this moment.

She was no longer just a New Yorker, or an American. This land was in her blood, part of her heritage, and she could feel it with every beat of her heart. Keely smiled to herself as she pulled the car door open. Though she'd been forced to drive in the wrong side of the car and on the wrong side of the road, she was getting better at navigating the country roads and narrow streets of the villages that she passed through. She nearly felt at home here.

A gentle rain began to fall and Keely ran to the car. She carefully turned around and started back down the lane, anxious to arrive in the little village she'd marked on the map. Ballykirk was only a few miles down the road, but as she came closer, her nerves got the better of her. She hadn't told her mother she'd decided to go to Ireland, or come to County Cork. She knew the idea would be strongly discouraged. But her mother had never given her a decent reason for her feelings and this was one impulse that couldn't be ignored. Besides, it had been a long time since she'd done anything to please her mother. She didn't dress properly, she didn't behave properly. And now, she didn't travel properly either.

"The past is in the past and it's best if it stays there," Fiona would have said.

As Keely had grown older, she'd asked more questions about her parents' past. And the more questions she'd asked, the more her mother had refused to speak—about her father, about Ireland, about relatives Keely had never known. "That was another life," she'd say. But Keely had remembered one bit of information: Ballykirk, her mother's birthplace in County Cork. A tiny village on the southwest coast, near Bantry Bay.

"So I'll find out for myself." Keely scanned the roadside for the landmarks on the hand-drawn map. She'd found the name in a phone book at the market in a nearby town. Quinn, her mother's maiden name. Maeve Quinn was the only Quinn in Ballykirk and when she'd asked the elderly clerk whether Maeve Quinn was related to the Fiona Quinn who married Seamus McClain about twenty-five years ago, he gave her a puzzled frown, scratched his head, then shrugged. "Maeve would know," he murmured as he scribbled a map to Maeve's home.

She found the place exactly where the clerk had said it would be. The tiny whitewashed cottage was set close to the road, a rose arbor arched over the front gate serving as a landmark. Keely could tell that the home had stood in the same spot for many years. An overgrown garden, filled with a riotous mix of wildflowers, filled the yard and nearly obscured the cobblestone walk to the front door. Had her mother lived here once, picked flowers in the garden, played hopscotch on the walk? Had she passed her father's home or was it just over the next hill on the road?

Keely sat in the car, her mind forming images of her mother as a child—racing out of the front door to play, weaving a garland of daisies for her head, chasing butterflies down the narrow lane. With a soft sigh, she stepped out of the car, anxious to get a closer look.

As she approached the stone fence that surrounded the cottage, the front door opened. Keely hesitated, then decided to explain herself to Maeve Quinn and hope for news of her family.

The slender elderly woman with hair the color of snow was dressed in a brightly flowered dress. She held her hand out to the rain, then waved. "Come in, come in, dear," she called, motioning to Keely. "Jimmy rang me from the market and told me you were on your way. Don't make me wait a minute longer to meet you."

Keely reached for the latch on the gate, unwilling to refuse such a friendly invitation. "I don't mean to disturb you," she said. "I'm Keely Mc—"

"I know exactly who you are," the woman said, her Irish accent thick in each word. "You are Fiona and Seamus's girl. You're family, that you are, come all the way from across the ocean. And I won't miss a chance to share a cup of tea with a relative." She held out her hand and it trembled slightly. "I'm Maeve Quinn. I suppose I would be your cousin then. At least I'm cousin to your father Seamus. So what would that make us?'' She waved her hand. ''Oh, never mind. It makes no difference at all, does it?''

Keely hesitated. Surely the woman had misspoke. Maeve was a Quinn. She would have been related to Keely's mother, not her father. Maybe she wasn't a relative at all. ''I think you must be mistaken,'' Keely said. ''My mother was Fiona Quinn.''

''Yes, yes,'' Maeve said. ''And she married my cousin, Seamus Quinn. She was a McClain, as I recall. From the McClains that lived down Topsall Road in that big house. Yes, that was it. Topsall Road.'' Maeve smiled, her eyes lighting up. ''She was the prettiest girl in the village and from a fine family. I was there at their wedding. And how is Fiona? Since her parents passed years back, we haven't heard a thing from her, or from Seamus, for that matter. But then you wouldn't have remembered your grandparents. You must have been just a wee child when they died. Donal and Katherine, God rest their souls, treasured each other until the day death separated them. Donal couldn't live without her and he died just a week after she did. Many say from a broken heart.''

''Donal and Katherine?'' Keely slowly sat down on the chair she was offered, trying to digest all the information. Katherine was her middle name! But it had been over twenty-five years since her parents had left. It was no wonder the elderly lady got things mixed up, names and places.

''I'll get tea,'' she said, as she hurried out of the parlor into the rear of the cottage. ''I have the pot on right now.''

Keely glanced around the tidy room, from the handmade lace doilies to the delicate crystal figurines, pretty landscape paintings and embroidered pillows. Tiny reminders of her mother's home were scattered around the room, knickknacks that she'd never known were of Irish origin. She reached out and picked up a delicate Belleek porcelain dish, examining the fine basketweave surface.

"Here we are," Maeve chirped. "Tea and a bit of gur cake." She set the tray down on the table in front of Keely and poured her a cup. "Milk or lemon?" she asked.

"Milk, please," Keely said. She took the cup and saucer from Maeve, along with the thin slice of fruit-cake tucked beside. She hesitated, then set the tea down in front of her. "There's something I have to clear up," she said. "It's about my parents. My mother's name was Fiona Quinn and my father's name was Seamus McClain. Maybe it's just a coincidence but—"

"Oh, no, dear. You must be confused."

Keely sighed in exasperation. "I can't be confused about my parents' names. They're my parents."

Maeve frowned, then quickly stood. "Well, we'll just have to sort this tangle out." She crossed the room, opened a cabinet, and withdrew a leather-bound album. "Here," she said, returning to Keely's side. She sat down next to her and opened the album. "Here they are."

Keely stared down at the picture. Her mother had never kept old photos around the house. She had never considered this odd until she'd grown older and asked about her long-dead father and her grandparents, suddenly anxious for any proof of their existence. There was even a time when she'd wondered if she'd been adopted or kidnapped by pirates or even left in a basket on the church…

Her gaze instantly froze on the pretty young woman standing near the sea. It was her mother, there was no doubt about that. She pointed to the photo. "That's Fiona Quinn," she said.

"Yes," Maeve said. "And there's your father, Seamus Quinn."

"My—father?" Keely asked, her voice dying in her throat. She ran her fingers over the faded edges. "This is my father."

"He was always a handsome devil," the old woman said. "A favorite of all the girls in the village. But he only had eyes for your mother, and though her parents didn't approve of the match, there was nothing that could stop them. I expect he still is quite dashing, though that black hair has surely turned to gray."

Keely's heart lurched and she felt the blood slowly drain from her brain. Her father was dead. Didn't this woman know? He'd been gone for so many years, since just after she was born. Her mother had to have sent the news in a letter or at least made a phone call. Or maybe Maeve had simply forgotten her relatives so far away. Though the woman didn't appear to be feebleminded, Keely decided to forgo the revelation about her father's death. The last thing she wanted was her new cousin to collapse from a heart attack at learning the sad fate of Seamus McClain.

Instead, Keely continued to stare at the only image she'd ever seen of her father. He was handsome, with his dark hair and fine features. Had she passed him on the street in New York she would have turned for a second look. Now she had an image to fix in her mind, a face to put with her father's name. "He *is* handsome," Keely murmured.

"All the Quinn men were," Maeve said. "And I do believe they knew it, too."

"Here's another photo taken that same day. I believe it was the day they left for America. Taken with the boys. I remember trying to get them all to stand still for a photo was nearly impossible."

"The boys?" Keely asked, following Maeve's finger to the next page of the album.

"And here they are again," Maeve said, pointing to another photo.

Keely glanced down at the picture, the color images washed out by time. This time Fiona and Seamus were surrounded by five young boys of various ages and sizes. "Are these your children?" Keely asked.

Maeve laughed as she pulled the photo from the album. "Then you don't recognize them? Why, these would be your brothers. Let me see if I remember correctly. The eldest was Conor. And then there was Brendan and Dylan, though I can't remember which of those two comes first. I suppose they're all grown and married now, with families of their own. And the twins. Now what were their names?" She turned the photo over. "I do believe your mother was pregnant." She pointed to the swell beneath Fiona's wind-blown dress. "That was probably you."

Keely quickly pushed to her feet. This couldn't be right. This wasn't her family. This wasn't her story. She didn't have brothers. She was an only child! "I really should go," she murmured. "I've already taken too much of your time."

"But you haven't touched your tea. Please stay and visit with me."

"Perhaps I'll come again tomorrow," Keely said, desperate to find a moment to herself, a moment to think about what Maeve had told her.

"Well, here, then. Take this with you." She handed Keely the photo, who reluctantly took it and tucked it in her purse before she hurried to the door.

"Tomorrow," she said as she stepped outside into the soft rain that had begun to fall.

By the time she reached the car, her mind was spinning with confusion. She wanted to believe Maeve Quinn was a crazy old lady who couldn't keep her facts straight. But every instinct told her that Maeve was in full possession of her faculties and *she* was the one who didn't have the story right.

Keely numbly started the car and steered it down the road. But her head pounded and her stomach roiled. A wave of nausea overtook her and she slammed on the brakes and stumbled out of the car. Bracing her hands on the front bumper, she retched, her emotions overtaking her body. When her stomach finally settled, she took a ragged breath and pressed her palm to her forehead.

Damn it, why did this always happen to her! This was what she got for acting so impulsively. Yet she couldn't be sorry she'd come. Ireland had revealed a past she'd never known, a past her mother had hidden from her for years. And if this wasn't the truth, then she'd be damn sure she'd get the truth, either here or back in the States. On wobbly legs, she slipped back into the car.

Keely withdrew the photo from the pocket of her purse and stared down at it. The faces of the five boys were undeniably familiar. If they weren't her brothers, then they were most certainly related. Minutes passed, but Keely couldn't take her eyes off the photo. A knock on the car window startled her out of her thoughts and she turned to find a grizzled old man staring at her with a toothless smile. A tiny scream burst from her lips.

"Are ye lost?" he asked.

Keely rolled the window down a few inches. "What?"

"Are ye lost?" he repeated.

"No," Keely said.

"Ye looked lost," he said. He rubbed his chest then hitched his thumbs in the straps of his tattered overalls and glanced up at the sky. "It's a soft auld day, that it is. You sure you're not lost?"

"I'm not," she snapped.

The old man shrugged and started down the road. But before he got more than a few yards from the car,

Keely jumped out and ran after him. "Wait!" she called.

He turned and waited for Keely, his hands now shoved in the pockets of his overalls.

"Have you lived in this village for a long time?" Keely asked.

"All me life," the old man replied. "Not long. But long enough."

"If I wanted to find out about a family that used to live here, who would I ask?"

"Well, Maeve Quinn would be the one. She's lived here for—"

"Besides her," Keely said.

The old man scratched his grizzled beard, then moved on to the top of his balding head. "Ye can try the church," he suggested. "Father Mike has tended this flock for near forty years. He's married sweethearts and buried old folk and christened every child in the village."

"Thank you," Keely said. "I'll talk to him." She turned and started back toward the car, but once she got back inside, she was hesitant to put the car back into gear.

Did she really want to know the truth? Or would it be better to just believe that Maeve Quinn was some crazy old lady? But if Maeve did have her facts straight, it would explain a few things. How many times had she walked in on her mother, only to find her lost in her thoughts, a quiet pain suffusing her expression? And why was Fiona so reluctant to speak of the past, unless that past was one big lie? Did

Keely really have five brothers? And if she had, what possible reason could there be for Fiona walking away from five fatherless boys?

Keely's heart froze. Could her father still be alive? Was the story about his accident at sea just part of one big deception? Another surge of nausea made her dizzy. So many questions and no answers.

There was only one thing to do. First, she'd have to prove that Maeve Quinn had spoken the truth. And if she had, then Keely would catch the next flight home. She had a few questions that needed answering. And only Fiona McClain—or was it Fiona Quinn?—could answer them.

SMOKE HUNG THICK in the air at Quinn's Pub, adding to the disreputable atmosphere already cultivated by spilt beer, loud music and raucous arguments. Rafe Kendrick sat at the end of the bar, a warm Guinness in front of him. The spot gave Rafe enough privacy for his own thoughts, yet also offered him a decent view of the patrons—and the men behind the bar.

That's why he'd come here to South Boston, to get a good look at the Quinns. By his count, there were seven of them, six sons and the old man, Seamus Quinn. Rafe had entire dossiers on each one of them, every detail of their lives outlined by his head of security at Kencor. But Rafe Kendrick always believed that it was better to study the enemy close up, to learn their faults and their weaknesses firsthand. All the better to exploit those weaknesses later.

Fortunately, all the Quinns spent plenty of time at

the pub. Over the past few months and three visits to the bar, he'd had plenty of time to observe each of them. There was Conor, the vice cop, quiet and serious, a man who took his responsibilities seriously, yet didn't always abide by the rules. Dylan, the fireman, was easygoing and gregarious, the kind of guy who laughed at danger and everything else in life. The third brother, Brendan Quinn, made his living as an adventure writer and seemed to be the most introspective of the trio. Rafe had read two of his books and found them quite riveting. He'd been surprised at the guy's talents.

Their professional talents were nothing compared to their talents with the ladies. An unending parade of women strolled through the front door of the pub, their sights set on attracting the attention of one of the bachelor Quinn brothers. If one of the older boys wasn't interested, they were left with three other eligible candidates—Sean, Brian and Liam Quinn.

Like their older brothers, they were awash in feminine attention, holding court with any number of beautiful females. Rafe had found the whole thing amusing to watch, the casual flirtation, the circling and advancing, and then the final denouement when one of the brothers would walk out the door of the bar with a woman at his side. And none of the brothers were seen with the same woman two nights in a row.

But then Rafe had never considered that particular trait a weakness, since he possessed the same. Rafe had been with his share of women in his life, though they came from a world very different from Quinn's Pub. They were cool and sophisticated, not nearly so obvious with their desires and their physical attributes. They were women who enjoyed the company of wealthy men, appreciating what money could provide, knowing how to play the game to their fullest advantage. And when Rafe became too busy or too bored, they'd accept the fact and move on to someone else without a second thought.

Rafe caught himself staring at a woman at the other end of the bar, a woman who had been flirting with Dylan Quinn until Quinn had focused his attention on her companion. Rafe looked away, but not soon enough. A few moments later, the woman slipped onto the stool beside him, tossing her honey-blond hair over her shoulder. She pulled out a cigarette and placed it between her moist lips, then leaned forward, offering a healthy view of her cleavage. Rafe knew what was expected. But he wasn't interested, so he simply slid the book of matches across the bar.

The woman didn't take the hint. She gave him a dazzling smile. "I'm Kara," she murmured. "Would you like to join me for a game of pool?"

Rafe didn't bother returning her smile. "I don't play pool," he said softly.

"Darts?" she said, arching her eyebrow and allowing her hand to brush against his sleeve.

Rafe slowly shook his head, then glanced over his shoulder. "I'm sure there are any number of men in this bar who'd enjoy your company tonight…Kara. I'm just not one of them."

She blinked in surprise, then, with a sniff, slipped off the bar stool and returned to her friends at the other end of the bar.

"Can I get you another Guinness, boyo?"

Rafe glanced up from his warm beer. The patriarch of the Quinn clan stood in front of him, a towel tossed over his shoulder. His thick gray hair dropped in a wave over his forehead and his face was lined from years of harsh sun and sea spray. "Or maybe ye'd like a bite to eat? Kitchen closes in fifteen minutes," Seamus added.

Rafe pushed the warm beer away from him. "Scotch," he said. "Neat."

Seamus nodded then went to fetch the drink. Rafe studied the old man coldly. How many times had he heard the name Seamus Quinn? His mother used to murmur it like a mantra, as if she had to remind herself over and over again that her husband was dead—and that Seamus Quinn was responsible.

Rafe glanced up when the old man returned with his drink. He couldn't ignore the surge of hate that heated his blood, better than any twelve-year-old Scotch could. But he had to push that aside for now, for reckless emotion had no part in his plans for the Quinns. It wouldn't be wise to tip his hand so early.

"You new around here?" Seamus asked, leaning an elbow on the bar.

Rafe took a sip of his Scotch and shook his head. "Not new to Boston," he said. "Lived here for a while."

"I know just about everybody in the neighborhood," Seamus countered, eyeing him suspiciously. "Haven't seen you around."

"I've got…business in the area," Rafe replied.

"Oh, yeah. Doin' what?"

"Tying up loose ends," he said with a shrug. He gulped the last of his Scotch, letting it burn a path down his throat. Then he stood up and pulled his wallet from his jacket pocket. Rafe tossed a twenty on the bar. "Keep the change," he muttered before he turned and headed toward the door.

He shoved the door open and walked out into the September night, the streets illuminated by the feeble light from the streetlamps. Though Quinn's Pub was located in a rough section of town, Rafe felt no qualms about walking the streets. He'd grown up on the streets and had learned to protect himself, first with his fists, then with his wits, and now with his wealth.

As he walked toward his car, he thought about the boy he'd once been, happy and carefree, certain of his parents' love. But that had all changed one fall day, much like this one. Even now, a sick feeling twisted his gut at the memory of his father's friends— the men who had worked the swordfishing boats with Sam Kendrick—walking up the front steps of their tiny house in Gloucester.

They hadn't had to speak. Rafe knew what they'd come for. But still, he listened to the details of how his father had met with an unfortunate accident at sea. His father had been caught in a long line and yanked overboard on the *Mighty Quinn,* Seamus Quinn's

boat. By the time they'd gotten him back on deck, he
was dead. Drowned. Like every fisherman's kid, Rafe
knew the dangers of working the North Atlantic, but
he couldn't believe his father could make such a stupid mistake. Even Rafe knew to be watchful when
they were playing out the line.

That day had marked the end of Rafe's childhood.
Lila Mirando Kendrick, already frail of mind and
health, took the news badly. Though she'd hated her
husband's choice of occupation, she'd loved Sam
Kendrick. It had been an odd match, the rough-and-
tumble Irish American and the delicate Portuguese
beauty. But they had adored each other and the loss
of him was more than she could bear. What emotional
stability she had left was shattered along with the
family's financial stability.

Rafe had immediately gone to work to help sup-
plement the insurance settlement his mother received.
He had worked from the time he was nine years old,
first delivering papers and collecting aluminum cans,
until he could get a real work permit. After that, he
took anything that would pay at least minimum wage.
He worked construction to put himself through col-
lege, then parlayed a small investment in a crumbling
storefront into a fortune in Boston's booming real estate market.

By the age of twenty-five, he'd made his first mil-
lion. And now, at thirty-three, he had more money
than he could ever spend. Enough to make his life
easy. Enough to buy his mother all the help she
needed. And plenty of money to make revenge a sim-

ple matter. After all, that's why he'd come to Quinn's Pub—to avenge his father's death and his mother's grief.

Rafe turned back and looked down the darkened street to the neon lights blinking from the pub windows. He wasn't sure why he had to do this. A shrink might say he had a need for closure, or a desire to work out his childhood rage. But Rafe didn't put much stock in the science of psychiatry, even though he'd spent a fortune supporting the profession on behalf of his mother. His motive was much simpler.

He'd find a way to take something away from Seamus Quinn, the same way Quinn had taken something from him. An eye for an eye, wasn't that how it was supposed to be? Maybe he'd find the means to buy the pub out from under him. Or maybe he'd get to Quinn through his sons. Or maybe he'd finally find the proof he needed to put Quinn in jail for the murder of Sam Kendrick.

Whatever it was, Rafe was determined to make it happen. Once he rid himself of the demons in his past, maybe he could finally get on with his future.

THE LIGHTS OF New York glittered against a carpet of black night. Keely stared out the window of the 747, her cheek pressed against the cool surface. She'd left Ireland five hours ago and somewhere over the Atlantic she'd come to the realization that her life had changed forever.

Her visit to the parish priest had been even more illuminating than her tea with Maeve Quinn. Though he couldn't tell her if her father was still alive, Keely left believing that somewhere in the world, she at least had five brothers, and probably six. The baby that her mother was carrying when she left Ireland was more than a year older than Keely. She didn't want to believe that the baby had been a girl and her mother had kept a sister from her for all these years.

Her thoughts wandered back to all the romantic stories she made up about her parents, their enduring love, his tragic accident, her mother's grief. So what had really happened? If her father was still alive, he would have made some attempt to see her, wouldn't he have?

"So, he's not alive. That part of the story is the truth," she told herself. "He would have made an attempt to see me if he could." Seamus Quinn had died and her mother was left with five, or maybe six children. She couldn't take care of them and she…put them into foster care? That would explain her mother's melancholy moods. But why keep that all from Keely? And why, once she made a decent living at the cake shop, didn't she find her sons?

Keely moaned softly, then rubbed her temples, working at the knots of tension that kept her head in a vice.

"Are you all right?"

She turned and looked at the businessman who sat next to her in first class. She hadn't even noticed him, so preoccupied was she with her thoughts for the past five hours. "No," she murmured.

"Can I get the flight attendant for you?"

"No," Keely said. She forced a smile. "I'll be fine, once we land."

"It'll be good to be home," he said. "I don't know about you, but I hate traveling. Not in the U.S., but this foreign travel is too much. The hotels are too small and the food is the worst. And I have to tell you…"

Keely smiled and nodded as the man prattled on and on, but she wasn't listening to a word he said. She pulled the photo out of her purse and stared down at it. Where were her brothers now? Had they all been split up after her father had died? Did they remember her or had they been too young?

A tiny smile curled the corners of her mouth. They were handsome boys. No doubt they'd be handsome men. "Conor, Dylan, Brendan," she murmured. "Brian and Sean."

"Is that your family?"

Keely dragged her gaze from the photo. "What?"

The businessman pointed to the picture. "Your family?"

"No," Keely said. She swallowed hard then forced a smile. "I mean, yes. This is my family. My brothers. And my parents."

He took the photo from her fingers and she fought the impulse to snatch it back and hide it away where it would be safe. For now, all she had was the photo. But the idea of family—her family—belonged out in the open. She wanted to know these brothers she had lost. She wanted to know what really happened to her father and why she'd been forced to grow up an only child.

A different person would be stepping off the plane in New York. She'd gone to Ireland believing she knew who and what she was. She'd been content with her life. But now she was more than just Keely McClain—she was a sister and an only daughter to a man she didn't know. She was a Quinn.

But she was also less. Everything she'd believed she was had been negated within the span of a few hours. All her memories of her childhood were now tainted with her mother's betrayal. The woman she thought she knew better than anyone in the world had become a complete enigma.

"Ladies and gentlemen, we're cleared for landing at JFK. We'll be on the ground in about fifteen minutes."

The flight attendant leaned over and grabbed the wineglass from Keely's tray table, then asked her to fasten her seat belt. Keely accepted the photo back from the man next to her, feeling her stomach flutter nervously. For a moment she thought she might get sick the way she had that day outside Maeve Quinn's cottage. She grabbed the airsickness bag from the pocket in front of her. But she couldn't face the humiliation of losing her honey-roasted peanuts in front of everyone in first class.

Keely pushed out of the seat and hurried to the bathroom. The flight attendant tried to stop her, but she waved her off and locked herself inside. Leaning over the sink, she drew a deep breath and tried to calm her nerves. This was the second time this had happened! It had been years since her nerves had gotten the best of her. But now panic and nausea seemed to descend on her without warning.

"Calm down," she murmured, staring at her reflection in the mirror. "No matter what the truth is, you'll deal with it."

She splashed some water on her face and ran her fingers though her short dark hair. She hadn't told her mother that she was coming home early. Right now, she could only think a few minutes ahead. Once they landed, she'd decide how to approach Fiona.

A knock sounded on the bathroom door. "Miss? We're on our final approach. You have to take your seat."

Keely closed her eyes and took a deep breath. "I'll be right out." She reached for the latch, then pasted a smile on her face.

She found her seat moments before the plane descended to the runway. The next hour passed in a blur, her mind numb with fatigue and pent-up emotion. Like a robot, she walked through customs and immigration, flipping open her passport only to wonder whether she was reentering the country illegally. After all, her name wasn't really McClain but Quinn. Then she dragged her luggage down the concourse to the taxi stand.

She gave the cabbie her address, then decided at the last minute that going home would be useless. She wouldn't get any sleep until she'd talked to her mother. "No," she said. "Take me to 210 East Bel-

tran in Prospect Heights. There's construction on Atlantic, so take Linden.''

Keely settled back into the seat, knowing that the
ride could be excruciatingly long or mercifully short.
Luckily, it was the latter and the cab pulled up in
front of her mother's place after only a half-hour ride.
The bakery looked quite different from the building
it had been in Keely's childhood. It now had a dis-
tinctly sophisticated look, with a fancy sign hanging
over the door that proclaimed it McClain's—Fine
Cakes and Pastries.

Anya had retired years ago, selling the business to
Fiona. So she and Keely had carried on. After Keely
graduated from high school, she had attended classes
at nearby Pratt Institute, honing her artistic talents in
design and sculpting. And four years ago, she'd taken
over the day-to-day business from her mother. Just
last year, as her popularity as a cake designer boomed,
she had finally moved out, finding a loft with room
enough for a small studio in a trendy location in the
East Village. But the everyday baking and decorating
was still done in Brooklyn.

Fiona worked at the shop every day, discussing
cake designs with nervous brides and picky mothers.
Keely rarely had time to get out of the kitchen, decorating cakes for lavish birthday parties and corporate
receptions, movie premieres and store openings, as
well as high-society weddings. She'd reached a landmark last month, selling a single wedding cake for
the same amount of money that her mother had made
in an entire year working for Anya. It still stunned

her what a little bit of flour, sugar and butter was worth if it looked pretty enough.

Though she'd never intended to follow in her mother's footsteps, she loved her job. She loved the excitement of making a crowning centerpiece for a wedding or birthday party. But all the way back from Ireland, she could barely even think of the work she had waiting for her. How could she possibly spend hour after hour, elbow-deep in buttercream, after what had happened?

The cab pulled up on Beltran and screeched to a halt. Keely paid the cabbie, then grabbed her bags from the trunk and hauled them to the front door of her mother's flat. She fumbled for her key and unlocked the door, then left her things in the tiny foyer.

She slowly climbed the stairs. When she reached the top, Keely knocked softly, then pushed the door open. She found her mother standing near the door, her hand pressed to her chest.

"Keely! Lord, you frightened me! What are you doing here? You weren't due home for another two days."

Her mother's voice sounded strange to her ears. Keely had always thought she had an accent, but compared to Maeve, her mother spoke with barely a hint of Ireland left in her voice. Fiona stepped up and drew her into a warm hug, but Keely stiffened, then pulled back. "I went to Ballykirk," she murmured.

Fiona's breath caught and her gaze met Keely's. "What?"

"You heard me," Keely said. "I visited Ballykirk.

I thought I'd go to learn a little more about my ancestry. I thought it might be interesting. Little did I realize.''

Her mother's face had gone pale and she pressed trembling fingers to her lips. "You know?"

"I want you to tell me," Keely said, her voice filling with anger. "Tell me they all died in a terrible accident and you couldn't bear to talk about it. Tell me they never existed and Maeve Quinn was wrong. Tell me because those are the only two reasons that I can accept for you lying to me all these years."

"I can't tell you that," Fiona said, her eyes downcast. "It would just be another lie."

"And of course lying is a sin, isn't it, Ma? But then maybe that's why you go to confession every week, so you can wipe away a lifetime of sin." Keely drew a ragged breath. "For once, tell me the truth. I need to know who I am."

She flopped down into one of her mother's overstuffed chairs, ready to listen to the real story of her life. And once she had the whole truth, then she'd decide what to do next.

CHAPTER TWO

"WHY CAN'T you understand? All my life, I've believed I was an only child. Do you know how that feels?" Keely snatched up a pastry bag and began to scoop icing into it. "There's no one else in this world that I can call family except you. And what happens when you're gone? Who will I have?"

"A nice thing, that," Fiona murmured, a haughty arch to her brow. "Putting me in my bloody grave so soon, are you?"

Keely sighed, then tossed the spatula back into the bowl and began to pipe the Italian meringue icing over the first layer of the wedding cake. "Why shouldn't I be angry with you? I have a father and six brothers. And you kept me from them."

"How many times have we gone over this? It's been a week since you got back from Ireland. When are you going to forgive me?"

"When you bloody well give me a good reason to," Keely shot back. "I want to know everything. Why you left him, how you could walk away from your children, why you never told me. Until you're honest about everything, then I'm going to keep bringing up the subject."

Fiona sighed softly. "I wanted to keep you from being hurt. There are reasons I left your father. Good reasons."

"I can understand that. Marriage is difficult. But how could you leave your sons? They were your children."

As she had so many times over the past week, Fiona refused to explain further. At first, Keely had been furious with her, lashing back with anger and accusations. Then after a few days, her anger had abated and was replaced by cool intolerance. But now she was frustrated by her mother's silence, curious to know more but stymied at every turn. Keely knew from the look in her mother's eyes that the memories still brought back overwhelming pain. But she didn't care! She picked up the bowl of buttercream and heaved it across the room. It bounced off the wall, then spattered all over the floor.

"Well," her mother muttered, "that's a fine way to behave."

"If you won't talk to me about this, then I have no choice. I'll have to go to Boston and find out for myself."

Her mother drew in a sharp breath. "You'll only get hurt."

"Why?"

"Because," Fiona said.

"That's not a reason!"

"They don't even know you exist."

Her words were barely a whisper, but they were like a dagger to Keely's heart. She blinked as emotion welled up inside of her. "They—they don't know about me?"

"I left Boston right after I learned I was pregnant with you. Your father didn't know. I came here to get away, just for a little while, to decide what I wanted to do with my life. And I just never went back. When I had you, I put my maiden name on your birth certificate and started using that name. Anya was the only person who ever knew the truth. So if you're determined to find them, you have to understand. They won't know you. And they might not believe you."

"I have a right to know them!" Keely cried, brushing a tear of frustration from her cheek.

"And what can I say to stop you?" Fiona asked. "If I tell you everything, you'll still go."

Keely shrugged. "So why not tell me?"

Fiona closed her eyes and tipped her head back. "It was a long, long time ago. Another life."

"And you've made no move to contact them in all these years?"

"I was protecting you," Fiona explained. "I thought my marriage was over. I knew that Seamus would never change. And when I walked out, I never intended to stay away for so long. I decided I'd go back after you were born. But by then, it was even more difficult to leave New York. I had a good job. I'd built a life for us."

"But your sons," Keely said. "How could you—"

Tears flooded Fiona's eyes. "Do you think it was

easy leaving them? I thought it would force Seamus to grow up if he had to be responsible for the boys for a while, if he had to pay the bills and take care of the house. I kept in touch with a neighbor for a time, just to make sure the boys were all right.'' She paused. "I didn't want to leave. But I was trapped. I would have taken them with me, but didn't have a way to provide for the boys, and Seamus did. I'd never worked in my life before I took the job in the bakery.''

"I used to make up all sorts of stories about my father," Keely said. "He was so heroic and brave and he died in a very tragic way. You see, I had to make up stories since you never told me anything.''

"Would you have been happy with the truth? Your father was a dirt-poor Irish fisherman who spent most of his time on a swordfishing boat out in the North Atlantic. When he was home, he was usually drunk. He gambled away most of what he earned. And when he went back out to sea, I was glad for it.''

Keely laughed softly. "And I imagined the reason that you never married again was that you never stopped loving him.''

"I'm a Catholic and divorce wasn't an option.''

Keely gasped. "You're still married?''

"I am," Fiona said. "I'm not sure about your father. He could have another wife. I suppose that would make him a bigamist.''

Keely stared down at the piping on the cake, noticing that her work had become uneven and sloppy. With a soft curse, she picked up her spatula and smoothed the decoration out, preparing to start all over again. "I have to go," she murmured. "I have to know who they are."

"Even if it means you'll get your heart broken? Please, Keely, don't turn this into some romantic fantasy," Fiona warned. "It's more likely to be a disaster."

"And maybe it won't be. Maybe they'll be happy to meet me."

A long silence grew between them. "When will you go?" Fiona finally asked.

"I've asked Janelle and Kim to take care of the jobs for this weekend. You'll have to do the Wilkinson cake and the Marbury cake. They're both decorated with marzipan and I've made all of that ahead of time. You'll just need to frost the tiers and do a little simple piping. I should only be gone about a day or two."

"Then, you'll need this," Fiona said. She reached into her pocket and pulled out a chain with a jewel-encrusted pendant. She held it out to Keely. "Take it," she said.

Keely twisted the chain around her fingers and examined the necklace. "What is this?"

"It was given to me on my wedding day by my mother. It's a McClain family heirloom. A claddagh. The Irish symbol of love. The heart is for fidelity, the hands for friendship and the crown for loyalty. I was saving it to give to you on your wedding day." She paused. "Seamus knows this pendant. If you show it to him, he'll know where it came from." Fiona laughed softly. "In truth, this necklace was the reason I left your father."

"It was?"

Fiona nodded. "He'd just come home after two months away. He was drunk and he'd just gambled away most of his pay down at the pub. He took the necklace to a pawn shop and sold it for gambling money. He said he needed to win back what he'd lost. Before I left Boston, I convinced the pawnbroker to let me buy it back over time. It took me three years." She stared at the pendant, dangling from Keely's fingers. "That's the kind of man your father was...the truth be told."

"Maybe he's changed," Keely said softly. "People can change, you know."

"And maybe he hasn't," Fiona countered.

Keely slipped the necklace into her apron pocket. "I guess I won't know for sure until I meet him myself."

She turned back to her cake and studied it critically. Suddenly she didn't have the patience for piping the delicate basket weave. Now that she'd decided to go to Boston and find her family, she wanted to pack her bags and leave right away. A tiny wave of nausea gave her pause, but she fought it back. She was brave enough to face whatever might happen in Boston.

And once she did, she'd be able to figure out who she really was—a McClain or a Quinn.

A CHILLY WIND stung Keely's face as she walked down the rain-slicked sidewalk, her hands shoved into her jacket pockets, her gaze fixed a few feet ahead of her. She was almost afraid to look up, afraid to face what she had come to see.

The weather was cold for early October and a nasty storm was bearing down on the East Coast, the prospect of rain heavy in the air. But that hadn't stopped her from driving to Boston. Since she'd returned from Ireland just over a week ago, Keely had dreamed about this day, going over it in her head, then with maps spread out on her bed. She had plotted how long it would take to drive from New York to Boston and back again.

She'd wanted to go the day after she'd returned from Ireland, the moment her mother told her that Seamus Quinn was in Boston. She'd found his address on the Internet and was ready to pick up the phone and call him. But she'd stopped herself, unwilling to act impulsively this time. For once in her life, Keely was determined to think before she acted and not rush headlong into something she knew might be dangerous.

Up until this moment, that had been the story of her life—impetuous decisions, impulsive actions, always leading to a severe reckoning. Like the time a friend had dared her to steal money from the offering basket at church. She'd tossed in a quarter and palmed a five-dollar bill, only to be caught by the old lady sitting next to her. Keely had been forced to clean the church bathrooms for six months to pay for that little lapse.

Then there was the time she'd run away with the

drummer from a sleazy garage band. She'd been six-
teen and had made it as far as New Jersey before the
guy dumped her. Fiona hadn't let her out of the house
for almost six months for that unwholesome adventure. And just last year, she'd been hauled into jail
for punching a policeman who'd been trying to roust
a homeless man who lived in the alley behind her
apartment. That had gotten her a substantial fine and
a genuine police record.

But her trip to Boston, though risky, wasn't really
reckless. She had no other choice but to come. Only
now that she was here, her only thought was how easy
it would be to turn around and go home, to take the
safe way out and resume her old life. But curiosity
drove her forward, in spite of her pounding heart and
her quickened breathing. Maybe her mother had been
right. *The past was the past,* Fiona had said. *Leave it
alone.*

The past that Keely had believed was *her* past had
been nothing but a lie, a fabrication devised to quell
a curious child's questions. The father she thought
had died in a commercial fishing accident was really
alive. And the siblings she'd always longed for were
living in a city just a few hundred miles from her
home in New York, living lives that she could only
imagine. Keely drew a shaky breath, then turned and
looked across the street.

It was there, right where it was supposed to be,
neon beer signs blazing in the plate-glass windows.
Quinn's Pub. She'd gone to her father's house,
screwed up her courage and knocked on the front

door, only to have a neighbor tell her that Seamus Quinn was at the pub he owned, just a few blocks away.

"Seamus," she murmured as she stared at the pub. "Seamus, Conor, Dylan, Brendan, Brian, Sean, Liam."

Until a month ago, the names were those of strangers. But in just a few moments of shocking revelation in Maeve's cottage in Ireland, they'd become her family. Now, she repeated the names over and over again, hoping the mere sound of the syllables would conjure up images of the men who belonged to them.

"All right," she murmured. "What's the plan?"

Maybe it would be best just to get a feel for the situation first. She'd go inside and order a beer, maybe get a look at her father. She crossed the street, but as she approached the bar, a man pushed open the front door and stepped outside, then another right behind him. An Irish tune drifted into the night from the interior of the pub, then disappeared on the wind. The lights flooding the front facade provided enough illumination for Keely to see both men, but her gaze was caught by the taller of the two.

It had to be him, though she wasn't sure which him it was. His features were so unique, the dark hair, the strong jaw and the wide mouth, the very same features she looked at in the mirror every morning—only hers were softened to a feminine form—the same features she'd seen in the old photograph, now altered by age.

Keely had no choice but to continue walking. To

turn and run would only draw attention to herself. As she passed the pair, she glanced up and her gaze locked with his. The recognition she felt was reflected in his own expression and, for a moment, Keely was sure he was going to stop and speak to her. A jolt of panic raced through her and she opened her mouth. But a casual greeting was too much. Instead, she just kept walking...walking until she felt a pang of regret at the missed opportunity.

"Keep walking," Keely murmured to herself. "Don't look back."

When she reached the front door of the pub, she started up the steps, but her courage had already been severely shaken. If this was how she reacted to a stranger on the street—a stranger who might not even be one of her brothers—then how would she react when she spoke to her father for the first time in her life?

Another wave of panic overwhelmed and she spun on her heel and hurried back down the steps. She kept going until she reached the shadow of a panel truck parked along the curb. Then Keely turned and watched the two men as they got into an old car parked halfway down the block. Had he recognized her the same way she'd recognized him? Had he seen the same family resemblance that she'd noticed?

The car pulled away from the curb and the two men drove past her. At the last second she stepped into the light. "Wait!" Keely called, raising her hand to wave at them.

But her voice caught in her throat and the words

were barely more than a sigh. "Wait," she murmured as the taillights of the car disappeared into the rain and darkness. Keely stood on the sidewalk for a long time, letting the raindrops spatter on her face and the cold seep through her jacket.

A shiver skittered down her spine and Keely blinked, forced to admit that she had failed. With a softly muttered curse, she started back in the direction from which she had come. When she reached the safety of her car, Keely closed her eyes and tipped her head back, trying to ignore her disappointment.

"It was just a first step," she murmured as her heart began to slow to its normal rhythm. "The second step will be much easier."

She flipped on the overhead light and grabbed her purse from the floor, then pulled out the precious photograph. An Irish family—her family—standing on a rocky cliff overlooking the Atlantic. The five boys were so young. Conor, the oldest, was just seven or eight. Liam hadn't even been born yet. They all looked so happy, so hopeful, ready to set out on the their grand adventure to America. Life was supposed to hold such promise, yet it had all gone so horribly bad.

As Keely rubbed her thumb over the photo, she tried to imagine her mother in those days before she walked away from her family. The notion of leaving her sons behind was impossible to imagine. And even worse was the realization that Keely had been to blame. That perhaps if her mother hadn't been pregnant again, she might have stayed and tried to work things out.

Slouching down in her seat, Keely turned her gaze toward the door of the pub, watching as patrons walked in and out, hoping that she'd see another man who resembled a boy in the picture. "Conor, Dylan, Brendan," she murmured. "Brian, Sean, Liam."

Who were they? What kind of men had they grown up to be? Were they kind and understanding, compassionate and open-minded? How would they react to her sudden appearance in their life? She had grown up not knowing they existed. Would they accept her into the family or would they turn her away?

"Conor, Dylan, Brendan. Sean, Brian, Liam." She paused. "And Keely."

A tiny smiled curled the corners of her mouth. "Keely Quinn," she said. It sounded right. Though she'd spent her life calling herself Keely McClain, Keely Quinn was her real name and it was time to start thinking of herself as someone with a real family—a father, a mother and six brothers.

She quickly formulated a timetable for herself, a habit that was a necessity in her career and now came in handy in her personal life. In a few weeks, she'd come back to Quinn's Pub, walk inside and buy a drink. And a few weeks after that, maybe she'd speak to her father or one of her brothers. Now was the time for restraint, not recklessnesss.

By Christmas, Keely was determined that her family would know she existed. They didn't have to accept her at first. In truth, she didn't expect a tearful reunion and declarations of love. She expected shock and confusion and maybe a bit of resentment. But sooner or later, she would have the family that she always wanted.

With a soft sigh, Keely took a final look at the front door of Quinn's Pub. This had been enough for one day. She'd found her father's pub and maybe even seen one of her brothers. She'd go back to her hotel and get a good night's sleep and come back to Boston another time. But the excitement of her discovery was too much to keep to herself. She'd made a promise to her mother to call as soon as she found her father and brothers. Keely reached into her purse and grabbed her cell phone, then punched in the phone number of her mother's apartment.

Fiona would have left the shop around six. By seven, she was usually preparing her dinner and, by eight, she had settled comfortably in her favorite chair with an Agatha Christie mystery. Keely's mind raced as she tried to decide what she'd say. Should she sound excited or should she keep her tone indifferent? Her mother picked up the phone on the other end.

"Mama?" Keely said, her voice trembling. "Mama, I found them."

There was a long pause on the other end of the line. "Then you talked to Seamus?" Fiona asked.

"No, not yet. But I will. Soon."

"Come home, Keely."

"You know I can't. I have to go now, Ma. I'll call you tomorrow."

She snapped her phone closed and tossed it on the

seat beside her. Then Keely reached for the ignition. But at the last minute, she changed her mind. She'd come all this way. Why not go inside now? She could walk through the door and ask to use the ladies' room. Or maybe pretend to make a phone call. What did she have to lose? And if everything went all right, she'd just introduce herself.

The impulse was too strong to resist. "I can do this," she said as she grabbed the keys and stepped out of the car. "I've come this far."

She hurried back across the street, then smoothed her hair before starting up the front steps. But, suddenly, her doubts got the better of her. The second step was almost painful. When she reached the third step, she could see through the wide plate-glass window into the interior of the bar. Her gaze scanned the crowd and then came to rest on a white-haired man behind the bar.

The door opened and a couple stumbled outside, allowing voices to drift out into the night. She stepped aside, her gaze still fixed on the older man. Then Keely heard a patron shout the name of Seamus and the white-haired man raised his hand and waved to an unseen patron on the other side of the bar.

The reality of the situation hit her. Seamus was a flesh-and-blood man, not just a fantasy. Her stomach lurched and she grabbed the railing and hurried back down the steps. She only made it halfway down the block before her nausea overwhelmed her. "Oh, bloody hell," she murmured as she bent over against a nearby car and tried to breath deeply.

If she ever expected to meet her father and brothers, she'd have to get control of her nerves! She wasn't a child anymore, plagued with doubts and confusion. And she wasn't a teeanager, riddled with guilt. This wasn't like letting the air out of Father Julian's bicycle tires or dropping a rotten tomato off the roof of the school at Sister Bertina or smoking cigarettes in the janitor's closet. She deserved to be able to meet her family and know them without all this upset.

Keely turned away from the car, but her head began to swim. She closed her eyes. "Breathe," she murmured to herself. "Breathe."

RAFE SAW HER as he walked down the street toward his car. He stopped and glanced back over his shoulder, then slowly looked around. There was no one else on the street. Though he didn't think twice about his own safety in Southie, a single woman on a dark street was a much more vulnerable target.

She was bent over, leaning back against the side of a car, her hands braced on her knees. He slowly approached and stood in front of her. "Are you all right?"

She glanced up at him, her wide gaze meeting his. For an instant, his breath caught in his throat. He'd expected one of the women who'd been hanging out at the bar. But this woman—or maybe "girl" was a more appropriate description—wasn't exactly the type who hung out at Quinn's. She wasn't dressed in skintight jeans. She wore a black leather jacket, a tapered black skirt that showed off a fair amount of leg, and a T-shirt that clung to her curves.

The harsh light from the streetlamps revealed a flawless complexion, untainted by heavy makeup and bright lipstick. And her hair, damp from the rain, was actually a color that appeared to be quite natural. "Is there anything I can do for you?"

She held out her hand and opened her mouth as if to speak. But then she moaned softly, bent over, and immediately threw up on his Italian loafers. "Oh, hell," she murmured. "Oh, bloody, bloody hell. I'm so sorry I—I didn't mean to do that."

Startled by her response, Rafe had no choice but to reach into his pocket and pull out a handkerchief. His mother had taught him from a young age that a gentleman always carried a handkerchief and it had been advice he'd never truly understood—until now. A guy never knew when a beautiful woman might throw up on his shoes.

She slowly straightened, then took the handkerchief from his fingers. She pressed it to her lips. "I don't know what's wrong with me," she murmured.

"Maybe you've had a little too much to drink?" Rafe suggested.

She shook her head. "No. It's just…nerves."

He nodded. "Right."

"No, really," she insisted. "I've just been a little upset lately. And I haven't been eating well, or sleeping at all. And between all the antacids and the coffee, I just…all my stress seems to end up in my stomach."

She paused. "But then you're really not interested in that, are you."

"Can I call you a cab?" Rafe asked.

She shook her head. "No. I'll be all right. My car is just down the street."

"I'm afraid I can't let you do that," Rafe said.

"Do what?"

"Drive," he said. "Either you allow me to call you a cab or you allow me to drive you wherever you're going."

"I'm perfectly able to—"

Rafe held out his hand to silence her. "Come on. It's cold out here. We can wait in my car for the cab." He reached down, grabbed her hand, and tucked it in the crook of his arm. Then he slowly walked with her down the block. When they reached his Mercedes sedan, he turned off the alarm and opened the passenger side door. She hesitated for a moment.

"I'm not going to hurt you," he said. "If you want to, we can stand out here. Or we can go back inside the bar."

"No!" she said. "No, I don't want to go back to the bar." She shivered, then rubbed her arms. Suddenly, she looked like she was going to throw up again. "Put your head down," he suggested. He gently pressed his hand against her back until she bent over at the waist. Then he took his cell phone out of his pocket and dialed the number for his security office at Kencor.

"This is Rafe. I want you to send a car around to Quinn's Pub in Southie. Have the driver look for my

Mercedes. I'm parked about a block away." Rafe
flipped the phone off, then slipped it back into his
pocket. "It'll just be a few minutes." He leaned into
the car and grabbed a bottle of water, then handed it
to the woman. "Here," he said. "To settle your
stomach."

"Thanks," she said, still bent over.

"What's your name?"

She straightened and took a tiny sip of the water.
"Keely. McClain." She swallowed hard. "Keely
McClain. What's yours?"

"Raphael Kendrick," he replied. "Rafe."

"Raphael. Like the artist." She took another sip,
then drew a deep breath. "Well, thank you, Raphael.
But I feel much better now. I think I can drive back
to my hotel on my own."

"I've sent for a car."

"But how will I get my car back?" Keely asked.

"I'll take care of that. Where are you staying?"

"Downtown. At the Copley Plaza."

"And what were you doing in this part of town?
Southie is a long way from the Copley Plaza."

She looked away, staring off down the street. "I
was here to meet someone." She glanced back at him.
"How about you?"

"I was just having a drink at Quinn's Pub."

"Really? Do you drink there often?"

Rafe chuckled and shook his head. "No, not often." He stared down at her for a long moment.
Christ, she was beautiful. The more he looked at her,
the more he was struck by that fact. He usually wasn't

attracted to her type, a quirky bohemian. But for some reason, he found himself fascinated by the color of her eyes, her upturned nose and her Cupid's bow mouth, the way her short-cropped hair curled against her face.

She was small, no taller than five-five, and he was certain he could have spanned her waist with his hands. Her hair was tousled by the wind and damp, making it appear as if she'd just stepped out of the shower and arranged it with her fingers. And her features were nearly perfect, delicate and refined, from the tip of her nose to her impish smile. Though she looked young, he guessed she was about twenty-three or twenty-four, tops.

"So, why don't you tell me what you're doing here in Boston, Keely McClain?"

"I'm here on personal business," she said. "Family business."

"That sounds a bit mysterious."

"It really isn't," she replied. She held out the handkerchief. "I can get back on my own. Really, I'm not drunk and I'm feeling much better now."

Rafe was loath to let her go. But he had to admit that she didn't appear to be drunk at all, just a little bit queasy. His mind scrambled for a logical reason to make her stay, but at some point in the last few minutes, he'd lost his ability to think clearly. "All right," he said. "But you have to promise that if you start to feel sick again, you'll pull over."

"I don't think I'll have much choice on that," Keely said.

Rafe took her hand. "Where's your car? I'll walk you there."

Keely pointed down the block. They walked slowly and when he sent her a sideways glance, he caught her looking up at him.

"What is it?" Rafe asked.

"I don't know. It's just that you're…nice. I didn't think there were men like you left in the world. You know, chivalrous?"

"You puked on my shoes," Rafe said. "What was I supposed to do? Keep walking?"

Keely winced, and in the meager light he saw a slight blush color her already rosy cheeks. "Your shoes. Oh, I'm sorry. I'll buy you a new pair. Tell me, how much did they cost and where did you get them?"

Rafe shook his head. "That's not necessary."

"But it is," Keely insisted. "You can't wear them after I threw up on them."

"I have plenty of other shoes at home that I can wear," Rafe countered.

"But I insist," Keely said.

God, she could be exasperating! But she was so damn beautiful when she was, her eyes bright, her color high. He was almost tempted to yank her into his arms and kiss her just to get her to shut up and accept his refusal. "All right," Rafe said. "They're handmade Italian. I think I paid a couple of thousand for them in Milan."

Keely stopped short and her jaw dropped. "What? I threw up on two-thousand-dollar shoes? Oh, shit."

She clutched her stomach and bent over. "Two thousand dollars? I'm going to be sick again." While she was bent over, she tried to wipe at the shoes with his handkerchief.

Rafe pulled her upright. "I was teasing," he lied. "I think I got them downtown. And I never pay more than a couple of hundred for shoes."

"And handkerchiefs?" she asked.

"I'll toss that one in for free."

They reached her car much sooner than he wanted to. He took the keys from her fingers, unlocked the driver's side door, and pulled it open. She stepped around the door, then turned to him, her fingers clutching the top. "So, where should I send the money for the shoes?" she asked.

Rafe reached in his pocket for his wallet and withdrew one of his business cards. She stared at it for a long moment then smiled. "All right then, Rafe Kendrick. I guess I should thank you for your kindness."

"No problem," Rafe said.

"Good. Well…goodbye." She quickly slipped into the car before he had a chance to consider kissing her. Reluctantly, he closed the driver's side door and stepped away from the car. She started the Toyota, gave him a little wave, then pulled away from the curve.

Rafe stood in the street and watched as the taillights of her car disappeared down the street. He'd met a lot of women in his life in a lot of different places, but he'd never met a woman quite like Keely McClain. There had been no seductive flirtation, no coy glances and come-hither stares. She'd humiliated herself in front of him, yet he somehow found it charming. With her defenses down, he'd dropped his own. He'd been completely at ease with Keely McClain and he'd never really felt that way with a woman in his life.

"Then why the hell did you let her go?" Rafe asked himself. He started toward his car, and by the time he reached the Mercedes, he'd already decided. He wasn't going to let her go. Nor was he going to trust her to contact him again. He wouldn't be satisfied until he was certain that he'd see her again.

He pulled a U-turn in front of Quinn's, then floored the accelerator, racing down the street after her. He'd just make sure she got back to her hotel safely and wish her good-night. And then, he'd casually ask her out to dinner. He'd never worried much about a woman accepting a date with him. If they did, he was usually pleased, and if they didn't, he moved on to someone else.

But as Rafe drove toward the lights of downtown Boston, his thoughts weren't on the Quinns or his need for revenge. Instead, he went over in his mind how best to ask Keely McClain out, the exact words he'd use to get her to say yes. Because, for the first time in his life, the answer would matter.

CHAPTER THREE

"YOU ARE SUCH a nitwit. A gorgeous hunk of man walks into your life and you just drive away. Have you forgotten that you haven't had sex in nearly a year? That you've been reduced to watching music videos and wondering which of five guys in some boy band would be the best in bed? If you don't take advantage of moments like those you're going to end up lonely and completely celibate and turning to your seventeen cats for companionship. Come on, Keely, get a grip!"

She stared out the windshield of her car, waiting for the light to change, tapping her fingers impatiently on the steering wheel. His card was in her jacket pocket. At least she had his name and number. If, after the excitement of the evening had worn off, she decided she wanted to see him again, she'd just call. Or maybe she'd personally deliver a new pair of shoes to his office.

"That won't work," she murmured. "I don't know his size."

One thing she did know was that Rafe Kendrick had nice taste in shoes. In truth, everything about Rafe was pretty nice, from his dark, smoldering eyes to his nearly black hair to his devastating smile. But it wasn't just the way he looked. Rafe Kendrick was a true gentleman. After all, how many men would have been so kind and understanding?

She'd ruined a perfectly good pair of his shoes. And she knew they weren't department store knock-offs. Rafe Kendrick dressed like a man who didn't have to worry about maxing out his credit card on fine Italian footwear. From his leather jacket to his body-skimming sweater to his shoes, his appearance shouted sophistication and wealth.

She'd passed men like him every day on the streets of Manhattan, but she'd never considered those men her type. They were too handsome, too confident, too unattainable, the kinds of guys who made her feel naive and unschooled and clumsy.

There had been plenty of men in Keely's life. Maybe that was the problem, there'd been too many and not a single one worth remembering. Once she'd reached legal age, she'd decided to wrest control of her social life from her mother and she'd never looked back. Along the way, there'd been a few serious re-lationships, but Keely had always grown bored and restless, certain there was a prince out there ready to replace the frog she was sleeping with.

She always went into a relationship looking for true love but she never seemed to find it. Her most recent "frog" had simply stopped calling and when she had finally got hold of him, he'd told her he was being transferred to New Zealand. Keely didn't believe him and expected to see him any day now, shopping for fresh artichokes at D'Agostino or walking his dog in Central Park.

For some reason, the men in her life just never lived up to her fantasies…until now. Rafe Kendrick was pure fantasy material. A naughty, sweaty, erotic fantasy.

As she wove through downtown Boston, Keely replayed their encounter over and over again. He seemed to like her. In fact, he seemed to find her outrageous behavior charming. He'd been concerned for her safety and her health, and had teased her through one of the most embarrassing moments of her life. And when he'd touched her, her knees had gone all wobbly and her heart had begun to pound. Keely smiled to herself and began to hum a tune. When she realized it was "Someday My Prince Will Come," she forced herself to stop.

After everything she'd been through the last month, she should know better than to allow herself to slip into another silly fantasy. Rafe Kendrick was just a man with all the flaws that came with his sex. All his money and good looks would soon fall away and she'd come to know him as the jerk he probably was. No doubt he'd charmed hundreds of women, promised to call the next day, then never had. And Keely was willing to bet that he had a date with two or three underwear models this very weekend.

She pushed those thoughts out of her mind and tried to focus on her next move with the Quinns. But images of Rafe Kendrick kept creeping back into her mind until she was certain she'd made the biggest mistake in her life by driving away from him.

Keely pulled the car up to the front entrance to the Copley Plaza and stepped out. She handed her keys to the parking attendant, then gave him a generous tip. As she turned to walk inside, she noticed a dark Mercedes pull up right behind her car. For a moment, she hesitated. There were a lot of black luxury sedans in Boston. She slowly walked toward the car. The door opened and Rafe Kendrick stepped out.

A tiny thrill raced through her. He'd followed her here. He was even more handsome than she remembered. And that memory was only minutes old! ''I thought I told you I could get back on my own,'' Keely said, unable to keep a smile from curling the corners of her mouth.

''I was just making sure you were all right,'' Rafe countered. He leaned against his car and sent her a rakish smile. ''Are you all right?''

Keely felt her blood warm and a flush creep up her cheeks. Here was her chance. ''Would you like to join me inside for a drink?''

''A drink?'' His eyebrow arched up. ''Only if it's a club soda.''

She laughed and patted her stomach. ''That sounds good to me.''

''I'll just park my car and I'll meet you inside.''

A parking attendant jogged up to him. ''I can park your car for you, sir.''

Rafe nodded, handed him the keys and then walked up to Keely. He placed his hand on the small of her back, the gesture oddly possessive. His touch sent another thrill coursing through Keely's body and she steadied herself. Though she was as nervous as she'd been all day long, she didn't feel sick now. She felt…exhilarated, full of anticipation. It felt good to have a man touch her again.

They walked inside, the doorman holding the door open for them both, then headed for the bar. The lobby of the Copley Plaza was as opulent as the rest of the hotel and one of the most elegant in Boston. Keely had decided she could afford one night there, especially since she'd come to Boston for such an important reason. But maybe it was fate that she'd made such a choice, rather than followed her usual practical impulse to find the cheapest room available at the nearest motor lodge.

The Plaza Bar was an inviting spot, furnished with leather chairs and comfy sofas and intimate tables. A jazz pianist played softly from a corner and Rafe steered her toward a sofa, then motioned to a cocktail waitress. He whispered something in the waitress's ear and she nodded, then walked away.

Keely slowly sat down and he joined her, casually draping his arm over the back of the sofa. "This is a nice place," she said, leaning into him ever so slightly, just until her shoulder touched his arm. "Have you been here before?"

Rafe nodded. "For business meetings. Are the rooms nice?"

"They're very elegant."

The waitress reappeared with their drinks. She set

two crystal champagne flutes on the coffee table in front of them, then poured sparkling water from a small bottle into the flutes. Then she set a silver dish of strawberries and whipped cream down next to the drinks.

Keely giggled as she picked up one of the glasses and took a sip. "A very fine vintage. French, is it?"

"I thought you'd like it," Rafe said. He leaned back and took a sip from his own glass. "So, I guess you should tell me something about yourself, Keely McClain. What do you do when you're not throwing up on men's shoes?"

"I bake cakes," Keely replied as she munched on a strawberry.

"Cakes? A person can make a living baking cakes?"

"Sure. There's no shortage of weddings and birthday parties and grand openings. And I have quite a reputation for designing unusual cakes. It's kind of a family business. We have a bakery in Brooklyn. And what do you do?"

"Nothing quite so interesting," he said. "I'm a businessman. I buy and sell buildings." His fingers toyed with a strand of her hair, and for a moment, Keely couldn't think. "You know, I'm a big fan of cake," he murmured.

"Then I'll have to bake you one." At first, she regretted the offer. She was acting as if they'd see each other again after tonight. But why hide her desire? She *was* attracted to Rafe Kendrick and she shouldn't be afraid to let him know. "What's your favorite flavor?'' Keely held up her hand. ''Wait, let me guess.'' She studied him for a long moment. ''I'm usually very good at this. It's obvious that yellow cake would be too ordinary for you. Most people would automatically think that you're a chocolate man, bold and intense, but everyone loves chocolate and you're a guy who doesn't follow the crowd. You don't look like a coconut man—too trendy. I'd peg you as a banana man.''

''A banana man?'' Rafe asked with a laugh.

''A man who likes banana cake,'' Keely explained. ''A bit exotic but still comforting. Am I right?''

''Actually, you are,'' Rafe admitted. ''Right now, I have a couple of Sara Lee banana cakes in my freezer at home. And I do find them very…comforting.''

Keely sent him a flirtatious glance. ''After you taste my banana cake, you'll never eat another frozen cake again.''

''I look forward to that,'' he murmured. He dipped a strawberry into the whipped cream and offered it to her. A long silence spun out between them. His gaze fell to her mouth and Keely held her breath, afraid to move, afraid to speak. All her silly talk about cake! How could a man like Rafe find her even remotely interesting?

She took a bite of the strawberry as she tried to think of a witty, sophisticated response, anything to break the silence. But it didn't matter. Rafe slowly leaned forward to touch his mouth to hers and all thought of conversation ceased.

The kiss was incredibly sensual, his lips brushing hers, tasting the strawberry and the whipped cream before he drew away. Keely swallowed hard. What was she supposed to do now? She fought an impulse to throw her arms around his neck and drag him down on the leather sofa. That would be way too aggressive, but it would certainly keep her from babbling on about cake. Maybe she could comment on the kiss, but Keely was afraid she'd start blithering.

In the end, she just smiled. And relaxed. And stopped thinking so hard about what she was doing. The conversation resumed and Keely was surprised at how easily Rafe moved between subjects. He asked personal questions yet never pressed for more details when she'd give him vague answers. Keely didn't mention anything about her new family. That conversation would have been too complicated and Keely wasn't even sure how she felt about it all.

As Keely had suspected, Rafe was quite well travelled. He'd spent time in Europe and the Orient and when she told him about her recent trip to London and Ireland, he remembered the exact stone circle she'd seen from a trip he'd made a few years ago. They moved from travel to books to art to music, and before Keely knew it, the pianist had stopped playing and the lights had gradually come up in the bar.

"What time is it?" she said, glancing around.

Rafe looked at his watch. "Past two," he said.

"In the morning?"

He nodded. "Maybe we should call it a night?"

Rafe stood and held out his hand. "Come on, I'll walk you to your room."

Keely forced a smile. It was now or never. If seduction was in the forecast, she'd have to decide to make it happen. Somewhere between the lobby and her room, she had to find a way to kiss him again, to make sure that the idea came to him before she'd have to make the suggestion herself. And twelve years of Catholic girls' school had made that possibility nearly impossible.

As they walked to the lobby, Rafe didn't rest his hand on her back. Instead, he laced his fingers through hers. Keely expected him to say goodbye at the elevators, but he followed her inside. She pushed the button for the eleventh floor, then fixed her attention on the numbers blinking as they went up.

When the elevator doors reopened, she stepped out, then paused, wondering if this would be the place to say good-night. Rafe looked both ways and Keely took that as a hint that he'd accompany her to her room. "I'm in 1135," she said. "Down this way."

As she walked, her heart slammed in her chest and she could barely breathe. Was he going to kiss her? Should she invite him in? What did he expect? By the time she reached her room, she felt light-headed with confusion. "This is it," Keely said. She leaned back against the door as Rafe slipped his hands around her waist.

"When are you leaving?" he asked, staring down at her with an intense gaze.

"Tomorrow," she said. "I have to get back to New York."

"Is there anything I could say to convince you to stay another night? I'd like to have dinner with you tomorrow evening. I have to fly to Detroit in the morning on business, but I'll be back by six."

Play it cool, she said to herself. *Act pleased, but not too pleased.* "I think I can stay. I haven't really finished everything I came here to do."

"Good," Rafe said. "Then I'll call you tomorrow after I get back and we'll go out."

His grip tightened on her waist and he gently pulled her toward him. Keely knew he was about to kiss her and kiss her thoroughly, but all she could think about was throwing up on his shoes. "Wait," she said, pressing her hands against his chest.

"Wait?"

"I—I just have to do something," Keely said. "I'll be right back. Just give me a few seconds." She turned and opened her hotel room, then closed it behind her, leaving him out in the hall. Then she raced to the bathroom and leaned over the toilet, the strawberries tumbling around in her stomach. Good grief, she was only going to kiss him!

She drew a deep breath and waited until the wave of nausea passed. Then she rinsed her mouth with water, splashed a bit of water on her face and looked into the mirror. "Loosen up and enjoy yourself," she murmured. "And for God's sake, don't throw up again. He may be sexy but I don't think he's kinky enough to find that attractive twice in one night."

RAFE STOOD in the hallway staring at the closed door of Keely's room. This wasn't exactly what he had planned. He leaned forward and peered through the peephole, but he couldn't see anything inside. Was she sick again? She'd seemed fine in the bar. Maybe a little edgy in the elevator, but, overall, he'd assumed the evening was headed in the right direction.

Rafe raked his fingers through his hair. This had really been a strange night. He'd never met a woman quite like Keely McClain. He wasn't sure what it was about her that made her so intriguing. Maybe it was because she was so…real, so unaffected. That probably had to do with the way they met. It would have been difficult for Keely to put on airs after what had happened in front of Quinn's.

He had to say, he liked that in a woman. She was honest and direct, sweet and funny. She was perfectly natural and, with her, Rafe could let down his guard. He could put aside all his responsibilities and his strategies and enjoy himself. Hell, he hadn't even thought about the Quinns since he'd met Keely on the sidewalk.

The door opened in front of him and Keely reappeared. She gave him a winsome smile. "I'm sorry. I just had to…well…never mind."

Rafe chuckled, then slipped his arm around her waist and pulled her against him. "Would it be all right if I kissed you?"

"I think so," Keely said. She paused. "Yes. That would be nice."

Rafe didn't bother to ask twice. He hooked his finger beneath her chin and tipped her face up to his. Her skin was flawless, like porcelain. And for the first time, he had a chance to really appreciate the color of her eyes—an odd mix of green and gold. ''You really are beautiful,'' he murmured as he brought his mouth down on hers.

The contact was electric and intense, much more than the casual kiss they shared in the bar. Heat raced through his body, his heart pumping hard, the blood singing in his head. Usually when he kissed a woman, it was more of an obligation, something that had to be ticked off the list before he could take her to bed. But kissing Keely, deeply and completely, was the only thing he had on his mind right now. And he was going to enjoy it.

With a low groan, he cupped her face in his palms and teased at her lips with his tongue. She tasted sweet, like strawberries. And he wanted more. Just a little bit more. Her mouth opened and Rafe sighed deeply as he accepted her unspoken invitation, savoring her taste like he would a fine Bordeaux.

When her fingers skimmed up beneath his leather jacket and smoothed over his chest, Rafe realized he'd been fooling himself. He wasn't going to be satisfied with just kissing. He already wanted to touch her, to explore her body, to learn more about this impossibly intriguing woman. It was as if he'd discovered a hidden treasure and he wanted to possess her before anyone else realized what he'd found.

Reluctantly, Rafe reached up and took her hands in his, then held them up on either side of her head. He looked down at her flushed face. "I should go," he said before he stole one more quick kiss.

"Yes, you should," Keely teased, pushing up on her tiptoes and capturing his mouth again.

Her hands fell to his nape, her fingers furrowing through his hair. Rafe took some satisfaction in the fact that Keely wanted him as much as he wanted her. He pressed her back against her room door until he could feel her body against his, her thighs, her hips, her breasts, warm flesh and inviting curves. This was crazy! Why not just seduce her? He'd never been one to deny his desires. Why the hell should he start now? Rafe Kendrick took what he wanted and didn't look back.

He couldn't help himself. Rafe reached down and grabbed her thigh, then pulled it up along his hip. Her skirt slipped up to her hips and he slid his hand beneath, grasping her backside and pulling her even closer. His hard-on was hot against her lacy panties and when she moved against him, he felt the heat build. If they weren't standing in a public place, her panties would be history by now and he'd be deep inside her. But Rafe was going to let this seduction play out at her pace, not his. And if she made any move to call an end to it, he'd do his best to walk away.

His fingers twisted in the lace at her hip and he tugged her panties, aching to touch the skin beneath, fully prepared to make love to her in the hallway. A tiny sigh slipped from her lips beneath his kiss and she tipped her head back. Rafe dragged his mouth along her jaw, his teeth raking her silken skin, then found a spot at the base of her neck. He gently sucked, as if the taste of her could somehow satisfy this hunger inside him.

Suddenly, she stiffened and the sound of the elevator bell registered in his muddled brain. He quickly shoved her skirt down and took a step back, but he didn't bother to remove his arm from around her waist. Keely pressed her forehead against his chest and he watched as a couple walked past them in the hall. He smiled and nodded, but they continued walking. And when they disappeared inside a room, she laughed softly.

Rafe figured it was over. Like cold water on a raging fire, the interruption had brought them both back to reality. Keely turned her back to him. She reached into her jacket pocket and removed her key card, then opened the door. When she stepped inside, Rafe waited. If he went inside with her, he knew what would happen.

She turned around and he expected her to bid him good-night. But instead, Keely grabbed the lapels of his jacket and yanked him into the room. Then she slammed the door closed behind him. The force of the door echoed in the silence, marking the exact moment when the risk of interruption was eliminated. And as if it were some signal to begin, they did.

His fumbling fingers worked at buttons and zippers. There was no method to his seduction, but he didn't care. This wasn't some game; this was lust, pure and simple. As soon as tempting skin was revealed, Rafe stopped to explore, first her shoulder, then her hip, then her belly. And she did the same. They didn't bother to remove clothes fully, only pushed them aside.

"God, you are beautiful," he murmured, his mouth finding the swell of her breast. "And you taste good, too." Rafe was surprised he was even able to put together a complete sentence. His brain was no longer running the show. Instead, he was driven by instinct and impulse and experience, and the anticipation of moving inside her, slowly, patiently. He knew how to make a woman ache with need and he wanted like hell to make Keely need him. Need him so much that she'd have no choice but to surrender.

Rafe gently steered her toward the huge bed and when they reached it, they tumbled onto it in a tangle of limbs and half-discarded clothing. Only then did he slow down and enjoy the process of removing her blouse. At first, she seemed uncertain. In truth, Rafe knew she was. Unlike other women he'd known, she wasn't playing coy. She was simply being Keely McClain.

"Tell me something," he murmured, bracing his head in his hand as he toyed with the strap of her bra.

"Yes," she replied firmly, answering his question before it was asked.

"'Yes'?"

"Yes, I want to do this. That's what you were going to ask, isn't it?"

Rafe nuzzled her breast, his fingers slipping beneath the satin-and-lace scrap that hid her from his gaze. "No."

"All right, no."

"No," Rafe repeated. "No what?"

"No, I've never done this before," Keely said.

Rafe froze, his fingers still twisted in her bra strap. He bit back a groan. "Never?" he asked.

"Never," Keely replied.

"Then, you're a—"

"Oh, no!" she cried. "I thought you meant had I ever—done this. Brought a man to my hotel room. A strange man. Not that you're strange. You're a stranger. Although you're not really that, either, because I feel like I've known you for a long time." Keely took a ragged breath and reached for the front clasp of her bra. "Can we please stop talking now?"

His gaze drifted down to the necklace she wore. The pendant hung at a spot between her breasts and he picked it up and distractedly slid it back and forth on the chain. "I think that might be best," Rafe said. And when her bra fell away, he couldn't help himself. He knew he had to taste her again, and this time, he found the sweet tip of her breast. With his tongue, he slowly brought her nipple to a peak. Satisfied, he moved to the other side, determined to keep the pace slow.

But Keely wasn't quite so patient. She pushed her hands up beneath his sweater, insistently, until he was forced to tug it off over his head. Her fingers splayed over his naked chest and he watched her, each movement, each caress driving him closer to the brink. But when she dipped lower, to his belly, then to his belt, and to the button on his trousers, he brushed her fingers aside and stripped off his clothes himself, stopping at his boxers. And then he finished undressing her.

When nothing stood between them but lacy underwear and silk boxers, Rafe paused. This was no longer about him and his needs, this was a chance to finally share something intensely intimate with a woman. He was almost afraid to go any further, afraid that he might screw it all up, afraid that he might fall back on old habits.

But the moment she touched him, ran her hand along his erection, Rafe's past became just that—past. Every ounce of his need was focused in the present, in the feel of her fingers closing around him, the warm dampness between her legs, the delicate weight of her on top of him. When she was finally ready and when he could wait no longer, Rafe grabbed the lone condom from his wallet and she slipped it over him. Her touch as she put it on nearly pushed him over the edge and he groaned inwardly, willing himself to hold back.

The sensation of entering her was a revelation, a moment that he wanted to savor. Yet, again, his instincts took over. He thrust hard, and then once more, testing her, needing to know how she wanted it. She wrapped her legs around his hips and shifted until he touched her so deeply that a tiny gasp slipped from her lips. ''Yes,'' she murmured breathlessly. ''Yes.''

Rafe pushed back until he was on his knees, yet

still buried inside her. He watched her every reaction as he moved. But when he touched her sensitive nub, her eyes flew open in surprise. Her lips were swollen from his kisses and her gaze clouded with passion, but she met his gaze as he rubbed his thumb against her. Every pleasure, every sensation was reflected in those golden-green eyes and Rafe knew when she was near.

He let her reach her peak slowly, thrusting hard, then withdrawing far enough so that the tip of his erection rubbed against her, before sinking deep again. He was so close and when he felt her swell around him, when she closed her eyes and arched against him, he gave up the last shred of his self-control.

Rafe held his breath and froze, letting himself enjoy the full effect of his explosion. A groan slipped from his throat and he tumbled down on top of her, yanking her legs up around him. And as the spasms racked his body, she was there with him, losing herself in her own orgasm.

As his heart slowed and his breathing returned to normal, an instant of crystal-clear thought struck him. Rafe realized that this was a new experience for him. He never wanted to leave this room. Hell, he didn't care about work or the Quinns or anything that was once important to him. This was all he needed, sweet, soft, beautiful Keely.

Rafe rolled over onto his side and drew Keely close, burying his face in the curve of her neck. He felt the need to say something, to tell her how incredible it had been between them. But then, she'd been right there with him and he was certain she knew. He closed his eyes and sighed. Rafe had always considered obsession with sexual pleasure to be a weakness in a man.

But now he understood that it wasn't a weakness at all, especially when the pleasure had been shared with the right woman.

KEELY SLOWLY opened her eyes. At first, she wasn't sure where she was. Then, as her head cleared, she realized that she was in Boston…in her hotel room…with—

Keely cursed softly. She slowly slid her hand out to her side, searching for the warmth of a body next to her. But the sheets were cold. She turned her head, holding her breath, to find the bed empty. Resting on the pillow was a folded sheet of hotel stationery. She sat up and snatched the paper from the pillow, then quickly skimmed the note from Rafe. He had to leave before daybreak to catch his flight to Detroit and didn't want to wake her. He'd see her that evening when he got back.

Keely ran her fingers through her hair and groaned. "What was I thinking? As if I didn't have enough crap going on in my life already." She'd never—not once—done anything quite so impulsive and reckless as she had last night. She usually waited until she got to know someone before she jumped into bed. After all, she was a good Catholic girl!

A shiver skittered down her spine at the thought of

what had happened last night. The passion, the need, was so undeniable, so powerful, that she'd been unable to resist. The moment Rafe had kissed her, she'd lost all capacity to deny him—or to deny herself. Keely had always enjoyed sex, but never as much as she had last night.

She'd actually experienced what all the magazines talked about. Multiple orgasms—shattering, breathtaking, the kind that made her dizzy just remembering them. And she hadn't had to do anything to make it happen except close her eyes and enjoy the ride. She wondered exactly how she'd handle that little revelation in confession.

Keely covered her face with her hands, feeling her cheeks warm. The things she'd done last night were so wonderfully sinful. Yet she couldn't feel an ounce of guilt. For once, she'd followed her impulses and gotten exactly what she wanted—pure unadulterated pleasure.

But this wasn't the time to throw herself into a passionate affair. Ever since returning from Ireland, her life had been turned upside down. She wasn't even sure who she was or where she belonged. Maybe last night had been a reaction to that—the ultimate rebellion.

Or maybe hopping into bed with a stranger was something that came from the Quinn side, those wild, unpredictable strains of DNA lurking in her body. Maybe they didn't go to church every Sunday, maybe they hadn't been to confession in years. And maybe they followed their own wanton desires. The apple didn't fall far from the tree, did it?

She flopped back on the bed and covered her eyes with her arm. She didn't really care what other people thought of her. The only real horror was thinking about what Rafe Kendrick thought of her! No doubt, he'd experienced a number of one-night stands with a number of promiscuous women—maybe even two at a time. He was a sophisticated and worldly man. She must have appeared so…eager.

But that wasn't the worst. She was, in her mother's words, a— "Slut," she muttered. "My mother was right. A man won't value what you give away for free." It was the old cow and milk story, but the original was too crude for Fiona McClain to pass along to her innocent daughter.

Keely sat up and tossed aside the covers. She wasn't going to wait all day long for the inevitable. Men didn't call back after one-night stands. They didn't take their one-night stands to dinner and they certainly didn't date them. As for love and marriage, that was one fantasy she knew would never follow a one-night stand. After all, what were you supposed to say to the wedding guests when they asked how the happy couple met? "Oh, we ran into each other on the street and hopped into the sack a few hours later," Keely murmured. "What a sweet story."

"Be practical," she muttered. "We'll have dinner tonight and come back here and do it all over and then there'll be that uncomfortable moment when nei-

ther one of us will know what to say." And then
she'd never see him again.

She crawled out of bed and began to gather up her
clothes. Three hours' sleep was not enough, but it
would have to be. She was going to leave Boston and
this fantasy that she'd stumbled into, and return to
reality in the Big Apple.

"It was a wonderful little detour," Keely assured
herself. "But I have more important things to think
about right now."

She'd go home, regroup, and try to put Rafe Kendrick out of her head. And then, when she was ready,
she'd come back to Boston and introduce herself to
her family. She anticipated a big "I told you so" from
her mother. But why did she have to tell her mother
anything? Fiona had kept her share of secrets. And as
far as her parish priest went, what happened between
her and Rafe was exactly that—between her and
Rafe!

A knock sounded at the door and Keely froze, her
underwear clutched in her hand. She tiptoed over to
the door and peered out the peephole, thinking that
perhaps Rafe had returned. But a uniformed bellboy
was standing outside with a small white box. Keely
hurried back to the bed, grabbed a sheet and wrapped
it around her. Then she opened the door.

"Miss McClain? This was delivered for you."

Keely took the box, then glanced over her shoulder.
"Wait, I'll get you a—"

"No need," the bellboy said. "It's been taken
care of."

Keely shrugged, then closed the door. She walked slowly back to the bed, then sat on the edge as she opened the box. Her breath caught as a glorious scent drifted into the air. A perfect bouquet of sweet peas in pretty pastel colors was nestled in the box. Last night, she'd mentioned that sweet peas were her favorite flower, but she'd never expected him to remember that. She pulled the bouquet out, only to find a lacy handkerchief folded beneath with a card resting on top.

Keely pulled the card from the envelope. "Until tonight," she read. "Rafe." She fingered the fine handkerchief and smiled. It was a perfect memory of their meeting.

She flopped back on the bed and groaned. Just when she thought she had this all figured out, Rafe had to do something romantic. Why couldn't he act like all the other one-night stands out there—scared, guilty, and ready to move on to the next woman? Grabbing the bouquet, she held it to her nose and inhaled. As the scent filled the air, her thoughts drifted back to Rafe. She wondered what he was doing at exactly that moment. Was he staring out a plane window, reliving last night in his mind? Or was he already trying to figure out a way to gracefully cancel their dinner date?

"You're not making this easy, Rafe Kendrick," she murmured. "Not easy at all."

CHAPTER FOUR

"MR. KENDRICK, I've got Mr. Arledge on the line from Telles and Associates."

Rafe stared out the window of his office, his gaze fixed on a scull as it skimmed over the gray water of the Charles. The weather was turning colder and, before long, even the most die-hard rowers would be off the river.

Kencor occupied an entire floor of the high-rise, and from various vantage points in the office suite, he could see across the river basin to Cambridge, or out into Boston Harbor, and even across the harbor to Logan. When he first bought the building, he felt as if he were on the top of the world. But now the views didn't seem to hold much interest. Maybe he'd become too jaded to appreciate how high he'd climbed.

"Mr. Kendrick?"

Rafe turned around. His secretary, Sylvie Arnold, stood in the doorway. Sylvie had been with him from the start, his very first employee when he opened his first office. They'd developed an efficient working relationship and an odd personal relationship. If he had had a big sister, that sister would probably have been a lot like Sylvie. She was coolheaded in contrast to his mercurial moods, sympathetic when he was unforgiving, laid-back when all he could do was drive himself harder and harder.

Though they'd both grown up in blue-collar families, he'd worked hard to fashion himself into a worldly man. Sylvie still had a bit of neighborhood in her, a feisty, scrappy attitude that he respected. She was only a few years older, but there were times when he felt like a kid next to her. She'd already experienced so much more of life than he had. She had a life outside work, a husband and two kids.

"Mr. Kendrick?"

He tipped his head back and closed his eyes. "Yes, I know. Can you tell him I'll call him back later?"

"I'm sorry, but you're the one who called him. Or I did, at your request. You wanted to know about that property in Southie. You told me to call him at 3:00 p.m. and it's three now."

Rafe slowly turned. "I don't want to talk to him, Sylvie. In fact, I really don't want to talk to anyone right now. Hold all my calls. And cancel all my meetings."

She nodded, then walked out of the office. Rafe stared after her, a frown furrowing his brow. He'd known Sylvie for nearly ten years. She was a beautiful woman, yet he'd never once found himself attracted to her in any way beyond platonic or professional. What was it that made one woman undeniably alluring while another caused nothing more than brief consideration?

His mind returned again to Keely McClain, to the night they'd spent together nearly a month ago. He cursed softly at the unbidden images that flashed in his head. How many times had he thought of her over the past weeks? And how many times had he pushed those thoughts right out of his head, hoping to forget her?

His desk was covered with computer printouts and department reports. He sat down and began to sort through them, determined to focus on current business rather than old…pleasures.

"I'm sorry to interrupt again."

Rafe glanced up. "No, it's all right, Sylvie."

She held up a box. "These just arrived." She walked in and closed the door behind her, then set the box on his desk. "I thought you might want to see if they fit before you took them home."

Rafe reached out and pulled the top off the shoe box. Beneath the tissue paper was a brand-new pair of loafers he'd ordered from Milan, to replace the shoes Keely had ruined. Christ, as if he didn't have enough reminders of her already, now he had fine Italian footwear. If he were a superstitious man, he might think she was haunting him. "I'll try them on later." He pushed the box aside.

"Is there anything I can help you with?" Sylvie said. "Because you've been having a hard time getting things done lately. And you've been in a black mood for a month."

"I've been busy," Rafe said.

"You were supposed to review that stack of reports

by last Friday and you haven't. Both Elliot and Samuelson have called wondering if they have the go-ahead on their projects.''

''Maybe if you'd take that damn promotion I offered you, then *you* could read the damn reports,'' Rafe muttered.

Sylvie clucked her tongue, shook her head, then held out her hand. ''Pay up,'' she said. ''Ten dollars times two.''

''*Damn* is not a curse word,'' Rafe said. ''We've had this discussion before.''

She wiggled her fingers. ''Pay up, Rafe.''

''That's Mr. Kendrick to you,'' he corrected as he pulled out his wallet and withdrew a pair of ten-dollar bills.

Her brown eyes sparkled with amusement. ''Only when I'm within earshot of other employees. Remember, I knew you back when you owned three properties and couldn't get a bank to loan you a nickel so you'd have two to rub together.'' She paused, her expression turning serious. ''Is it your mother?''

''She's fine.'' He shook his head. ''And I meant to thank you for the flowers you sent for her birthday.''

''Then is it the business?''

Rafe shook his head. ''Really, it's nothing. I've just been traveling too much lately. Too much time sleeping on planes. Too many strange hotel rooms. I just need some rest.''

In truth, whenever he tried to sleep, he found himself thinking about Keely. She was like a drug. Now that he'd had a taste, he wanted more. But he thought

if he fought the cravings hard enough, they'd
go away.

He'd gone over that night again and again in his
head. It wasn't the sex, though that had been pretty
great. And it wasn't because she was some gorgeous
piece of ass, though she was nice to look at. It was
how she'd made him feel. For those few moments in
just a single evening, he'd let down his guard, he'd
forgotten all his anger and he'd been happy.

And then, he'd left for Detroit and returned to find
her gone. There had been no answer in her room and
when he had inquired at the desk, the clerk had informed him that Keely McClain had checked out
early that morning. The note she'd left him only said
that she had to get back to New York and that she'd
call him the next time she was in Boston.

So she had waltzed out of his life as quickly as
she'd waltzed in. And look where it had gotten him.
This was the end of it. From now on, Keely McClain
was part of his past, a past not worth dwelling on.
"You know, you could help me out," Rafe suggested. "Make some dinner reservations for tonight
for two. Someplace quiet…romantic. Then call Elaine
Parrish and tell her I'll pick her up at seven."

The only way to put Keely McClain out of his head
would be to replace her with another woman, someone prettier, more adventurous in bed. And the sooner
the better.

"I'm afraid that wouldn't be a good idea," Sylvie
said.

"Why not?"

"Elaine announced her engagement three months ago. I read it in the paper."

"Then find someone else. Anyone, I don't care."

"Maybe that's your problem," Sylvie commented.

Rafe sent her a stern look. "Just do it. And take these shoes. Give them to your husband. If they don't fit him, give them to the Salvation Army. Just get them out of my sight."

She grabbed the box and tucked it under her arm. "Right away, Mr. Kendrick."

But before she got to the door, Rafe stopped her. "One more thing. They're having a party at my mother's hospital," he lied. "I told the staff that I'd arrange for the refreshments. I thought a cake might be nice. And some of that...you know, you put it in a big bowl and—"

"Punch?" Sylvie asked.

"Right." He paused. "And I was reading about this person in New York who makes unusual cakes for parties. I think the name was McClain. I'm pretty sure her bakery is located in Brooklyn. Can you see if you can track down a number? But don't call—let me. I'd like to discuss what she can do."

Sylvie's eyebrow shot up. "Since when do you talk to cake decorators?"

"Just find out more," Rafe ordered. "And if I were you, I'd think about taking that promotion. Before I fire you for insubordination."

"You've been offering me a promotion for five years and I've been giving you crap for twice as long. And you haven't fired me yet."

Rafe held out his hand and wiggled his fingers. "Ten dollars. If *damn* is a curse word then so is *crap*."

She slapped a ten into his hand, then stalked out of the office. He was glad Sylvie didn't want another job. He wasn't sure he'd be able to get along without her. Rafe leaned back in his chair and closed his eyes. But a few seconds later, his intercom buzzed. He reached over and punched the button. "Yes, Mrs. Arnold. What is it?"

"I have a number. I found a McClain's Bakery in Brooklyn and they do make party cakes."

Rafe sat up straight. He wasn't sure whether he wanted Keely's number. Just a few minutes ago, he'd decided to move on, to find another woman to occupy his thoughts.

"Mr. Kendrick?"

"Just hold on to it for a while," Rafe finally said. "I'll let you know if I need her—I mean, it. The number."

He sighed, then raked his fingers through his hair. His gaze fell on a stack of file folders sitting on the corner of the desk. "Quinns," he murmured. He'd collected all the information he needed to put his plan into action, yet in the past month he hadn't done anything to further his aims.

From now on, he intended to keep his eye on the ball. Nothing, not even Keely McClain, would keep him from his plans this time.

KEELY FINGERED the claddagh pendant hanging around her neck, running her thumb over the emeralds as if they might bring her good luck. She'd come back to Boston to meet her family and tonight she'd do just that. She'd walk into Quinn's Pub, have a beer and introduce herself. And no matter what happened, she'd live with the consequences.

Smoothing her palms over the wool jacket she wore, she started toward the entrance to the bar. "Hi, my name is Keely Quinn and I'm your daughter." She groaned. "I can't just blurt it out like that. I have to have a more subtle approach. Maybe I can get him talking about his family. I'll ask him about his wife and then when I see an opening, I'll take it."

Her stomach did a little flip, but she refused to allow it to get the better of her. Instead, she paused and took a deep breath until the nausea passed. She hadn't had any coffee for a whole week, choosing milk instead to stave off the threat of throwing up in public. Gritting her teeth, she yanked open the door of the pub and stepped inside.

The place was crowded, noisy and hazy with cigarette smoke. No one bothered to look at her as she walked over to the bar. And she tried not to look at the patrons, wanting to stay as anonymous as possible. An empty stool near the end of the bar beckoned and she quickly took a seat, placing her purse in front of her.

She held her breath, waiting for someone behind the bar to notice her. Seamus was there, along with two younger men she knew were two of her brothers. The resemblance was striking, the same dark hair that she had, the same golden-green eyes. She saw her mother in each of them, in the playful way their mouths quirked up when they smiled. Seamus was the one who approached and she sat up straight and prayed that her voice wouldn't tremble when she spoke.

"What can I get ya, lass?"

Even now she could see the man that her mother had fallen in love with. If he had been half as handsome as the other two behind the bar, then he must have been irresistible. Keely swallowed hard. "I'd like a beer."

"A Guinness, then?"

"Yes. A Guinness would be fine."

He returned a few moments later with a huge glass of dark brown brew, topped by a head of pale foam. With a flick of his fingers, he tossed a coaster down in front of her and set the glass on top of it. "That's a lot of beer," Keely said with a weak smile.

"It's a pint. You look like a lass who can handle it," he said, his Irish accent thick. "Drink up now."

He made to walk away and Keely scrambled to find something to say to keep him at her end of the bar. "So is this your place?" she asked.

"That it is," Seamus said. He grabbed a towel from behind the bar and began to polish a rack of glasses. "Quinn's Pub. That's me. Quinn." He cocked his head at the two younger men at the other end of the bar. "My sons. They help me out."

"Have you always had the pub?"

He shook his head. "I used to captain a long-liner. Fished for sword on the Grand Banks."

"A fishing boat," Keely said. "That must have been dangerous."

"It was a good life for a younger man," he said in a wistful tone.

"Hey, Seamus, ya ol' gombeen! Gimme a pint!"

Seamus glanced over his shoulder, then walked away from Keely without another word. She sighed softly before taking a long sip of her Guinness. "Well, that went pretty well," she murmured. He didn't seem like such a bad guy. After her mother had painted a picture of a dissolute, irresponsible husband, Keely wasn't sure what to expect. But Seamus seemed like the kind of man who might welcome her arrival. After all, she was his only daughter.

Irish music blared from the jukebox and Keely gradually felt more comfortable in her surroundings. She drank her Guinness as fast as she could so that she could order another glass. Sean and Liam prowled the length of the bar—she'd gleaned their names from shouting patrons anxious for a refill. Liam was the youngest, the closest to Keely in age, and she felt a special connection to him. Had they spent a childhood together, they may have become best friends.

"Another?" Liam asked.

Keely pushed her glass toward him. "Make it a half-pint this time." If she didn't slow down, she'd be drunk before she said another word to Seamus.

But when Liam returned, he wasn't carrying a glass of Guinness. Instead, he placed a champagne flute in front of her and filled it with sparkling water. "What's this?" Keely asked, an uneasy feeling settling in her stomach.

"That guy down there wanted to buy you a drink." Liam shrugged. "This is what he said you'd like."

Keely leaned over the bar and looked down the length of it. Her heart stopped the moment her gaze met his. "Oh, God." She quickly leaned back and cursed softly. Rafe Kendrick was the last person she expected to see.

Her heart slammed in her chest and for a moment she wasn't sure what to do. A decision didn't come quickly enough. A few seconds later, Rafe slipped into the narrow space next to her stool, his body brushing up against hers. A tremor raced through her and she closed her eyes as she remembered the feel of his hands on her body.

Why hadn't she ever considered this possibility? She had met Rafe outside Quinn's Pub that night a month ago. It didn't take a rocket scientist to realize that he might show up again. But she'd been so focused on meeting her father and brothers that she'd completely ignored the prospect that she might see Rafe there.

"So are you going to pretend that I'm not standing here?" he asked.

Keely felt a flush creep up her cheeks. The scent of his cologne touched her nose and she recognized it immediately. Her pillow had smelled of it the morning after he'd left. "Hello, Rafe. How are you?"

"Hello, Keely. I'm fine. And how are you?"

His voice was deep, his mouth so close to her ear she could feel his breath on her neck. Still, she couldn't bring herself to look at him. "Fine." Her voice cracked and Keely winced inwardly. She wondered what would happen if she turned to him. Judging by the sound of his voice, that would put her lips about an inch from his. Maybe they wouldn't have to go through this uneasy conversation. Maybe they could just lose themselves in a very long and very deep kiss. All she'd have to do was lean forward and—

"I'm surprised to see you."

She caught a trace of anger in his voice and suddenly she felt as if he were playing a little game with her. "Why is that?"

"Oh, maybe because that note you left said you'd call the next time you were in Boston. And here you are, without a word to me."

Now Keely was sure he was toying with her. His tone dripped with sarcasm, setting her nerves on edge. What did he want? An apology? An explanation? A long silence spun out between them, filled with the raucous sounds of bar music and loud patrons. She'd imagined seeing him again, but the fantasy had never been colored with animosity; it had always been rife with passion and lust.

"I didn't expect to see you here tonight," Keely finally said.

"That's your explanation?"

She looked up at him, surprised at the hard gaze

that met hers. She felt her defenses rise. Rafe was spoiling for a fight. "Are you angry at me?"

"I'm not used to being stood up," he said.

Keely forced a laugh. "Is that what this is about? Your ego?"

Oh, wasn't that exactly like a man. It was fine for him to walk out and never call again, but let her do it and he felt as if she'd sliced off his manhood. His attitude tweaked her temper. She knew the prudent choice would be to get up and walk away, but impulse told her otherwise. Keely turned on him, answering in a low voice, "It was a one-night stand. That's all. If you're trying to make me feel guilty that I left, it's not going to work. You know better than I do that it began and ended in that hotel room. You may have come back that night and we may have had dinner and another romp in bed, but it would have ended shortly after that. I just saved you the trouble."

He reached out and smoothed his fingers over her face. Her pulse quickened and her breath caught in her throat. To a casual observer, it might look like a seductive caress. But Keely knew exactly what he wanted. He wanted to prove that his touch still affected her, that all he had to do was remind her of that night and she'd want him again. Well, she wasn't going to fall into his trap! Not this time. She regarded him with a bland expression, ignoring the desire that surged up inside of her.

"Tell me, Keely. How many times have you thought about that night? I'd wager you're thinking about it right now." His voice dropped to a low tone, still rife with mockery. "And wishing for a repeat performance."

Keely grabbed the champagne flute and tossed the sparkling water into his face. "We had sex! It was incredible. End of story. Are you satisfied now?"

Only after the words came out of her mouth, did she realize the impromptu beverage toss had rendered the patrons sitting at the bar silent—silent enough to hear her evaluation of their night together.

Liam moved from a spot a few feet away, ready to intercede. Mortified, Keely laid some money on the bar, grabbed her purse and headed toward the door. The last thing she wanted was to cause a scene, especially in front of her father and brothers. They'd think she was some low-class hussy before they even got to know her.

When she reached the street, she drew a shaky breath and tried to keep her hands from trembling. How dare he? Both of them knew what they were getting into that night. If he had any illusions about her feelings, she'd done nothing to confirm them.

Keely heard the door open behind her and turned around. Rafe stood on the top step. She swallowed hard. Why did he have to be so incredibly sexy? Why couldn't she have had a one-night stand with an ordinary guy? "Stay away from me," she warned.

He slowly walked toward her, his hands held out in mock surrender. "I'm sorry. I don't know why the hell I said that. Go ahead—go back inside. I'm leaving. End of story."

"What's wrong with you?" Keely demanded.

''What gives you the right to be so angry at me? We shared a pleasant evening together and that's all. I'm sure you've spent pleasant evenings with lots of women before.'' Even so, Keely wanted to believe that their evening together had ranked right up there near the top.

''You're absolutely right,'' Rafe said. ''Just forget you ever saw me tonight. I'm leaving.''

He walked past her and headed into the darkness. Keely stared after him, fighting the urge to call out to him, to rush into his arms and do it all over again. What right did *he* have to be so angry? She'd done exactly what she was supposed to do after a one-night stand, hadn't she?

A sudden realization made her heart skip a beat or two. Unless Rafe Kendrick didn't consider what they'd shared a one-night stand. ''Oh, bloody hell.'' She bit her lip to keep a few more juicy expletives from coming out of her mouth.

''Well, you've done it now,'' she murmured. ''Your very first one-night stand and you completely screw it up.'' She walked down the steps. ''Someone should write a manual, record all the rules.''

She stared down the street, wondering if she should go after him and apologize. But what was she supposed to say? Sorry, I thoroughly enjoyed our night together, but I didn't think you enjoyed it as much as I did, so I left? She'd thought about him so many times over the past month, yet never once, even in her wildest fantasies, did she think he might actually feel something more for her than temporary lust. After all, her relationships with men usually tended to be one-sided. Either she cared too much or they did. There was never a mutual meeting in the middle.

She stopped halfway down the sidewalk and screamed in frustration. "This is not what I came here for," she shouted. "I'm not here for my sex life—I'm here to find my family." Keely turned to go back inside, but she knew she'd only be greeted with stares and whispers and speculation about her behavior.

She had planned to stay overnight and drive back to New York in the morning, but it was only ten. If she left now, she'd be back home by one. "Next time," she reassured herself. "The next time I come, I'll tell them."

As she walked toward her car, she half hoped that she'd find Rafe waiting. But the street was empty. She walked around the back of her car, then noticed that one of her tires was flat. Keely bent down and examined it closely. She found a perfect slice near the rim. She stood and glanced up and down the street. Someone had cut her tire deliberately. But who?

Rafe had disappeared in the direction of her car, but she couldn't believe he'd do anything so petty. What would his motivation be? To rescue her again? Or to force her to deal with her problems without his help? With a soft curse, Keely opened the trunk and began to rummage around for tools to change the tire.

She began with a tire iron and tried to work the lug nuts loose. But no matter how much she twisted and tugged, the nuts were frozen in place. "Damn it!" She kicked the tire.

"Can I help?"

The sound of a voice behind her caused her to jump and a tiny scream slipped from her lips. She turned, clutching the tire iron in her fist, but recognized the man immediately. She'd seen him that first night in front of Quinn's, right before she'd met Rafe.

He held out his hands as if to calm her. "It's all right. I'm a cop. I can help you."

Keely clutched the tire iron tighter. Though she suspected that this might be one of her brothers, she wanted to be sure before she put down her weapon. "Let me see your badge," she demanded, trying hard to remain calm.

As requested, he reached into his back pocket and produced a leather case. When he held it open in front of her, Keely squinted to see his name in the dim light.

"See. Detective Conor Quinn. Boston P.D."

She'd been right that very first night. This was her oldest brother! "Quinn?"

"Yeah," Conor said. "My da owns Quinn's Pub." He paused, his gaze examining her face shrewdly. "You look familiar. Have we met?"

"No. Never," Keely answered, shaking her head.

He asked her question after question, until she felt as if he were interrogating her, trying to get to the truth of why she was alone on a dark street in Southie so late at night. Thankfully, he finally decided she wasn't a criminal and offered to help her fix her tire.

Keely stood back and watched him, marveling at the ease at which he completed the task. "You know, you could have just come into the bar," he suggested, "and used the phone to call a friend. You shouldn't be out on a dark street like this alone." He stood up, brushed off his hands, then walked to the trunk and grabbed the spare.

"I don't have any friends," Keely said "I—I mean, not in the neighborhood. Not home. They're all...out." Maybe if she began asking him questions, he'd stop asking her. "So is the bar a family business?" She tried to make her tone casual, as if she was just mildly curious and not starving for the tiniest bit of information about her family.

Conor glanced over his shoulder. "Me and my brothers all take turns working on the weekends."

"Brothers? You have brothers? How many?"

He frowned as he slowly replaced the lug nuts. "I have five brothers," he said.

Keely smiled. "Five brothers. I—I can't imagine having five brothers. What are their names?"

He stood, wiping grit from the knees of his jeans. Then he released the jack and the car slowly came down. "Dylan, Brendan, Sean, Brian and Liam. They're all inside waiting for me. Why don't you come in? You can wash your hands and I'll buy you a soda."

Keely had already decided to call it a night. But the offer was tempting. She could walk into Quinn's with her eldest brother and introduce herself and get it all over with. "No." She was not going to be guided by impulse. Telling her family would take time and careful planning. "I have to go. I'm late."

Keely took the tire iron from his hand then quickly yanked the jack from beneath the bumper, tossing them both in the trunk before hopping back inside her car.

As she pulled away, she released a tightly held breath. For a night that had started so simply, it had certainly ended with high drama. She'd been caught in the middle of her own little soap opera—the secret daughter, a newfound family, a spurned lover. All she really needed was a touch of amnesia and a disfiguring accident and she'd have a complete plot.

KEELY PEERED into the mixing bowl as she dropped a blob of butter into the icing. The paddle spun round and round and she watched it, hypnotically, glad for the chance to give her mind a rest. Since she'd returned from Boston last night, she'd been plagued with thoughts of Rafe, wondering whether she ought to contact him again or just let it go.

She couldn't deny the attraction she still felt for him, the little shiver that skittered down her spine when she first met his gaze, the thrill that raced through her when his body brushed against hers. Even in his anger, he was still an incredibly sexy man.

She'd sat in her kitchen last night, sipping herbal tea and making a list of the pros and cons of calling him. His business card was still hanging on her refrigerator door, right under a watermelon magnet. But a phone call would have been too uncomfortable, filled with uneasy silences. And sending a letter would have been too impersonal. So she'd decided on the best alternative she had—a cake.

When the icing consistency was perfect, she shut off the mixer and put a spoonful of the buttercream into a small bowl. She needed just a tiny bit of black to finish her creation.

"What is that?"

Keely glanced up, the pastry bag hovering over the cake. Her mother stood in the doorway of the kitchen, her hands braced on her hips. She wore a green apron with the McClain's logo emblazoned on the bib. "I'm working on a new design."

Fiona approached the huge worktable. "We've got to deliver the Wagner cake before ten tomorrow morning, three tiers with your Edwardian lace decoration. And you haven't even put the crumb coat on yet."

"I'll get it done—don't worry."

"If you don't want to do the cake, just tell me. I'll have one of the other girls decorate it. It will take two of them to finish it but—"

Keely ground her teeth. "I said I'll do it. I've got the rest of the afternoon and all night."

"I don't think you realize how complicated that cake is."

Her mother knew full well that Keely was capable of finishing the cake with time to spare. "I designed the bloody cake, Mother. I know how complicated it is."

"Don't use vulgar language, Keely."

"Why? You do. You're not always the proper Irish lady that you pretend to be."

Fiona ignored the provocation and stared down at the cake her daughter was frosting. "Are those shoes?"

"Italian loafers," Keely said. "It's for a…" What should she call Rafe Kendrick? Lover? Acquaintance? "A friend."

Keely scooped the icing into a pastry bag and carefully begin to add stitching to the top of the left loafer. "Was there anything else?"

"Do I always have to ask you? Couldn't you volunteer to keep me informed about your trips to Boston? I was expecting you for dinner last night. I thought we had plans."

"I'm sorry. I decided to go at the last minute. I had a free day."

"Did you talk to your father?" Fiona's tone was indifferent, but Keely sensed that she was curious.

"Yes, and I met three of my brothers. Conor, Liam and Sean." Keely shook her head. "Actually, I didn't meet them, but I spoke to them."

Her mother fell silent and when Keely looked up again, she saw tears swimming in Fiona's eyes. She silently scolded herself for acting so childishly. Her mother had lived without news of her six sons for twenty-five years and now her daughter was hoarding information like some petulant brat. "They're very handsome," Keely offered, her voice softening.

Fiona smiled tremulously. "Really? Are—are they good men? I mean, are they polite? I always tried to teach them manners. Their father was so rough and unschooled but I wanted my boys to be more than just hooligans.''

"They're very nice,'' Keely said. "Conor is a policeman. I had a flat tire and he helped me change it. He was kind and considerate. Sean and Liam were tending bar at the pub. Sean is tall and handsome, but he's very quiet. But Liam is friendly and kind of a flirt.''

"Are they married? Do they have children?'' She paused. "Do—do I have grandchildren?''

"I don't know,'' Keely replied, meeting her mother's watery gaze. "I didn't see any of them wearing a wedding band, but that doesn't always mean anything.'' She turned back to her cake and smoothed a section of icing near the heel of the right shoe, then studied it critically. "You haven't asked me about Seamus.''

"I'm not sure I want to know," Fiona said.

"I can understand how you fell for him.'' Keely laughed softly. "When he smiles, his whole face lights up. His hair has gone white and his face is a bit weathered, but he's still very handsome.''

"I think you're doing the right thing.''

Keely froze. "Do you?''

"You should know your father and brothers.''

"I'm glad you feel that way, because I've made a decision. I think I'm going to go to Boston. Not for a weekend, but maybe for a month or two. I want to get to know them all first before I tell them. That way, they'll get to like me before they know who I really am.''

Her mother gasped. "But you can't leave the business for such a long time. We have jobs and clients.''

"I'll still do the designs. I'll just put together more explicit instructions for decorating. Both Janelle and Kim are willing to put in some extra time—I've already asked them. And they're both anxious to prove themselves. They'll have some nice photos to put in their portfolios when they start their own cake-decorating businesses. I've also offered them both a raise and authorized hiring another kitchen assistant if they need one.''

"Can we afford that?''

"I can afford it," Keely said. "The business is doing well. And you'll be here to watch over things. Besides, I'm not going to leave for another month or so.'' She paused. "You could always come to Boston with me.''

Fiona shook her head. "No. That wouldn't be possible.''

Keely set the pastry bag down. "Ma, you're going to have to see your sons sometime. After they find out about me, they're probably going to want to see you.''

"They didn't want to see me before, why would they change their minds now? Not one of my sons has ever tried to find me. They probably all hate me.''

"You don't know that. You have no idea how they feel. And maybe they have tried to find you. Or maybe Seamus discouraged them. But I think you need to make the effort. After all, you're the one who left them.''

''What if they refuse to speak to me? I'm not sure I could bear that.''

''What do you have to lose?''

Fiona thought about that for a moment, then nodded. ''All these years, I've tried so hard to believe that they were all right. It would be nice to know for sure.''

Keely circled the worktable and stood in front of her mother. She grabbed Fiona's hands and gave them a squeeze. ''I know this is difficult for you, but I also know that everything will be all right. Going to Ireland was a good thing.''

Fiona nodded, then pulled Keely into her embrace. ''You're a sweet girl, Keely McClain.'' She pulled back and took Keely's face between her hands. ''Keely Quinn. You've always been a sweet girl—a little bit headstrong and reckless at times—but when your father and brothers meet you, they'll recognize what a treasure you are and they'll learn to love you as much as I do.'' Fiona kissed her cheek, then hurried out of the kitchen.

''Sure, I'm a good girl,'' Keely said. She sighed softly, then shook her head. In truth, she had no idea who she was anymore. She wanted to believe she had control over her behavior, but her encounter with Rafe had proved that wrong. He could simply look at her and she got all crazy for him, wild fantasies racing through her mind.

She stared down at the cake. Was the cake really

an apology, or just another invitation to sin? After all, didn't she hope that he'd get the cake, pick up the phone and call her? Keely couldn't deny that she'd like to repeat her night with Rafe Kendrick. But now was not the time to fall into some crazy love affair. It would only distract her and she had more important things to do.

She picked up the cake board and carried it over to the trash bin, then tossed it inside. It was a bad idea and a bad design. She had enough emotional upheaval to look forward to in the next months without throwing herself into the path of a devilishly handsome but ultimately dangerous man.

Maybe when she finally figured out who she was, she might allow herself to fall in love. But not until then.

CHAPTER FIVE

"RUM AND COKE, two drafts and a—a—" Keely looked down at her notepad. "A piña colada?"

Seamus chuckled and wagged his finger at her. "We don't make fruity drinks here," he said. "They're just givin' you the business because you're new, lass. Who wanted the piña colada?"

Keely turned and pointed to a burly, bearded man sitting in a booth, wearing a motorcycle jacket and red bandanna. "I think his name is Art."

"Art's a good Irish lad. He drinks nothing but Guinness. And when it's Christmas Eve and the Guinness is free, he drinks a lot." Seamus drew a pint and set it on her tray. "You tell him this is a piña colada. And if he's looking for a fruit garnish, he can look in the mirror." Seamus chuckled at his own joke as he filled the rest of her order.

Meanwhile, Keely slipped off her shoes and stretched her toes. She was not cut out to be a waitress, much less a waitress who slung drinks in an Irish pub. It wasn't difficult to remember the orders— nearly every patron preferred Guinness. But avoiding the wandering hands of customers, the slippery puddles of beer on the floor and the blinding clouds of cigarette smoke took the athletic ability of an Olympian.

She'd noticed the Help Wanted sign when she'd paid another visit to Quinn's in November and decided if the job was still available when she returned in December, she'd take it. She'd been a waitress at Quinn's for a week now, and here she was spending Christmas Eve with the Quinns—her family. It had been a perfect plan.

And she wasn't such a bad waitress. So far, she hadn't made too many major mistakes—beyond dumping an entire tray of drinks on herself the first night. And then there had been the second night, which had been capped with a practical joke from Liam. He had secretly pasted a sign on her back with the words Pinch Me printed in big letters. She'd gone home so jumpy she hadn't been able to sleep. By the third night, she'd gotten wise to their tricks. It had only taken her two hours to realize the customers wiping drops of beer off her face actually had black marker on their fingertips. But the tricks made her feel even more a part of the family.

As soon as her tray was filled, she hustled over to the booth and delivered the drinks. Ed, a good-natured regular at Quinn's Pub, handed her a ten for the round and told her to keep the change—a three-dollar tip with the free Guinness. Keely quickly checked in with the rest of her tables, then took a spot at the end of the bar where Liam had poured her a diet soda.

As she sipped at the cold drink, her mind wandered to where it had so many times over the past week—

Rafe. It felt odd to be in the same city as him, yet not know where he was or what he was doing. She'd thought about contacting him but had always come up with an excuse not to—the holidays, her job at Quinns, her confusion over what they'd shared. And the realization that if she saw him again, she'd probably fall victim to his charms once more.

Though just the thought of sex with Rafe Kendrick caused her pulse to quicken and her toes to curl, there were more important things on her agenda than wildly passionate intercourse and earth-shattering orgasms. Still, she couldn't help but look up each time another patron entered the bar, wondering if it might be Rafe…and wondering what she'd do if it was.

Keely turned her mind to more somber thoughts. Though the pub was filled with Christmas cheer—colored lights, a dancing Santa, and holiday music—she couldn't help but think of her mother, home alone. To make up for her first Christmas away, Keely had treated Fiona to a nightly phone call with little tidbits of news about the Quinn brothers. In her heart, Keely hoped that next Christmas all the Quinns could celebrate under one roof.

She'd come as close as she could this Christmas. Sean and Liam had been working the bar since early afternoon, doing double duty ladling out free bowls of Irish stew and drawing free pints of Guinness. Conor had arrived at three with his new wife, Olivia, and moments after that, Dylan had burst in with his fiancée, Meggie, and her brother, Tommy. Now they all waited for Brendan's arrival, though no one was sure that he'd put in an appearance.

Keely was anxious to meet the last of her brothers. She already knew Dylan was a fireman and Meggie owned a coffee shop. And Conor and Olivia had been married on Thanksgiving weekend. Brendan was a writer and Seamus kept copies of his books behind the bar. And just last night, everyone in the bar had gathered around the television as Brian did his first on-air segment in his capacity as a reporter for one of the Boston television stations.

As for Liam and Sean, they worked when they could, Sean as a private investigator and Liam as a freelance photographer for the *Boston Globe*. The three youngest brothers were still unabashed bachelors and from what she could glean from the pub's female patrons, they didn't lack for feminine companionship. They had quite a reputation with the opposite sex, so Keely kept her distance, unwilling to explain why she was single, but unavailable.

Keely took another sip of her soda then let her gaze wander from one brother to another. This would be the perfect night to tell them. Once they were all here, she could make her announcement and hope that the holiday spirit would carry her through. And what better Christmas present than to find a little sister under their tree?

"And there's the man of the hour! Come on, Bren, we've been waiting for you!"

Keely spun around on her stool as Dylan shouted, her heart leaping in anticipation. There he was! Brendan Quinn. The last of her six brothers stood in the doorway with a pretty woman on his arm. He took the woman's hand and drew her over to the group gathered at the bar. Keely kept her gaze on her newest brother, anxious to learn more about him, to gather information to tell her mother when they spoke later that night.

The big news came almost immediately when Brendan introduced his companion, Amy, as his fiancée. As good wishes were given all around, Keely's heart twisted. Another family moment she'd never share. And another reason not to come forward with her own news. It wouldn't be fair to steal Brendan and Amy's thunder.

Keely looked over at Seamus and noticed he was the only one not celebrating. He sat on a bar stool a few feet from Keely, sipping at a small glass of Guinness. Brendan walked over and slipped his arm around Seamus's shoulders. "Well, Da. What do you think?"

Seamus shook his head. "Ah, geez. Not another one. Have I taught you boys nothing? Our Quinn ancestors are rolling over in their graves, they are."

Suddenly, the night which had begun with such anticipation turned into a vivid reminder of the fact that she was not a part of the Quinn family. They all shared a camaraderie that she might never know, an ease that came with having a history together. Keely's attention turned to the three women in the group—Olivia, Meggie and Amy. They'd come into the family as strangers, but they'd been accepted. Could she hope for the same?

"Keely!" Seamus called. "You've got some folks out there with empty glasses. Step lively, girl."

Keely grabbed her tray and hurried over to the row of booths on the far side of the bar. Over the next few minutes, she didn't have time to think about her family until Conor asked her to deliver a bottle of champagne to Brendan and Amy. As Keely approached the newly engaged pair, she smiled at her brother and his fiancée, making sure she didn't stare too hard. Brendan was as handsome as the other five Quinns with his dark hair and his golden-green eyes.

"Conor sent this over," she murmured. She set the champagne flutes on the pool table and handed Brendan the bottle. "Congratulations. I hope you two will be very happy."

"Thank you," Brendan said, sending her a warm smile.

Keely nodded then hurried away. But she stopped halfway back to the bar when Seamus pointed impatiently to a new patron at one of the booths. She fumbled with her pad and pencil and when she finally looked up, ready to take the order, her heart came to a dead stop. "Rafe."

He was just as stunned to see her. "Keely. What are you doing here? And why are you carrying a tray?"

Keely's heart fell. How was she supposed to explain this? She'd never expected Rafe to return to Quinn's, especially after their last encounter. "I—I took a job as a waitress." She tried to remember what she'd told him about her work. She decorated cakes and she owned a bakery. Why would she sell her business, move to Boston and take a job in a pub? "I—I—"

"I thought you lived in Brooklyn and worked in your family's bakery."

"I did," Keely said, relieved. "But I quit and decided to move here. You know, I needed to get out on my own. I've been trying to find a job in a bakery, decorating cakes, but it's been tough. So I took this job."

Rafe didn't seem to be buying her story. "Why Boston?"

"Why not?" She paused. "Oh, I didn't come here for you if that's what you're worried about."

He smiled. "I'm not. After our last meeting, I've been avoiding this place. But I guess I didn't expect to find you here on Christmas Eve."

"Can I get you a drink? What would you like? We have free Guinness and free Irish stew."

"Scotch on the rocks," Rafe said. "The best you've got."

As she walked over to the bar, Keely tried to calm her racing pulse. She'd thought about him so many times since the last time she'd seen him. But each time she'd stubbornly put those fantasies out of her head, determined to focus on her new family. But now that he was here, Keely couldn't help but be pleased. He was really the only person she knew in Boston. And he didn't seem angry at her anymore. In truth, he was acting almost pleasant. "Holiday spirit," Keely murmured.

When she returned, she placed his drink in front of him. "Can you sit down for a while?" Rafe asked.

Keely glanced around the bar. "I really shouldn't. We're getting pretty busy."

"What time do you get off?"

"The pub closes at five."

Rafe nodded. "I suppose you'll be heading back to New York to spend the holidays with your family."

"No, I'm spending Christmas here. Alone. Just me, a cup of hot cocoa and a good book."

"No," Rafe said. "You're coming out with me. I'll treat you to dinner. As an apology for my behavior the last time we met."

"If that's the offer, then we should probably go dutch. I was as much to blame as you were. But you must have plans with your family."

"No plans."

Keely considered his invitation for a moment or two, then nodded. "All right. I'd like that. I'd like that a lot."

As she went back to work, Keely couldn't keep herself from smiling. Though she'd tried to ignore her attraction to Rafe, seeing him again had only proved how fruitless that effort had been. Maybe it was only a physical thing, but what was wrong with that? There was something to be said for really great sex.

And if, by some chance, it led to something more, then she'd deal with that when it came. Right now, she had plans for Christmas Eve and that was enough.

RAFE SLOWLY SIPPED his Scotch, his gaze fixed on Keely as she moved around the bar from table to table. Every now and then, she'd look over at him and smile and he found himself lost in idle contemplation of her beauty.

In this atmosphere of rather overblown feminine pulchritude—of big hair and red lips and artificially enhanced bosoms—she stood out as something special. She wore very little makeup and her hair was cut short in a tousled style that made it appear as if she'd just crawled out of bed. Rafe couldn't quite figure out her clothes. They were fashionable with a funky edge, causing a few raised eyebrows in the rather conservative atmosphere of the pub.

Tonight, she wore a lime-green sweater and a little black skirt that gave every man in the place a tempting view of her legs. Knee-high boots made the look even sexier. God, he loved black boots, Rafe mused.

A loud shout from the bar drew his attention to Seamus Quinn, and Rafe's mood immediately darkened. Everything was in place. The day after Christmas, Seamus was going to learn that his mortgage on the pub had been sold. A building inspector would visit the day after that and discover the pipes and heating system in the place were covered with asbestos. Quinn's Pub would need to be closed down until the removal was completed. And the day after that, a fisherman who'd been on board the *Mighty Quinn* the day Sam Kendrick died would go to the police with a story of murder on the North Atlantic.

Ken Yaeger had told the story many years ago.

He'd visited Rafe's mother shortly after the funeral
and told her how her husband had really died. Rafe
had heard the tale from his mother in disjointed
pieces, always with Seamus Quinn painted as the vil-
lain. Over time, Rafe had managed to figure out the
truth of the story. And when he found Yaeger a few
months ago, that story was confirmed. Seamus Quinn
was responsible for Sam Kendrick's death. He'd gotten away with murder.

If all went as planned, by the start of the New Year,
Seamus Quinn would be sitting in jail and there'd be
nothing any of the Quinn boys would be able to do
to rescue their father from justice. Rafe leaned back
and took another sip of his drink. His only regret was
that Keely would lose her job. But then, she didn't
belong in a place like this. He'd have to find a way
to make it up to her, beyond a Christmas Eve dinner.

By the time Rafe finished his Scotch, Seamus had
made last call. Keely hurried from table to table to
settle tabs, and when she finished, she tossed her
apron behind the bar and met him at the door. When
they got outside, she looped her arm through his as
they walked to Rafe's car.

"Tired?" he asked.

"I've only been working since noon. A five-hour
shift isn't so bad."

"How do you like your new job?"

"It's nice. A little hard on the feet. And when I
leave, I smell like cigarette smoke and stale beer. But
the customers are nice. Very Irish."

"And the people you work for?" Rafe probed.

"I don't know them very well," Keely said offhandedly. "But I like them so far. Where are we going?"

"I have one stop to make before we get dinner. I have to deliver a Christmas gift. But I should only be a few minutes."

They spent the rest of the drive chatting, Rafe hardly able to keep his eyes on the road with Keely in the car. He wasn't the kind of guy to believe in fate, but something had brought him to Quinn's that night. He had to believe he was meant to satisfy this craving he'd had for Keely over the past few months.

Now that he knew what she expected, he wasn't going to make the same mistakes twice. She wanted a physical relationship, wild and uninhibited, with no strings attached. Any expectations for a relationship beyond pure pleasure were to be checked at the bedroom door. Hell, that's all he'd ever really wanted from the opposite sex and now he'd found the perfect woman to provide it.

They chatted about her job as Rafe turned off the highway into Cambridge. A few minutes later, he swung the car into the Oak Terrace Convalescent Hospital and pulled into a parking spot near the front door.

"Why are we stopping here?" Keely asked.

"My mom lives here. I won't be long."

Keely gasped. "But it's Christmas. You should spend some time with her."

"Lately she hasn't even recognized me," Rafe said. "She has some problems and she kind of drifts in and out. Around the holidays, she always seems to be worse. I think she misses my dad.''

"He's dead?''

Rafe nodded. "For almost thirty years. But to her it was just yesterday. Emotionally, she's been a little…fragile since he died.'' He reached into the back seat for an elaborately wrapped Christmas gift. "I'll be back in a minute.''

"I'd like to come with you,'' Keely said softly. "I'd like to meet your mother.''

Stunned by her offer, Rafe wasn't sure what to say. His mother was hard enough for him to handle; he couldn't imagine a complete stranger taking that on. But then Keely continually surprised him with the depth of her character. "All right.''

He hopped out of the car and circled to Keely's door to pull it open for her. She stepped out and gave him a smile. "I'll have to thank her for teaching you such good manners.''

Though decorated festively, the home was quiet when they entered. Rafe nodded to the nurse at the front desk, then started down the long hall. Keely stayed at his side, unfazed by the residents who stared at her with vacant gazes and expressionless faces. When they reached Lila's room, Rafe turned to her. "Sometimes she gets a little upset, so feel free to leave if her behavior bothers you.''

"I'll be fine,'' Keely assured him.

Rafe wasn't sure where the urge came from, but he leaned forward and kissed her gently, their lips barely touching before he drew away. He couldn't find the words to tell her how sweet she was, so he'd chosen to show his appreciation. He turned and knocked softly on the door.

Lila didn't look up as they entered. She sat in a chair near the window, staring out into the winter darkness with a strange smile on her face. Rafe crossed the room and kissed her on the top of her head. "Hi, Ma. Merry Christmas."

"He should be home by now," Lila said. "He's never so late."

"He will be home soon, Ma. Until he gets here, would you like to open this present?"

She finally glanced up at him, her gaze taking in the gift. But then it shifted to Keely and her smile faded slightly. "Are you my nurse?" she asked.

Keely slowly approached the chair, then bent down until she stood at Lila's level. "No, I'm not. I'm a friend of Rafe's. Merry Christmas, Mrs. Kendrick."

Lila stared at Keely for a long time, her expression melting into a frown. "I know you," she said.

"No, Ma, you don't."

"I know you. You have those eyes."

"You have very pretty eyes," Keely said, deftly changing the subject. "And beautiful hair. Would you like me to fix your hair for you?"

Rafe watched as Keely fussed with his mother's hair, all the while talking softly to her, chatting about fashions and perfume and all the things that ladies enjoyed. Lila seemed to relax in her presence and she even laughed once or twice. For the first time in many years, Rafe saw the mother he'd once known—the

mother who had taught him to dance to old 45s playing on the console stereo in their living room, the
mother who had been proclaimed "hot" by all his
friends at school; the mother who told him he could
be anyone, do anything, he set his mind to.

And now he'd set his mind to ruining the Quinns.
"You did so much for me," Rafe murmured to himself. "And now I'm going to do this for you, Ma."

Nearly an hour had passed before Rafe decided it
was time to leave. His mother was getting tired and
when she grew tired, she became even more irra-
tional. He motioned to Keely and she took the responsibility of announcing their departure. But she
assured Lila that she'd enjoyed their chat and hoped
to visit her again soon.

As she walked out to the hall, Rafe sat down across
from his mother. "It was nice to see you again, Ma."

She reached out and held on to his hand, so tightly
that his fingers hurt. "Christmas is coming soon,"
Lila said. "You will come to see me at Christmas-
time, won't you?"

"I will. I love you, Ma." Rafe bent forward to kiss
her goodbye, but she suddenly grabbed the front of
his shirt and yanked him closer, her gaze turning wild.

"Tell her I'm sorry," she pleaded. "Tell her I
didn't mean it. She doesn't have those eyes. *He* has
those eyes. Seamus Quinn does. Evil eyes. I made a
mistake. Be sure you tell her. Promise me."

He gently untwisted her fingers from his shirt. "I
will, Ma."

When he joined Keely in the hall, he gave her a

hesitant smile. Then he took her hand and drew it to his lips, pressing a kiss just above her wrist. "Thank you," he said.

"For what?"

"For giving me my mother. She doesn't wander back to reality very often. It was the best Christmas gift I've gotten in many years."

Keely stared at him, her expression tinged with confusion. Then she gave him a small smile and started down the hall. Rafe watched her, struck dumb by the flood of emotion that raced through him. What bit of luck had brought Keely McClain into his life? And what would he have to do to keep her there?

"I DIDN'T EXPECT all my favorite restaurants to be closed on Christmas Eve," Rafe said.

"That's all right," Keely replied. "We can have dinner another time."

"I promised you dinner and I'm going to deliver," Rafe said. "There's one more place we can try. And it's just a few blocks away."

Keely snuggled down in the heated front seat of Rafe's Mercedes. She was glad they'd have a dinner table between them because, right now, all she could think about was kissing him again. The brief kiss in the hallway outside his mother's room had done nothing to satisfy the need building inside her. She felt as if every nerve in her body crackled with electricity. And if he touched her in just the right way, she might spontaneously burst into flames.

If she didn't want to get herself into trouble tonight,

she might do best to make her dinner selection on the basis of the quantity of garlic in it. Keely frowned as Rafe reached up to his visor and pressed the control for the door of an underground garage. "What kind of food does this restaurant serve?" Keely asked.

"It's not exactly a restaurant. It's a kitchen with a great view."

"You live here, don't you?" Keely said.

Rafe smiled and shrugged. "I make a mean omelette."

Keely groaned inwardly. She knew exactly where this would lead. When it came to Rafe she had absolutely no control over her desires. There must be something in the air here in Boston, she mused. Something that turned a nice Catholic girl into a raging sexaholic. Or maybe it was her Quinn genes asserting themselves. Her brothers weren't known for self-control when it came to the opposite sex, so why should she?

They rode up the elevator, Keely keeping her gaze fixed on the numbers as they flashed higher and higher. They finally stopped at the top floor and Keely stepped out. "How did you get the top floor?"

Rafe slipped his key into the door of his apartment. "I built the building."

He lived in understated luxury, the imprint of an interior designer evident in every perfect accessory, in the colors and the textures of the European-style furniture. Compared to her little bohemian loft in the East Village, Keely felt as if she'd stepped into a spread in *Architectural Digest.*

She fought the urge to turn around and leave. There were times when she felt completely out of her league with Rafe. He was wealthy and sophisticated, and he held an undeniable power over her desire that she couldn't explain. But, at the same time, Keely trusted Rafe.

The apartment was dimly lit and Keely was immediately drawn to the wall of wide windows on the far side of the living room. She stood in front of them and looked down on the harbor, the shape of the shore outlined by the lights of the city. "It's beautiful," she said.

"Would you like something to drink? A glass of wine, perhaps?"

"That would be nice," Keely said.

Rafe disappeared into the kitchen. Keely wrapped her arms around herself, trying to calm a shiver. The first time they'd been together had been so spontaneous, she hadn't had time to think. Now, she had all the time in the world to consider her actions. There would be no chance for impulsive decisions this time.

And the one-night stand excuse wouldn't work tonight. If she fell into bed with him, she'd have to deal with the consequences in the morning. Keely closed her eyes and tipped her head back. She couldn't deny her attraction to Rafe. Images of him constantly invaded her waking thoughts and plagued her dreams.

She turned at the sound of his footsteps and forced a smile. He held a bottle of champagne in one hand and two flutes in the other. "I thought maybe this time we'd have the real thing." He poured Keely a glass, then handed it to her. Their hands touched for a moment and it was as if she'd touched lightning, a dangerous current racing through her body. She clutched the glass, afraid she might drop it. Even after all this time she remembered the exact feel of his hands on her body, the way his mouth trailed after, searching and exploring.

He filled his own flute, then held it out. "Merry Christmas, Keely McClain."

"Merry Christmas," she said, touching her glass to his.

Rafe watched as she took a sip of her champagne. He reached out and drew his finger along her jawline, a caress that was both tantalizing and overwhelming. "Are you hungry?"

Somehow, she didn't think he was talking about food. But she was willing to play along. "I am. Can I help?"

Rafe nodded and she followed him through the dining area and into the kitchen. He flipped on the lights and the room came alive, all smooth granite and stainless steel and halogen lighting. Keely looked around at all the high-tech gadgetry. She pointed to a professional-grade mixer, the kind she used to make icing at the bakery. "Have you ever used that?"

Rafe chuckled. "No. But I guess the decorator thought it was important." He grabbed a sauté pan from the rack above the cooktop. "I'll need eggs and bacon," he said. "And there should be a green pepper in the fridge. And some cheese."

Keely pulled open the refrigerator door, expecting

to find it thinly stocked, but it was full of both staples and snack food. "Wow. You must do a lot of cooking at home."

"Not much. My housekeeper does the shopping. And since omelettes are the extent of my cooking skills, the shopping list isn't very long."

She set the ingredients next to him on the counter, then leaned back and watched. But when he reached for the eggs, he had to reach around her. As if it were the most natural thing in the world, he bent closer and brushed his mouth over hers. This time he lingered, teasing and tasting before moving away.

As he cracked the eggs into a bowl, Rafe smiled. "I needed to do that."

"I wanted you to do that," Keely said. "Maybe you could do it again sometime?"

She stared at him, already resigning herself to complete and unconditional surrender. Good Lord, how long had it taken her to capitulate—five or ten minutes?

Rafe dropped the fork into the bowl of half-scrambled eggs. "Maybe I could."

With exquisite care, he wrapped his arms around her waist and lifted her up to sit on the edge of the counter. Then he pushed her knees apart and stepped between them, all the time looking deep into her eyes. Keely felt every nerve in her body ready itself for the sensation of his touch. And when he ran his hands along her thighs and brought her legs up around his waist, she slowly released a breath.

"I like these boots," he said, running his hands from her knees to her ankles.

His hands shifted in the other direction, all the way up her legs as he bunched up her short skirt around her hips. He hooked a finger around her panties and tugged at the lace. "And I like these, too."

His exploration moved on to her waist and he grabbed the hem of her sweater and slowly tugged it over her head. After tossing it aside, he smoothed his palms over her shoulders. A flood of desire coursed through her body, making her heart pound with the effort.

Rafe toyed with her bra straps, but he couldn't seem to settle in one place. "You're so beautiful," he murmured, his voice deep and raw. He ran his tongue along the crease of her lips, then drew away. "I love the way you taste. Better than champagne."

With a slow and deliberate pace, he moved from spot to spot, the base of her neck, the skin beneath her ear, the swell of her breast and then her nipple. And each time his tongue touched her, she shuddered with pleasure. But then he moved lower to her belly and then to the inside of her thigh. "Let me taste you," Rafe murmured. "All of you."

Keely leaned back onto the counter, closing her eyes and bracing her arms behind her, anticipating his assault. He moved up her thigh and she moaned, knowing the next stop on his tour of her body. When he slipped his hands beneath her skirt and tugged at her panties, Keely sighed. He stepped away for a moment as the lace made its way over her boots and then to the floor.

The lights of the kitchen blazed. Rafe parted her legs and Keely turned her head toward the windows. This corner of his apartment looked out on another high-rise directly across the street, so close that she could see people in their apartments. Rafe glanced over at the windows. "Are we going to have an audience? Or would you like me to shut the blinds?"

He didn't give her a chance to answer. Instead, he hooked her legs over his shoulders, bent lower and took his first taste. The touch of his tongue sent shock waves through her body, causing her to cry out in surprise. Keely was sure anyone looking in the window would know what they were doing. But she didn't care. The sensation of his mouth on her sex was devastating, crumbling the last of her inhibitions.

Again and again he penetrated her with his tongue, then withdrew to tease and suck. She wasn't sure when she lost the ability to think clearly, or when reason was replaced by desperate gasps and soft moans. But suddenly the sensations intensified and her mind cleared. Her need for release grew more acute, the tension setting her nerves on edge, every flick of his tongue nearly unbearable. Keely wanted to make it last, but the only way to do that was to make Rafe stop. And making him stop was beyond her capability. She was so close...he was so good...so—

It hit her quickly, the tension snapping like a taut rubber band. One moment, she was on her way there, and then her need exploded in a powerful orgasm. Keely cried out, her arms collapsing beneath her. Spasms rocked her body, but he didn't stop. He took the last ounce of her release, bringing her down slowly, giving her a chance to recover.

Rafe was ready to begin all over again, but Keely sat up, then raked her hands through his hair and drew him away. He knew what she wanted the moment he looked up at her. He straightened and, without a word, pulled her off the counter and wrapped her legs around his waist, carrying her toward the door.

As they passed the window they both looked out and noticed a few figures in the apartments across the street watching them. Keely felt a blush warm her cheeks and she buried her face in the curve of his neck.

Rafe chuckled softly. "I think we gave them a good show, don't you?"

He took her to the bedroom and slowly undressed her in front of windows that overlooked the harbor. When he'd stripped off his own clothes, he joined her in bed and they made love, slowly, gently, until they both shared their release, two bodies arching against each other, two strangers giving in to an attraction that couldn't be denied anymore.

HOURS LATER, they were still awake, talking softly across a pillow. Rafe toyed with the necklace she always wore, rubbing the pendant between his fingers as he stared into her golden-green eyes. He was surprised at how easy it was to open his soul to her.

They talked about everything and nothing, the subject of their conversation of no consequence. It was enough just to listen to the sound of her voice, to see her smile at a joke or to hear her laugh. "So tell me, Keely McClain. What's the real reason you came to Boston?"

She pushed up on her elbow, reaching over to brush a lock of hair from his eyes. "I told you. I wanted a new start."

"Is that all?"

"No," Keely said. "There is another reason, but I'm not sure I should talk about it."

"Secrets should be nothing after what we just shared," Rafe teased.

She hesitated for a moment. "Well, it would be nice to talk to someone about it."

He had wanted to believe that she'd come back to see him, but that was wishful thinking. Now that he knew the reason she'd given him earlier was false, his curiosity was piqued. "Tell me."

"I'm here to find my real family."

"Your family? Aren't they in New York?"

"My mother is. But my father and my brothers are here in Boston. My parents separated when I was just a baby and I never knew my father or my siblings. We're kind of alike that way. We both lost our fathers early on."

But Keely's father was still alive. And he hadn't bothered to go into the truth behind his own father's death.

"So you're working at the bar until you find them?"

"Oh, no, I've already found them," Keely said. "I just haven't introduced myself yet. That's why I'm working at the bar." She rubbed a hand over her eyes and then yawned into her palm.

Rafe started to get an uneasy feeling in the pit of his stomach. "You're working at Quinn's Pub."

Keely nodded and nestled into his body. She closed her eyes and sighed softly. "Seamus Quinn is my father. And his sons are my brothers."

Rafe froze, afraid she might sense his reaction. He kept his voice quiet and indifferent. "So your name isn't Keely McClain. It's Keely Quinn."

"Umm. Keely Quinn," she murmured drowsily.

He closed his eyes and cursed inwardly, rage surging up inside of him. Christ, this couldn't be happening to him. He'd been planning his revenge for months and everything had been set in motion just a few days ago. He couldn't stop now. Seamus Quinn had murdered his father and he'd have to pay!

But Seamus wouldn't be the only one to pay. Keely would barely meet her father before he'd be carted off to prison where he'd spend the rest of his life. Rafe turned to gaze into her face. She'd fallen asleep, her lashes dark against her pale skin, her lips still swollen from his kisses.

He'd kept the details of his father's death from her for a reason—he didn't want her to hear the anger in his voice, to catch a glimpse of his dark purpose. But how could he possibly continue, all the while knowing how she'd feel once she learned the truth? But wasn't that all part of the plan, for the Quinns to know exactly who had done this to their family and why?

Keely was a Quinn. And, with the exception of his mother, she was also the first woman he'd ever cared about. Rafe carefully slipped out of bed and walked to the windows. Streetlights still twinkled around Boston Harbor as the deep-blue sky gave way to blazing orange and pink. He pressed his palms against the cold glass as he tried to bring order to the chaos raging in his head.

He had thought finding Keely again had been an incredible stroke of luck. But now, after her rather startling revelation, Rafe could only wonder if falling into bed with her was poetic justice. He'd just made love to the daughter of his father's killer. And now he felt himself wavering in his resolve to destroy Seamus Quinn.

He'd lived with this anger for so long, his need to set things right consuming his life lately. How could he put it aside? The truth had to be told and the guilty had to pay. But that had been easy to justify when Seamus was nothing more than the shadowy figure behind Sam Kendrick's death. Now, he was a father with a daughter who wanted nothing more than a future with him.

Even if Rafe wanted to stop it all, he couldn't do it without making it look like he was covering up a crime. And it wasn't as if he'd fabricated evidence. Everything he was doing was legal and aboveboard. He had a witness who had a story to tell. So why not leave it up to the law? If Seamus wasn't responsible, then he'd be exonerated. If he was, then he'd serve his time.

Rafe turned and looked at Keely, curled up in his bed, the sheets twisted around her slender body. She looked so naive, so innocent, her hand splayed over his pillow—such a stark contrast to the woman who had driven him mad with lust just hours before. He'd come to crave that contrast, the sexy siren trapped inside an innocent's body.

But how much longer could she possibly want him? How much time did he have to make her want him more than she wanted her own family?

CHAPTER SIX

KEELY WOKE UP slowly, stretching beneath the fine cotton sheets and squinting against the bright morning light. She saw the outline of a tall, broad-shouldered figure standing at the window and smiled. Rafe. As her eyes adjusted to the light, he came into focus. He was naked, his smooth skin burnished by the glare of the sun.

Keely snuggled into her pillow and relished the chance to appreciate his body—the sculpted arms and muscular back, the narrow waist, long legs, a study in masculine perfection. He seemed to wear that perfection in such a casual way, as if he didn't know—or didn't care—about the effect his body had on a woman's libido.

Keely ran her hands through her tangled hair. "Good morning."

He turned around, startled by her voice. "Good morning. Did you sleep well?"

Keely sat up and stretched her arms over her head, the sheet dropping away from her breasts. But she made no move to cover up. With him, she felt more comfortable naked, more aware of her sexuality and the power it gave her. "Fine. How about you?"

"Great," Rafe said.

Her gaze wandered down his body, following the fine dusting of hair that began at his collarbone and ended below his belly. A tiny shiver raced through her as she thought of him in full arousal. "You look so handsome standing there in that light. If I had some paper, I'd draw you just like that."

"You draw?"

Keely nodded. Though they knew each other's bodies by heart, knew exactly how to make the other moan with pleasure, they were still learning the basics. She felt as if she knew him intimately, yet didn't really know him at all. "I have an art degree. I used to paint. But I really liked sculpting more. I could do you in bronze."

"That might be interesting."

"I always enjoyed drawing nudes," she continued. "For a nice Catholic girl who went to an all-girls high school, art school drawing class was an eye-opening experience. I'd only been with one boy and I'd never actually seen, you know…the equipment."

His eyebrow arched. "And why was that?"

"We were afraid to turn on the lights. Lord, I wasn't sure what I'd see, but I knew I'd probably be struck blind from seeing it." Keely grinned and covered her eyes. "Maybe you better put some clothes on. I've grown rather fond of my eyesight."

Instead, Rafe climbed back into bed, stretching out beside her and pulling her against his body, becoming aroused almost immediately. His expression was se-

rious, his gaze intense. "Who are you, Keely Mc-
Clain? And why are you doing these things to me?"

Keely stared at him. He was in a strange mood this
morning, quiet and reserved, as if he had something
on his mind. "*What* am I doing to you, Rafe?"

"I'm not sure. But it feels pretty good."

Keely gently stroked his face, her fingertips running over the stubble on his jawline. "I don't know
what this is, Rafe. I don't know if it will end tomorrow or if it will last forever. So maybe we should just
let it happen and see where it goes. And if it doesn't
work, no regrets. On either side."

"That sounds like a good plan," Rafe said. Suddenly, he grabbed her around the waist and pulled her
beneath him. "Let's take a trip. It's Christmas—we
should be doing something special. We can leave today. We'll buy a couple of tickets to somewhere and
just take off. We can go to Hawaii or Paris or London.
You choose. Someplace far away from here."

His offer sounded so tempting. A week in a hotel
room with Rafe Kendrick was every woman's fantasy. "I can't," Keely said. "I have to work. The pub
opens at five tonight and I'm scheduled. I signed up
to work around Christmas because I wanted to be
with my family."

"Come on," Rafe said. "How could you possibly
choose that smoky, smelly pub over a pristine beach
on Maui? Or a sidewalk café in Paris? Or a cozy hotel
room in London? What's to think about?"

"You know why I have to stay," she said. "I need
to tell my family who I am. And I need to find just

the right time to do that. And I won't find it if I'm sunning myself on some beach in Hawaii.''

Rafe pressed his forehead against hers. ''I'm not sure I want to let you go. The last time I did, you disappeared.''

She reached up and touched his lips with her fingertips. ''Why don't I come back here tonight after work and we'll have a late dinner? This time I'll cook.''

''Are you a good cook?''

''Better than you,'' she teased. ''You lack focus. That's what it takes to make a good omelette. You can't get distracted by more…exotic tastes.''

''And what should we do until it's time for you to go to work?'' he asked, nuzzling her neck.

''You know what would be fun? Let's get up and get dressed and go to church. It's Christmas morning. I always go to Christmas services. And I missed midnight mass last night.''

''You really want to go to church?''

''After all the sinning we did last night, I think we should. We can stop at my place and I can change. And after church we'll go for coffee. And you know what else I'd like to do? I'd like to go ice-skating. Or maybe take a carriage ride. Or we could go for a nice long walk and window-shop. That would be the perfect Christmas.''

''All right,'' Rafe said grudgingly. ''But first I want the perfect shower. Care to join me?''

Keely smiled. ''I will in a minute. I really need to call my mother. Can I use the phone?''

Rafe kissed her on the tip of her nose, then crawled out of bed. "I'll be waiting for you."

He walked toward the bathroom while Keely stayed in bed and admired the view. When she heard him turn on the shower, she rolled over and grabbed the phone from the bedside table, then punched in her mother's phone number. Fiona picked up after two rings.

"Hi, Ma. Merry Christmas."

"Merry Christmas, sweetheart. I've been worried about you. You didn't call last night. I thought maybe you'd decided to come home after all. I tried your room at the bed-and-breakfast last night at nine, but they said you hadn't returned. I was afraid to call them after ten. I didn't want to disturb them so late at night. Are you all right?"

"I'm fine."

"Did you go to midnight mass?"

"No, but I'm going to church this morning with a friend."

"You have a friend in Boston?"

"Yes. Just one. But he's very nice."

"He?"

"I have news," Keely said, deftly changing the subject. "Brendan is engaged. He brought her to the pub last night and made the announcement. Her name is Amy Aldrich and she seems so nice, very pretty. And they look so happy together. My father didn't seem too pleased, but everyone else was. I wish you could have been there, Ma. With Conor married and the other two engaged, you should have grandchildren before too long.''

Her mother was silent for a long time before she spoke. ''When are you coming home?''

''Maybe a couple of weeks. I really plan to tell them soon. And I'm pretty sure they'll be all right with it. They're all so sweet to me, Ma. I wish you could know them. Maybe next Christmas, we can all be together.''

''Maybe,'' Fiona said.

''Keely! Get your pretty little ass in here!''

Keely winced, but luckily her mother hadn't heard the command. ''I have to go. I'm working tonight at five, so I'll call you from the pub when I get a chance. Maybe I'll get one of the boys to say hello.''

''Oh, Keely, I would love that,'' her mother said, tears evident in her voice. ''I—I'll talk to you later. Merry Christmas, darling.''

''Bye, Ma.'' Keely returned the phone to the beside table. She sighed softly, then rubbed the sleep out of her eyes.

''Keely!''

With a giggle, she jumped out of bed and padded to the bathroom. Like the kitchen, it was a marvel of technology, with a huge whirlpool tub and a shower stall made for two. She peered around the corner of the shower's glass-block wall and found a naked Rafe, fully aroused, his body slick with soap and water. ''You know, I'm really not a shower girl. I prefer baths.''

Rafe took a step toward her. His hand shot out and

grabbed her arm. He yanked her into the shower and pulled her beneath the rushing water, then kissed her thoroughly.

"I'm going to teach you to love showers," he said with a low growl.

RAFE SAT on the park bench on Boston Common, his cashmere overcoat open to the warmth of the noonday sun. He watched the skaters glide around in a circle on Frog Pond, remembering Christmas Day and the time he'd spent skating with Keely. If someone had told him he'd pass an afternoon wobbling around a frozen pond on skates, he would have called them a fool. But he'd actually had fun. By the end of the day, he had even become a passable skater.

He and Keely had shared so much in the past five days. But, above all, everything they'd done had been fun—from the uninhibited sex to the quiet dinners over a bottle of wine to their walks along the Charles. Rafe had never put much stock in "fun," but he had to admit that it added a new dimension to his life. He'd smiled more in the past week than he had in the entire year. In the annals of his affairs with women, Rafe knew that Keely would rank as his favorite. She was sweet and understanding out of bed, and wild and passionate between the sheets. And there was something about that contrast that he found completely captivating. Other women had tried to cultivate such an image, but with Keely it was real.

Still, a dark cloud continued to hang over them. Keely wasn't just any woman he'd brought to his bed—she was a Quinn. The daughter of his father's murderer. And he should be spending his time working up a decent case of disgust for his behavior with her, instead of wondering what new adventure they'd share in his bedroom that night.

So he enjoyed her body. Like she'd said, they had no claims on each other, no strings. It was purely a sexual thing and, before long, the desire would fade and they'd both move on.

"You have nothing to feel guilty about," he muttered to himself. Rafe cursed softly. He had to watch himself. There were times when he was starting to feel like a first-class sap, thinking about Keely at all hours, wondering what she was doing, who she was talking to, whether she was thinking about him. Though Rafe was quite certain he wasn't in love, he still couldn't define exactly what he was feeling. He liked Keely. She was beautiful and sexy and intriguing and he enjoyed spending time with her.

Hell, he'd always had a one-month maximum with women, averaging two dates a week and five decent nights in bed before boredom set in. He quickly tallied up his time with Keely and was surprised to find that he'd already surpassed his normal mark.

"Hey! Are you Sam Kendrick's kid?"

Rafe looked up, startled out of his thoughts. An older man stood in front of him wearing a battered jacket and faded blue jeans. Time had not been kind to Ken Yaeger. His face was deeply lined and his thinning hair was unkempt and his teeth were badly in need of a dentist. "I am."

Yaeger flopped down next to him on the bench and rubbed his hands together. "Why the hell did we have to meet here? This town is filled with heated taverns and decent whiskey. I spent enough of my life out in the cold—I don't need to spend more." He reached inside of his jacket pocket and pulled out a flask, then offered it to Rafe. "Care for a nip?"

Rafe pushed the flask away, shaking his head. "How did it go?"

Yaeger shrugged. "They were pretty interested in what I had to say. Asked why I was coming forward and I gave them some shit about my conscience. I wrote it all down for them and they told me they'd be calling me. They gotta figure out who's in charge."

"You didn't go in there drunk, did you?"

"What difference does it make? It doesn't change the truth."

"I want to hear it," Rafe demanded. "The whole story. Exactly the way you told it to the police."

Yaeger gathered his thoughts for a moment, took another swig from the flask, then cleared his throat. "Well, ya see, I'd been working on the crew of the *Mighty Quinn* for about three years. Seamus was looking for a sixth to make one last run out to the Grand Banks before the winter set in. Sam Kendrick and I knew each other from Gloucester and I knew he was looking for work. The boat he usually fished from didn't make late-season runs. And since your ma was...well, you know...sickly, Sam wasn't planning to head south that winter. So he signed on with

Seamus Quinn for one run.'' Yaeger paused and gave Rafe a toothless smile. ''Your dad was a good guy. He could have captained his own boat if he'd had the scratch to buy a rig.''

''He was planning to buy a boat,'' Rafe said. ''He and my mother were saving.''

''We'd been out for two weeks and the hold was about half-full. Then the weather reports started coming in. Seamus wanted to ride out the storm and continue fishing. Your dad wanted to head in. But Seamus's word was final. Still, Sam kept at him and the weather kept getting worse and pretty soon everyone wanted to go in. Something felt bad about this run and we all knew if we didn't get off the water, we'd end up under it. It spooked us. Pretty soon, it was us against Seamus.''

''A mutiny?'' Rafe asked.

''About as close as you could come. Your dad was out on deck, securing all the gear so the waves wouldn't wash it away. I was up in the wheelhouse. Seamus went out and they started yelling at each other. Sam threw a punch and caught Seamus on the chin. Seamus hit Sam in the stomach. Sam threw another cross and lost his balance on the slippery deck. Then Seamus went for him. He shoved him hard and Sam went over the side. It was black out and the storm was coming up fast. We tried to find him, but by the time we did, it was too late. That water's so cold. A guy can only last maybe ten, fifteen minutes before he's a goner.'' Yaeger shuddered, then took another swallow from the flask. ''I remember what he looked like when we finally found him and fished him out. That image just doesn't leave a guy.''

Rafe stared down at his hands, feeling anger surge up inside him, and his determination doubled. Seamus Quinn was going to pay. ''Why didn't you tell the truth back then?''

''Seamus convinced us to make it appear as if he got pulled over by the line. We tore up his slicker a little bit to make it look like that's what got caught. That way he would have been killed while he was working and your ma could collect more insurance. If Sam was even partially to blame for his own death, she'd get less. And he was the one who threw the first punch. He was the one talking mutiny.''

''So Seamus covered up his part in a murder. And he committed insurance fraud as well.''

''I s'pose you could say that. Yeah, I'd say that. Fraud.''

''Was there any investigation?''

''Fishing is a dangerous profession. That's a fact everyone accepts. And all the guys on the boat were straight with the story, so that was the end of it. I kept my mouth shut and collected my pay.''

''Is there anyone else who can back up this story?''

''The cops asked me that. Walt McGill died a few years back. Johnny Sayers went down with the *Katie Jean* in 1981. And the last I heard, Lee Franklin was working a charter business somewhere in the Florida Keys. But that was ten years ago. He'd back up my story though. Seamus was the one who pushed your father overboard that night.'' Yaeger paused and took another sip from the flask. "So I did my part. What am I going to get for telling my story?"

"What do you expect?"

"Well, I'm not doin' this for my health. I've got expenses."

"I thought you wanted to help my mother."

"Hey, that don't pay the rent."

Rafe reached in his pocket and pulled out his wallet. He withdrew all the cash he carried and handed it to Yaeger. "That's to cover your expenses for coming here. And once Quinn is in jail, then there'll be more to get you home. And more after you testify. But let me make one thing clear. I'm not paying for your testimony. I'm just covering your expenses because you're a friend of the family. And if you bring my name into this, the cash flow stops."

Yaeger gave him a grudging nod, then stood and held out his hand. "It's nice doin' business with you."

Rafe didn't return the gesture. Instead, he turned his attention back to the skaters. When Yaeger finally stumbled off, Rafe let out a tightly held breath. He was doing the right thing. He shouldn't have to convince himself of that fact anymore. Then why the hell was he so uneasy? Something about his plan didn't seem right.

"Keely," he muttered. This was all her damn fault. If she hadn't stumbled into his life and turned everything upside down, he wouldn't have any doubts about ruining Seamus Quinn for good.

All his life, he'd been focused on success, every

move calculated to make more money and acquire greater power. He'd thought that money and power would fill the empty spaces in his soul. And when it didn't, he'd decided those spaces could be filled by avenging his father's death. Now, if that didn't work, he'd have to look elsewhere. But he knew that surrendering power to Keely would never be the solution.

If he allowed himself to feel something for her, then she gained the advantage, she held all the cards. He'd change his life for her and, sooner or later, she'd walk away. His mother's psychiatrists might say that his father's death had instilled these fears in him, fears of abandonment. They might also say that, until he faced these issues, he'd never have a normal relationship with a woman.

But that's what he was doing with his campaign against Seamus Quinn—he was facing his issues and putting his life in order. And if Keely was an innocent bystander who got caught in the crossfire, then that was her problem, not his. The truth would set them all free.

Rafe stood up and took a last look at Frog Pond, pushing aside any thoughts of Keely Quinn. His course had been set. This afternoon, he'd drop her off at work and call an end to it. There was no going back. Losing an incredible bedmate was a consequence he'd have to live with.

Rafe just hoped it wouldn't take too long to find someone to replace her.

"PICK ME UP after work." Keely leaned over and kissed Rafe on the cheek. "I'll be done at six. We can go out and get something to eat and then catch a movie." She laughed softly. "Don't we sound like the ordinary couple? Maybe you should leave town without telling me. Or maybe when I get to your place tonight I should find a woman in your bed. That would shake things up, don't you think?"

Rafe ignored her teasing, his expression grim. He'd been in a dark mood since they'd gotten out of bed that morning. Keely couldn't help but wonder if he was tiring of their relationship already. She knew there was every chance that it would happen sooner or later, but she had hoped for later.

This was the risk she took, giving herself completely to him, with no sense of his feelings toward her. Yes, the sex had been good. It had progressed from incredible to earth-shattering and it didn't show signs of letting up anytime soon. Though Keely had enjoyed their time together, she'd also kept her heart well protected. She had refused to allow herself any fantasies of a future with Rafe and, to her surprise, it had worked.

"If you'd rather not do anything tonight, that's fine, too," Keely offered. "I could probably use a full night's sleep. And I have to do some laundry and run errands. I could take a cab home."

"When are you going to tell them?" Rafe asked as he stared out the window.

"I'm not sure. Maybe today, if the time is right."

"You can't put it off forever."

"This is my problem and my decision," Keely said, irritated at his interference. "I'll decide when I decide." She paused. "You know, maybe it would be better if I stayed at my place tonight. I'm paying for a room at the bed-and-breakfast and I haven't been there for almost a week."

"Do what you want," Rafe said.

"Then I will." Keely stepped out of the car and slammed the door behind her. She circled around the front then looked both ways before starting across the street. She turned when she heard Rafe get out of the car and, an instant later, he'd grabbed her arm and yanked her into his embrace.

He kissed her, hard and deep, refusing to allow her a chance to breathe. And when he finally released her, he smiled tightly. "I'll pick you up after work." With that, he turned around and got back into the car. When the engine roared to life, Keely stepped back. She watched him drive off down the street, her mind whirling with both the aftereffects of his kiss and overwhelming confusion.

There were times when she didn't understand Rafe Kendrick at all. Maybe that's what she found so attractive about him, that bad boy beneath the expensive Italian suits. That mercurial man who kept her guessing. She was living on the edge, never knowing what would happen next and she liked it.

Keely ran up the steps to the pub, turning her mind to thoughts of her family. Maybe Rafe was right. Maybe it was time to tell Seamus. She knew her father a bit better now and she was almost sure that he'd take the news well. "I'm going to tell him. I have fifteen minutes before the pub opens and by the time the first customer walks in, Seamus Quinn is going to have a daughter." She pulled the door open and walked inside.

Keely knew something was wrong the moment she saw her family gathered at the end of the bar. They were standing in a tight circle, their heads bent in an intense discussion. A sliver of fear shot through her when she saw the serious expressions on their faces. She searched the bar for Seamus, and when she didn't see him, her fear increased. Had something happened to him? Was he ill? She'd just assumed he'd be around when she was ready to tell him, but he wasn't a young man anymore.

She hung her jacket on the rack near the door, then stowed her purse behind the bar. Her brothers were all talking in heated tones and didn't notice her arrival. She strained to hear what they were saying, moving closer and closer. When Liam finally broke away from the group, she caught his eye. He walked to the end of the bar. "Is everything all right?" Keely asked, her heart slamming in her chest.

Liam turned back to look at his brothers, then raked his hands through his hair. His face was tinged with exhaustion and his brow furrowed with worry. "No," he said.

"What is it? Is it Seamus? Is he sick?"

"No," Liam repeated. "I mean, he's not sick. It's just—" He paused, obviously trying to decide what he would tell her. "He's in trouble. The cops came and got him early this morning and they're holding him for questioning.''

Keely gasped. "For what?"

He shook his head. "Nothing. You don't have to worry about it. It'll all get sorted out. But there's something else. Some bad news."

"Seamus in jail isn't bad news?" Keely asked.

"We had an unscheduled visit from the building inspector the other day and he found asbestos on some of the heating pipes. He's shutting us down until it's removed. With the bar closed down, my father won't be able to meet the mortgage. He barely does now and we all work for free. If the bank calls the mortgage in, he'll lose the pub."

"I can't believe this."

"Conor doesn't think this is all happening by chance," Liam said, lowering his voice so his brothers couldn't hear. "He thinks someone is out to get our da. We're just trying to figure out what to do. For now, I don't think we can keep you on."

"I'll work for tips," Keely said.

"It's not that. It's going to take at least a week to get workmen here and a few more weeks to complete the job and then we have to wait for a reinspection and that could take a week, maybe two. We've got to move everything out and move it all back in again. The bar could be closed for a month."

"I could help," Keely offered. A whole month without an excuse to see her father and brothers. This couldn't be happening. She had to find a way to stay in touch. Maybe she should tell them right now.

Liam shook his head. "No, this a family thing.
We'll deal with it. We're not going to open today,
but you can stay for your shift and help clean up, then
collect your pay. Sean will get you cash from the till.
We've got your phone number so when things get
straightened away, we'll call you. But we won't be
upset if you have to take another job. A month is a
long time to go without a paycheck." He wiped his
hands on a bar towel. "So, I guess that's it."

"Don't worry," Keely said. "Everything will be
all right. Why don't you go back to your brothers. I'll
wash these glasses and dust the bottles on the back
bar."

He reached out and gave her arm a squeeze.
"Thanks. You're sweet."

She waited until he rejoined his brothers before
grabbing Rafe's business card out of her purse. Rafe
would know what to do. He probably knew hundreds
of good lawyers. And a few contractors who could
get the job done in a few days rather than weeks. And
a guy like Rafe didn't get to where he was without
knowing a few people in the building inspector's office. He probably even knew the mayor. Keely put
the card back in her purse. It would be better to talk
to him about this in person. If there was any convincing to be done she'd be in a better…position.

She walked over to the sink beneath the bar and
grabbed a towel, then washed a glass and wiped it
dry. She was family and she was going to make a
contribution to solving this problem. As soon as she
finished a few tasks, she'd ask to leave, then go di-

rectly to Rafe's office to solicit his help. Until then, she'd pick up as much as she could about why her father had been taken into custody.

"None of us knows what happened on that boat," she overheard Brendan say. "And Da doesn't seem to be talking. Conor, you need to take care of the legal end of this. This is probably going to be a federal investigation, but they should be able to tell you something. I'll take care of what's going on with the pub. I've got plenty of cash to cover the mortgage and the contractor costs so we don't have to worry about that."

"You can count on me to help there," Dylan said.

"Me, too," Conor added.

"Brian, you've got some friends down at city hall, why don't you see if we can move that building inspector along. I don't think we can afford to be shut down for more than a few weeks."

"What about Da?" Sean asked. "What if he ends up being charged with murder?"

Keely's heart froze and a tiny cry slipped from her lips. She tried to keep her expression bland as she worked harder at washing the glasses, determined to cover her distress. Murder? Her father was being questioned about a murder?

"Did he say anything about this Kendrick guy?" Conor asked. "I got a look at the statement. This witness claims that Kendrick died on the *Mighty Quinn* and Da was responsible. There was some kind of fight and Kendrick went overboard. Da swears it didn't happen that way."

For a long moment, Keely didn't breathe. She must have misheard. They didn't really say the name Kendrick, did they?

Brian leaned forward. "Do we know anything about this guy's family?"

"Sam Kendrick had a wife and a kid. His widow was Lila and I don't know about the kid. I guess after he died there was some insurance settlement. But as far as I can tell, there was no investigation. I'm wondering if the family knows anything about this witness coming forward. Maybe we should contact them?"

Keely felt her body go numb all the way to the tips of her fingers. The glass she was holding slipped from her hand and smashed on the floor at her feet. Her brothers all turned to look at her and, with trembling hands, she hurried to pick up the pieces. But in her haste, she cut her palm with a shard of glass.

In an instant, Dylan had hopped over the bar and grabbed her hand. "Here," he said, pulling her toward the sink.

"I—I'm sorry. It just slipped. I didn't mean to—"

"Never mind," Dylan said as he rinsed the blood from her hand. He grabbed a clean towel and then pressed it to the cut. "There. It doesn't look deep. It should stop bleeding soon." He pulled a first aid kit from a nearby drawer and handed her a bandage.

The pain was dulled by the echo of the name in her head. Kendrick. Seamus was in jail because the police thought he murdered Sam Kendrick. And Sam Kendrick had been married to Lila Kendrick, the very woman she met on Christmas Eve. That meant that her father was suspected of killing Rafe's father.

A wave of nausea washed over her. "I—I'll just go take care of this in the ladies' room," she murmured as she rushed past him and through the bar.

When she reached the privacy of the bathroom, she leaned back against the door and swallowed hard, fighting the urge to throw up. What was she supposed to do with this news? And how could she tell Rafe?

A sudden realization struck her like a slap to the face. Maybe Rafe already knew. But if he suspected her father of murder, then why hadn't he said something that night when she'd told him her reasons for coming to Boston? Her mind spun back to that moment and Keely tried to remember his reaction. Rafe had been a bit distant at times since then, but she'd written that off as a bad mood.

For all she knew, Rafe had no idea of the connection between his father's death and the Quinn family. She drew a ragged breath. But what if he did know? Another realization hit her. Keely groaned softly and covered her mouth with her hand. Had Rafe known who she was all along? Even from that very first night on the street in front of the pub? Was their meeting a part of some plan?

"No," she murmured. She was reading way too much into the situation. She pressed the heels of her hands to her temples. The only way she'd know the truth was to confront Rafe.

Keely turned on the tap and splashed cold water on her face, then dabbed it dry with a paper towel. Before she walked out the door, she ran her fingers through her hair and pasted a smile on her face.

Her brothers were still in the same spot, still involved in their discussion, when she walked back behind the bar. Sean joined her and opened the cash register. "Liam explained to you what is going on, right? Rather than wait for your paycheck, I'll just pay you in cash. I'm sorry we can't keep you on, Keely. You were a good waitress."

"That's all right. I understand. You all seem so worried—I wish there was something I could do."

"It'll be fine," he replied. "It's just a family thing."

Tears of frustration pressed at the corners of her eyes and she fought them back. She was tired of hearing it was a family thing! *She* was family and *she* wanted to help. But with all that had happened to them today, she couldn't possibly reveal the news now.

Maybe she didn't deserve to be a part of the Quinn family. After all, she'd been sleeping with Rafe Kendrick. But was Rafe the enemy? Did he have anything to do with this whole thing? God, she couldn't think! Her mind was a mess of doubt and speculation. "I think I'm going to go home, if that's all right with you."

"No problem," Sean replied. "Not much to do around here." He handed her the cash and she tucked it in her pocket. "Good luck with everything, Keely."

"Thanks. Good luck to you. And give Seamus my best wishes." Her voiced trembled slightly and when she turned to grab her purse and jacket, she had to bite her lip to keep from crying.

"Bye, Keely," Liam shouted. The rest of her brothers added their farewells, and she turned and gave them a wave, then opened the door. When she reached the street, Keely yanked her jacket more tightly around her to still the tremors that racked her body.

The cold winter air cleared her head and she tried to sort out all she'd heard. But her initial suspicion kept coming back to plague her. Rafe had to be involved. Why had he been hanging out at the pub? And why, during all of their discussions, hadn't he told her about his father? Why was that such a big secret?

Keely glanced up and down the street, wondering how to get back to the bed-and-breakfast. There had to be a bus stop or a subway stop close by. She'd just have to walk around until she found one. And while she searched, she'd decide exactly how to handle her next encounter with Rafe.

One thing she did know—Keely Quinn wouldn't be falling into bed with Rafe Kendrick anytime soon.

CHAPTER SEVEN

KEELY SAT in the dark living room of Rafe's apartment, staring at an elaborate flower arrangement on the cherry coffee table in front of her. The doorman had happily let her in as he'd done a number of times since Christmas Eve. She shivered, then rubbed her arms through the sleeves of her jacket, trying to conquer the apprehension she felt.

The moment he walked in the door, Keely knew she had to confront him, so determined was she to have an explanation for his deceit. As she waited, she had thought about opening a bottle of wine, but then decided against it, certain that she'd need all her wits about her. Besides, with the level of her anger, the wine bottle could be used as a weapon.

The words were difficult to plan. She only knew how she felt—betrayed, confused, hurt. Funny, she'd thought she was immune to those emotions. If she didn't allow herself to fall in love with Rafe, then he couldn't possibly hurt her. So what did this mean? Was she in love with him or had the shock of the situation simply overwhelmed her?

The sound of his key in the lock startled her out of her thoughts. She didn't speak the moment he walked in, choosing instead to observe him from the shadows. He looked tired and tense as he threw his keys on a table and dropped his briefcase on the floor. And try as she might, she couldn't see him as the enemy. When he reached out for the light switch, Keely held her breath.

Rafe saw her immediately. "Keely! Christ, what are you doing here?"

"Where did you expect me to be?"

"I—I thought you were going to spend the night at your place. Shouldn't you be at work?"

She swallowed hard, unsure if she'd even be able to form a coherent sentence. "The pub's been closed. Does that come as a surprise to you?"

"What the hell are you talking about?" He raked his hand through his hair, then slowly approached. "Are you angry about something?"

"Should I be?"

"Damn it, Keely, if you're going to answer every question I pose with another question, we'll just quit talking. But if you have a problem, tell me what it is and we'll discuss it. I'm not going to play games with you."

She laughed derisively. "Oh, *you're* not going to play games? Tell me, what have you been doing from the moment we met? No, don't answer that. First, tell me, what were you doing at Quinn's the night we met?" She paused for a long moment, long enough for her to see the answer in his eyes. "You did this, didn't you? All this trouble for Seamus. You're the one who made it happen."

"Keely, I—"

Her heart ached a little more with every word she said. Suspecting him of such an act was one thing, but seeing the confirmation of it in his eyes was another. "You think Seamus had something to do with your father's death. I heard my brothers talking about it and when they mentioned your name—Kendrick—I couldn't believe it. But then it all fell into place. After all, what would a sophisticated, wealthy downtown guy like you be doing in a working-class pub in South Boston? Unless you had some reason for hanging out there."

He grabbed her hand and held on to it so tightly that she couldn't pull it away. "Just listen for a few seconds and I'll explain."

Keely jumped up from beside him, tearing her fingers from his grasp. "Tell me you didn't have anything to do with calling down the cops on my father. Tell me you didn't do something to bring the building inspectors out to the pub." She clutched her fists at her side, fighting the urge to punch him. "Tell me."

Rafe slowly leaned back into the sofa. "I can't," he murmured. "I won't. Everything you suspect is true. I found the witness against Seamus Quinn and I convinced him to go to the authorities. I called a friend I have in the inspector's office and asked him to take a look at Quinn's Pub. And when Seamus tries to find an asbestos contractor to take care of his problem, he won't find a single contractor in the greater Boston area who will take the job. Oh, and I now hold the mortgage on the pub, so if he defaults, the place belongs to me.''

His cavalier attitude was like a punch to the stomach, stealing the breath from her lungs and making it impossible to draw another. She opened her mouth, but no words would come. How could the man she'd been so intimate with now be so hateful?

"Before you tell me how much you detest me, maybe you should consider one point, Keely. What if it's true? What if your father really is responsible for the death of my father?''

"It—it can't be true," she said, her voice trembling.

"I think it is. All the evidence points that way, Keely.''

She walked to the window, then braced her hands on the sill, gripping it with white knuckles. "What about me? Was I all a part of this scheme? Were you going to use me against my own family?''

Rafe stood up, but she backed away as he approached, unwilling to allow him to touch her again. "That night in front of the pub, I didn't know who you were. Imagine my surprise when you told me you were really a Quinn.''

"And you didn't have any second thoughts about what you were doing? Even after you knew I was Seamus's daughter?''

"Why would I?''

Keely spun on him, then made to slap him across the face. But he caught her hand just in time and she slowly let it drop. "No, I guess you wouldn't,'' she murmured. "I was just the woman you were sleeping with. Well, that's the end of it then. You've chosen your side and I've chosen mine." She drew a ragged breath. "You're not going to win, you know. I'll do everything I can to make sure you don't hurt my family."

"That's not going to happen."

His voice was so coldly confident it sent a shiver down her spine. "Try me," Keely dared.

With a low curse, Rafe stepped forward and grabbed her by the arm, then pulled her toward the door. At first she thought he simply meant to throw her out of his apartment. But then he picked up his keys on the way out and punched the button for the elevator. No, he meant to embarrass her by throwing her out on the street.

"Let go of me," Keely demanded.

"No," Rafe said. The elevator descended, but it didn't stop in the lobby of his building. Instead, it went down to the parking level. "You and I are going to talk this out. And after you hear my side of the story, you're welcome to go running to the Quinns. But you are going to listen."

Twisting and turning, she tried to pull out of his grasp. "I don't want to listen to anything you have to say. It's all lies." But as she fought him, Keely secretly prayed that he did have an explanation for his behavior. Or that somehow, between the two of them, they'd figure out that this was all just a big misunderstanding.

He yanked open the car door. "Get in."

"No," she muttered.

"Get in," he repeated, his frustration tightly checked.

"If you want to talk, we can talk right here."

"No, we can't." He paused. "I need to show you something." He took her arm and gently pushed her into the car. Keely knew she should have fought him, knew that he'd suddenly become the enemy. But she also knew Rafe and he wasn't the kind of man to accuse someone of murder lightly. Did he have some kind of proof to show her?

Keely reluctantly slid into the passenger seat. She wasn't abandoning her family by going with him. She simply needed to know all the facts. But even that reassurance didn't make her feel any better. In truth, it made her ashamed. Her feelings for Rafe had overwhelmed her loyalty for her family. She was treading on thin ice and if she wasn't careful, she'd fall through.

"Where are we going?" she asked as Rafe got inside.

"Someplace where we can talk." He turned the ignition, then locked all the doors with a flick of a button. A few minutes later, they were out on the street, speeding through late-afternoon traffic. But when Rafe steered the car onto the northbound interstate, Keely frowned. "Where are you taking me?" she demanded.

He didn't answer her this time. Instead, he punched a number into his car phone, then picked it up. "Hi, it's Rafe. I'm on my way up to Aspen Lake. Make sure the kitchen is stocked and the heat is turned on. We'll be staying for a few days at the least.'' Rafe hung up the phone, then turned his full attention back to the road.

Keely's stomach tightened. She'd never seen Rafe in such a black mood, so filled with anger he was ready to explode. ''Where the hell is Aspen Lake?''

''It's in Vermont,'' Rafe replied.

''Vermont?'' she cried. ''*Vermont?* I don't want to go to Vermont.''

''I don't care. That's where we're going.'' His voice was cold and emotionless.

''You don't have anything to show me, do you? You lied to me to get me in this car.''

''You wouldn't have gotten in if I hadn't.''

''Are you kidnapping me? Kidnapping is against the law. If I don't want to go to Vermont, then this is kidnapping. I could have you arrested.''

Rafe shrugged. ''I suppose you could. But then, since I'm kidnapping you, I'm not exactly going to let you run to the police.''

Keely crossed her arms over her chest. ''Take me back to Boston right now.''

''No.''

She reached out and grabbed the wheel and the car swerved wildly. Rafe cursed as he brought it back under control, along with his temper. ''You and I are going to Vermont. Now you can either waste the next three hours shouting at me or trying to kill us both, or you can enjoy the ride. I'd prefer to enjoy the ride.'' He reached out and pushed a CD into the player. The sound of classical music filled the car.

Just as quickly, Keely reached out and shut it off. ''What do you think you're going to accomplish with this?''

''I don't know yet.''

''You can talk at me all you want and it's not going to change my mind. I'm still not going to believe my father capable of murder. Or do you think you'll gain an advantage by kidnapping me, that my family will somehow suffer because of it?''

Rafe glanced her way, then chuckled. ''Your family doesn't know you exist. It might be hard to collect a ransom on a daughter Seamus Quinn doesn't even know he has. Besides, I'm not after ransom. I have plenty of money.''

''Then what?''

''Time,'' Rafe said. He reached over and turned up the volume on the CD player.

But Keely was far from done with him. She pressed the Eject button on the CD player and when the CD popped out, she tossed it into the back seat. ''I'm not going to let you get away with this. The first time this car stops, I'm going to jump out. And then I'm going to call the police and have you arrested.''

He glanced over his shoulder as he changed lanes, the car accelerating smoothly. ''The one thing I required when I decided on vacation property was that it had to be quick to get to. You'll find it interesting that there isn't a single stop sign between here and

my place on Aspen Lake. Really quite amazing, don't
you think?''

Keely gritted her teeth and then growled in frustration. He had an answer for everything. God, why
hadn't she noticed before what a smug bastard he
really was? She eyed the car phone and wondered if
she might dial 911 before he had a chance to take it
from her.

But Rafe saw what she was looking at and grabbed
the phone. He unhooked the cord with one hand, then
rolled down the window and tossed it out. ''You can
add littering to that charge of kidnapping,'' he said.

Keely slouched down in the seat. She wasn't going
to win this round. But she had three hours to plot her
escape. Once she did that, she'd capitalize on the first
opportunity that presented itself. And in the process,
she'd make Rafe Kendrick pay for everything he'd
done to her. For those long, deep kisses and those
earth-shattering orgasms. For those quiet conversations over dinner and for the fun and games in the
shower. For making her doubt her loyalty to the
Quinns. For everything he made her…feel.

But as she thought about her own revenge, Keely
wondered if she'd be the one paying the greatest
price. Whether she wanted to admit it or not, she had
fallen in love with Rafe Kendrick. And that could be
the most costly mistake she'd ever made.

BY THE TIME they reached the cabin, Rafe was ready
to unlock the doors and let Keely jump out of the
speeding car of her own free will. She'd been nothing

but a shrew and a harpy and a royal pain in the ass the entire way to Aspen Lake and he seriously wondered at his decision to bring her to his weekend getaway. But all her demands for an explanation and threats of retribution didn't seem to quell his desire to strip her naked and make wild, uninhibited love to her.

In truth, the reason he hadn't answered her questions was that he didn't have answers yet. He wasn't sure why he'd decided to kidnap her, only that he was certain if he let her out of his sight again, something disastrous might happen. And trying to keep Keely locked in his apartment until he pleaded his case with her would be damn near impossible. At Aspen Lake they'd have the peace and quiet to sort everything out. And when he was satisfied that she understood his side of the story, they'd return to Boston.

The driveway into the cabin was difficult to find during the summer months, but in the dark of a winter night, it was nearly impossible. He slowed the car as they were getting close then spotted the wooden sign tacked up on a tree. "Kendrick" was all it said. Rafe carefully maneuvered the car between the snowbanks, then down a long hill to the cabin, which was set on the shore of the lake.

He glanced over at Keely to find her studying the surroundings carefully—no doubt planning her escape. But Kencor owned all the property around the lake as well as the lake itself. "The nearest neighbors are at least two miles away," he said. "And they're summer residents. You've got a four-mile walk into town, if you can find your way.''

The cabin hadn't been opened since Labor Day. Snow crusted the roof and icicles hung from the eaves, but the caretaker had managed to plow the drive and shovel the porch since Rafe's call. The porch light beamed brightly, welcoming them and reflecting the snowflakes that had begun to fall.

Rafe parked the car, then reached over and opened the glove compartment. He pulled out a flashlight. ''We're here.'' He pushed open his door and stepped outside.

Keely refused to get out of the car, stubbornly staring straight ahead, her arms crossed tightly over her chest. Rafe circled to her side, opened the door, then dragged her out. ''Come with me. I have something to show you.'' She trudged along beside him, eyeing the dark woods on either side of the path and struggling through deep snow.

''Where are we going now? Are you going to tie me to a tree so I can't escape?''

He stopped and considered her suggestion with a dramatic pause. ''Not a bad idea. But the wolves and grizzlys would get you within the hour. I have a much better way to keep you here.'' They walked up the snow-covered path to a small shack with a crescent moon cut in the door. ''This is the outhouse.'' Rafe pulled open the door. ''And these are my car keys,'' he added, dangling them in front of her nose. ''If you have any notion of driving yourself out of here, let me assure you, that's not going to happen.'' With precise aim, he tossed the keys through the hole and listened as they landed ten feet below with a slight jangle. "We leave when I say we leave."

Keely's eyes went wide. "How are we going to get out of here?" She took a step over to the hole and peered down into the darkness. Rafe handed her the flashlight and she shined it downward until she was convinced that the keys were irretrievable. "You're crazy," she murmured. "You throw away the phone, you throw away the keys. What if there's an emergency?"

Rafe snatched the flashlight from her hands. "There's always smoke signals." He started back down the path and was pleased when Keely followed close at his heels, obviously afraid of the wolves and the grizzlys, animals that hadn't been seen in this area of Vermont for years.

As he'd requested, the cabin had been stocked with firewood and a fire blazed in the large fieldstone fireplace. Though he had the luxury of electricity and running water inside the cabin, he hadn't gotten around to putting in a septic system. For a single guy, the outhouse hadn't posed a major problem, but Keely, his first female guest at Aspen Lake, might feel differently.

"Go ahead," he said. "Look around. The kitchen is back there. There are two bedrooms." He pointed to the doors on either side of the fireplace. "Take your pick."

Rafe sat down on the sofa in front of the fire and warmed his feet as he watched Keely wander through the cabin. He closed his eyes and leaned his head back, trying to fight off a yawn. All he needed was just a few moments of silence and he'd be all right. But the sound of the backdoor opening brought him to his feet.

She was already out the door by the time he reached the kitchen. Rafe sprinted out into the darkness, slipping on the snow-covered steps and bumping down the last two on his ass. He stood up and tried to regain his balance, but twisted his ankle in the process, going down hard for a second time and hitting his head on the railing for the steps.

"Sonofabitch!" he shouted as he struggled to his feet, his voice echoing in the silent woods. He tested the ankle and decided it wasn't broken. But there was no way he'd catch Keely now. Rafe cursed himself for even letting her out of his sight. With the cold and the snow and the dark, she was sure to lose herself in the woods. And when she was found frozen to death tomorrow morning, he'd be to blame.

Rafe felt something warm on his forehead and he reached up and came away with damp fingertips. By the light from the open door, he saw blood. "Sonofabitch!" he repeated. He sat down on the step and pressed his palm to the cut on his forehead.

"Are you all right?"

The voice came from behind a nearby tree. "Keely?"

"Well, are you?"

"No," Rafe lied. "I think I broke my ankle. And

I have a bad cut on my head. I'm bleeding, for chrissakes.''

The light from a flashlight flickered against the snow and, a few seconds later, Keely appeared. She observed him for a long moment, then cursed softly. ''I shouldn't be helping you,'' she muttered as she wrapped Rafe's arm around her shoulders and helped him to his feet.

He faked a serious limp until the moment they got back into the house. Before she could figure out what was happening, he grabbed the flashlight from her, removed the batteries and slipped them into his pocket. Then, he pulled her along to the fireplace.

''Your ankle isn't broken,'' Keely cried.

''Do you have any idea how long you would have lasted in the woods? That was a damn stupid thing to do. You would have been dead by morning.'' Rafe found a handkerchief in his pocket, then sat down on the sofa and dabbed at his forehead, which had already stopped bleeding.

Keely stood off to the side, watching him warily, waiting for her next chance to make a run for it.

''Take off your clothes,'' Rafe ordered.

Her eyes went wide. ''What?''

''You heard me. Take off your clothes. And your boots.''

''If you think we're having sex, you are sadly mistaken. If you're horny, you can go…fuck a tree!''

With a low curse, Rafe strode over to her, picked her up and set her on top of the coffee table. He bent down and unzipped her boots, then tugged them off

her feet. Without a word, he carried them over to the
fireplace and tossed them into the crackling blaze.

Keely cried out and scrambled to the fire, but the
flames licked around the black leather, too hot for her
to mount a rescue effort. "Those were my favorite
pair of boots. I spent a week's salary on them."

"I'll buy you a new pair. Hell, I'll buy you ten
pairs. But for now, you're not going to need them. It
will be harder for you to escape without shoes, don't
you think?"

Keely balled up her fist and hit his shoulder as hard
as she could. But he seemed unfazed by the pain.

"Now your clothes."

"No, I'm not letting you burn my clothes!"

Rafe leveled his gaze on her. "Take your clothes
off now, or I'll do the job for you."

She sent him a withering glare. But Rafe would not
be deterred. He wasn't going to take the chance of
her making another escape attempt and killing herself
in the process. He tried to grab her sweater, but Keely
held out her hand. She jumped down from the coffee
table, then slowly wandered over to his stereo system.
After picking through a stack of CDs, she chose one
and popped it into the player. A bluesy guitar solo
drifted out of the speakers.

As she stepped back up on the coffee table, Rafe
wasn't sure what she was up to. Then she started
moving to the music, swaying sinuously and doing
her very best imitation of a stripper. "You wanted me
to take off my clothes?" She slipped out of her jacket
and threw it at him, hitting him square in the face.

Rafe held his breath as the jacket dropped to the floor, unable to drag his gaze away.

Piece by piece, she removed her clothes, first tugging her sweater over her head, then shimmying out of her jeans. She dangled both items in front of his face before dropping them at his feet and continuing her dance. Rafe felt himself growing aroused—against his will. She'd wrested control of the situation from him in just a few seconds, proving that when it came to desire, she always held the winning hand.

The gold necklace she always wore dangled between her breasts in a tempting way, drawing attention to what he couldn't see. She reached behind her back for the clasp of her bra, but Rafe wasn't about to let her go so far. In one quick move, he grabbed her hand, then pulled her down onto the sofa. Stretching out on top of her, he trapped her body. Keely wiggled against him, trying to get free, but Rafe wasn't about to let her go. "I think that's enough of that," he murmured, pinning her hands above her head.

"You asked for it," Keely accused, still twisting against him. She arched her hips into his, rubbing up against the erection that had grown the moment she started her little striptease. "And I'd say you enjoyed it."

"And what do you enjoy, Keely?" He dipped his head to her breast and covered her nipple with his mouth, wetting the thin satin fabric of her bra. Then he pulled back and blew on the spot until her nipple peaked against the cold. "Do you enjoy that?"

She continued to twist against him, but Rafe noticed a marked decrease in her effort. "Let me go," she demanded.

Rafe caught both her wrists in one hand, then ran his hand along the length of her body. When he reached her panties, he delved beneath the scrap of satin and lace and touched the damp crease between her legs. "What about this?" he asked, drawing his finger against her again, probing deeper. Keely drew a ragged breath, then sighed softly.

"Tell me you want that," Rafe said. "Tell me you want me to make you come."

She turned her face away, refusing to answer him, but when he touched her again, she arched up against his hand. Rafe released his grip on her hands at the same time he began a gentle assault on her moist core. He watched her face as he touched her, watched the expression of intense concentration and pure pleasure as he brought her closer and closer.

When she stiffened and held her breath, Rafe slowed his seduction, wanting to draw her orgasm out, make it more powerful. And then she moaned his name once and collapsed into spasms of pleasure, her breath coming in deep gasps, her body trembling in response.

Rafe brought her down slowly, his hand wet with her desire. Again, she turned her face into his chest, refusing to look at him. Though he'd wanted to prove a point, Rafe suddenly regretted his choice of methods. He pushed back until he could look down into her face. And when he did, his heart twisted. A tear trickled down Keely's cheek and came to rest near her ear.

He rolled off of her and stood beside the sofa, suddenly realizing the impact of what he'd done. "Keely, I—"

"Don't say anything." She struggled to climb off the sofa, then bent to pick up her clothes from the floor. "I'm going to bed. You might want to think about sleeping with one eye open at all times, because the first chance I get, I'm out of here."

Rafe winced when the bedroom door slammed. He flopped back down on the sofa and covered his eyes with his arm. He knew what he'd done to her, humiliating her by turning her own desire against her. But when it came to Keely Quinn, he couldn't seem to think straight. His emotions always took control, overriding his logic and common sense.

She was right. He had kidnapped her and there was every chance a case against him would hold up in court. But he just needed the time to make her understand his side of the story, to make her see how much he…needed her.

"Oh, hell," he murmured. He might as well admit the truth because it was right in front of his eyes. He hadn't brought her here to convince her of anything. He'd brought her here because he was afraid to let her go, afraid that he'd never see her again. He'd fallen in love with Keely Quinn. And there wasn't anything he could do about it.

KEELY SNUGGLED beneath the thick down comforter, pulling it up to cover her cold nose. The morning light filtered through pretty country-style curtains and she tried to guess what time it was.

She'd tossed and turned restlessly for most of the night, listening to the wind rattle the windows. After exhaustion finally overwhelmed the chaos in her head, she drifted off, but her sleep was plagued with fitful dreams. She should hate Rafe for what he'd done to her, but, in truth, she'd taken every ounce of pleasure he'd given her and savored it. True and uninhibited passion had always been elusive in her previous relationships with men. But with Rafe, all it took was one caress to break down her inhibitions. Goodbye, Catholic schoolgirl. Hello, nymphomaniac.

Even now, after all she knew about his plans to destroy her family, she still couldn't control her desire for him. It was like a drug, insidious and addictive, destroying her self-control. Keely was certain if she looked for a lifetime, there would never be another man like him, a man who could make her ache with desire just by looking at him. Instead, she'd be left to compare each man who stumbled into her future with Rafe Kendrick and what they'd shared in the past.

A soft knock sounded at her bedroom door and Keely sat up, clutching the comforter to her nearly naked body. "I'm awake," she called out.

Rafe slowly pushed the door open, then stepped inside. He held out a pair of oversize boots as if they were a peace offering. "I thought you might want to use the outhouse," he said. "I shoveled a path."

Keely nodded. "Thank you. Are you going to accompany me or can I go on my own?"

"You can go on your own," Rafe said. "And I've filled the bathtub for you. It's in the kitchen when you're ready." He turned and walked out the door.

Keely jumped out of bed and quickly pulled on her clothes, then slipped her bare feet into the warmly lined boots. She clomped out into the living room and found her jacket, then hurried outside.

The snow that had begun on their arrival had continued through the night and the windblown drifts blocked the driveway and nearly buried one side of Rafe's car. Fat flakes still fell, so thick that she could barely see the outhouse or the end of the drive. She dismissed an impulse to run up to the road and flag down a passing car. Rafe would see her from the cabin window long before a car came by.

When she reached the outhouse, she slowly opened the door, checking for wild animals before she stepped inside. The keys were still at the bottom of the hole and she wondered how difficult it might be to fish them out. If she was successful, she could hop into his car and drive away right now.

But even if she could find a stick or something long enough to use, the task would take time and a strong stomach. And Rafe would come looking for her after she was gone for more than a few minutes. And with the drifts as high as they were, she'd probably get stuck before she even reached the road. Maybe she ought to resign herself to listening to his story. Once she did, he'd take her home and that would be the end of it.

"The end of it," Keely murmured.

Is that what she really wanted? To walk away from Rafe Kendrick and never see him again? She had to make a choice. Once her father and brothers made the connection between their troubles and Rafe's manipulation, they'd hate him forever. And Rafe already hated the Quinns. No doubt, she'd be caught in the middle of a terrible tug-of-war if she didn't make a decision. But then that was assuming she had a future with Rafe. She'd be better off putting her money on a future with the Quinns.

Keely quickly finished her business in the outhouse, then ran back down the path. When she got inside the cabin, she kicked off the boots and slowly walked into the kitchen. "It's still snowing out there," she called.

Rafe held a bucket in his hand and slowly dumped steaming water into an old-fashioned copper bathtub. The tub looked so inviting, the hot water a chance to chase away the early morning chill. But she would have to take her bath out in the open. She wondered if this was another one of his games.

"I hope this is all right. The tub came with the cabin. I think it's probably an antique. I built a shower in the back, but it's kind of cold and drafty. And I remembered that you liked baths." He poured another bucket into the tub, then stepped back. "That should do it." He pointed to the counter beside the sink. "Soap, shampoo, and towels. And there's a bucket here for rinsing. You can just fill it from the sink. I'll just be in the other room if you need anything.''

This wasn't a game. ''Thank you,'' Keely murmured, surprised by the generous gesture. She shrugged out of her jacket. ''You can stay if you want. It's not like you haven't seen it all before. And you can fetch more hot water for me.'' She started to strip out of her clothes and was surprised when Rafe turned his back to her as she did.

When she was completely naked, she slipped beneath the steaming water, sinking down until it touched her chin. ''Oh, this is wonderful.'' She closed her eyes and tipped her head back against the edge of the tub. A long silence grew between them and Keely opened one eye to find Rafe staring at her, an uneasy expression on his face. ''Would you like to tell me now?''

''Tell you?''

''About your father.''

''Are you willing to listen? With an open mind?''

Keely met his gaze. ''I'll do my best.''

Rafe grabbed a chair from the table and pulled it closer to the tub, then sat down. He braced his elbows on his knees and hunched over, silently contemplating what he was going to say. After a long while, he finally spoke.

''I remember the day that they came to the house to tell us my father was dead. They'd radioed in from the boat and the local sheriff came to break the news. We didn't know any details, but later, after the boat had come in, some of my dad's friends came by and explained how my dad got caught in the line and dragged under. From that moment on, I suspected it wasn't the truth. My father didn't make stupid mistakes like that.''

Rafe went on, telling Keely about the aftermath of his father's death, the funeral, his mother's emotional breakdowns, the insurance money that seemed to evaporate in the face of Lila's medical bills. ''When I was a teenager, my mother was rattling on and on about my father's death and she mentioned something about Seamus Quinn and murder. At first, I thought she was just delusional, but I was curious. I never forgot what she said, and when I got older and had a little more money, I started to do some investigating. A few months ago, I finally tracked down one of the crew members who was on that run with my father. And he told me what really happened on the *Mighty Quinn*.''

Keely listened closely as the rest of the story unfolded. Rafe told it in a cold, unemotional voice, as if he were recalling the death of a stranger rather than his own father. When he finished, he released a long breath. ''So you can see why I have to know what happened. My father's death changed my life—it made me the person I am today. And sometimes I don't like that person very much. There's this…rage that I can't seem to get rid of. If I finally know the truth, then maybe I can let it go.''

''Even though it means ruining another man's life?'' Keely asked.

"If he wasn't your father, would you feel the same way, Keely?"

Keely considered his point and was forced to concede. In any other case, she'd be behind him one-hundred percent. "Probably not. But the fact is Seamus *is* my father. And if you get what you want, I may never know him."

"When I started this, I wanted revenge. But now I just want the truth. If you can understand that, Keely, then I'll understand if you have to side with your family."

Keely nodded, then reached out her hand. "Shampoo."

Rafe stood up from the chair and grabbed the bottle. Keely slid down beneath the water to wet her hair, then popped back up. She waited for Rafe to hand her the shampoo, but instead he stood behind her and began to wash her hair himself.

"I don't believe my father is capable of murder," she said. "I know him. It's not possible. And nothing you say to me is going to make me believe that."

"I hope you're right," Rafe said as he lathered her hair.

Keely closed her eyes again and relaxed into the luxurious feel of his fingers in her hair. Though the feeling was incredibly sensual, the task was ordinary and it made her feel closer to Rafe than she ever had making love to him.

"I'm sorry about last night," he murmured.

"I know you are."

Keely tipped her head back and Rafe rinsed her

hair. Then he set the bucket down and wiped his hands on his jeans. "Well, I guess I should get things cleaned up around here. The plow should be coming soon to clear the drive and I'm sure you want to get back to Boston."

"How are we going to get back? We don't have any car keys."

He turned and reached into the kitchen cupboard, then withdrew a key ring. "I always keep an extra set up here. Just in case."

Keely couldn't help but smile. "And I was actually trying to figure out a way to retrieve the keys from the outhouse." She paused, playing with a mound of soap bubbles near her shoulder. Now that Rafe was ready to take her home, Keely wasn't sure she wanted to go. Somewhere, deep in her heart, she knew that this might be the last time she and Rafe would see each other.

He was right. She had to make a choice—either him or her family. But she wasn't ready to make that choice just yet. If they left now, she'd have a few more hours with him and that would be it. Keely closed her eyes. Now or later, it wouldn't make much difference.

"Good," Keely said. "I'm going to be glad to get back to Boston."

CHAPTER EIGHT

RAFE STOMPED his feet on the rug just inside the door, noting that his ankle only gave him a twinge of pain now. He carefully balanced the load of firewood in his arms as he kicked off his boots. Peering over the top of the wood, he found Keely where he had left her an hour ago. She was curled up on the sofa in front of the fireplace with a book she'd found—his dog-eared copy of Dickens's *Great Expectations.*

"The snow hasn't let up," Rafe said. "The roads are probably pretty bad. But we should be plowed out soon."

"It's going to be dark soon. If you hadn't thrown your phone away, you could have called and found out when he'd be here."

Rafe nodded. "Right." He wasn't going to tell her that he had a cell phone in his coat pocket in case of a real emergency. A drifted driveway wasn't worth a phone call. The more time he had with Keely the better.

Keely lowered her book to her lap, then turned to him. "Maybe we should just plan to stay," she said. "After all, it's New Year's Eve. It might be nice to ring in the new year in the peace and quiet of the north woods, away from everything going on in Boston.''

Rafe was happy that she'd come to that conclusion on her own. If he'd suggested it, she probably would have fought him all the way. ''There's food in the refrigerator. And I think I've got a bottle of champagne around here somewhere from last New Year's Eve.''

''Leftover from one of your other kidnap victims?'' Keely asked, one eyebrow arched.

''No. I've never brought a woman here before. You're the first.'' The smile faded from her face and her gaze shifted back to her book. Rafe cleared his throat. ''I was thinking of taking a walk. Would you like to come with me?''

Keely shook her head. ''I don't have any boots. Remember? You burned them up in the fireplace?''

He glanced over at the rug near the door. ''You could wear those.''

''I can't walk very well in those.''

''We'll walk slowly. And I have a down jacket you can wear and a decent hat. You'll be warm, I promise. And we won't go far.''

''All right,'' Keely said. ''I could use some fresh air.''

Rafe was glad for the company. Besides, if this day was their last together, then he was going to do all he could to make it memorable. He bent down and helped her put the boots on, then tied the laces tightly until her feet were secure inside. Then he helped her slip into his old down jacket. To top it off, Rafe pushed a plaid hat on her head, complete with earflaps.

"I bet I look beautiful in this getup," Keely said.

He stared down at her, fighting the urge to pull her into his arms and kiss her. "You always look beautiful."

"Let's go," she murmured.

The wind had died down, but snowflakes still drifted between the trees as they broke a pathway to the lake. The woods were perfectly quiet and, for once, Rafe felt as if the world had slowed down enough for them to relax. "I'm sorry I can't get you back to Boston today," he said.

Keely shrugged. "I'm a little nervous about what's going to happen when I get there. I guess I could use an extra day to figure out how I'm going to do this. It's so easy standing on the outside looking in. I know who I am and I know who they are. But to them I'm just going to be some stranger trying to barge into their lives. I'm worried about how they're going to react."

"Just barf on their shoes and they'll fall in love with you," Rafe said.

She glanced over at him and smiled winsomely. "Will they? I mean, just because we're family doesn't mean they have to accept me. I'm always going to be an outsider. I don't share the same memories as they do." She stopped walking and stared out at the lake. "And I'm afraid they might blame me."

"For not telling them sooner?"

"No. For making my mother leave."

"How is that even possible? You weren't born when your mother walked out."

"But I was the reason," Keely explained. "When she found out she was pregnant with me, she took off. If it hadn't been for me, she would have stayed."

Rafe reached out and tucked a windblown strand of hair beneath her hat. There were times when all he wanted to do was drag her into his arms and kiss away her worries. When she talked about her family, she seemed so vulnerable. "You can't blame yourself, Keely. I used to think it was my fault that my mother had her mental problems. Because I wasn't able to replace my dad. Because she didn't feel safe with me taking care of her. But her problems weren't my fault any more than your mother's choice to walk out on her family was your fault."

"Still, it's going to be hard telling them. I keep imagining their reactions. Dead silence would be horrible. If they don't believe me at all, I don't know what I'll do. They could yell at me." She brought a hand to her throat. "But I have proof." She pulled her necklace out from beneath her sweater, the necklace she'd worn since the very first time he'd made love to her. "My mother gave this to me. It's a claddagh. An Irish symbol of love and fidelity. My mother says Seamus will recognize it."

"Are you going to tell him first?" Rafe asked.

She shook her head, then slipped the necklace back beneath her sweater. "I don't think so. I think I'll tell one of my brothers and get his reaction before breaking the news to Seamus."

"And I suppose you're going to tell them about me," Rafe said.

Keely nodded. "I am. I think they need to know. Maybe it will help."

"It will be the end of us," Rafe said.

Keely nodded. "I know."

Her calm acceptance of the fact cut him deep. "Come on. I have something I want to show you." They headed off the main path through the woods, then up into a small clearing. The clearing offered a view of the entire lake, the dense forest that surrounded it, the windswept ice and a sunset that colored the sky pink and orange and purple. A hawk circled overhead, dipping and gliding on the cold air. "We're all alone up here. This cabin is the only place on the lake."

"No neighbors?"

"Nope. I own the whole lake and the property around it. Or Kencor does. We bought it about five years ago and we were going to develop it. Condos, maybe a resort, some larger vacation homes. But then I couldn't do it."

"I can see why," Keely murmured. "I wouldn't change a thing."

They sat down on a small boulder and stared out at the lake. "Whatever happens with your father, Keely, I want you to know that I never meant any of it to hurt you."

"I know," she replied. "And I understand what you need to do. We both have pasts that we need to fix. But my father is innocent. I believe that with all

my heart. And I'm going to help my family
prove it.''

He took her fingers and brought them up to his
mouth, pressing his lips against the back of her hand.
''I hope you do, Keely.''

KEELY PICKED UP the bottle of burgundy and sloshed
a bit more into the casserole. Though she prided herself on her cooking skills, she felt like the Iron Chef
trying to put together an elegant meal from the food
in Rafe's refrigerator. They had a choice of frozen
pizza, canned spaghetti, chicken Hungry-Man dinners
or T-bone steaks. ''Real manly food,'' she muttered.

Luckily potatoes qualified as manly food, as did
onions. She was able to make a passable beef burgundy with a bottle of wine she'd found. Whoever
had stocked the cabin had also purchased a bag of
romaine so she toasted bread for croutons and
whipped up a Caesar's salad—without anchovy or
Parmesan cheese. As for dessert, they had four different kinds of ice cream. So she'd melted down some
chocolate bars for ice cream sundaes.

As she was putting the casserole back in the oven,
the lights flickered and Keely waited for the electricity to come back on. It had happened four or five
times that afternoon, Rafe explaining that the snow
was heavy on the power lines. In truth, it frightened
Keely. She felt isolated enough without indoor
plumbing. She wandered into the living room and
found Rafe poking at the fire.

''Dinner smells good.''

"It's done. The power should be back on soon. In the meantime it'll stay warm, so we can eat whenever we want." She glanced over at Rafe. "What if the power doesn't come back on?"

Rafe straightened, wiping his hands on his jeans. "We'll just have to build a very big fire and snuggle up." He paused, then smiled weakly. "I think it might be off for good this time."

"For the rest of the night?" Keely asked.

"Maybe." He reached up to the mantel and grabbed a box of matches. "It happens pretty regularly up here. Let's hope the pipes won't freeze. The last time that happened I had a real mess." He lit the kerosene lamp on the coffee table, then brought it over to her. "Why don't you put this in the kitchen? I'll dig up some candles and find the rest of the lanterns."

"And I have to visit the powder room before it gets any colder or darker." Keely pulled on the oversize boots she'd grown used to wearing, then grabbed her jacket from a hook beside the door. The flashlight was where she'd left it after her last hike to the outhouse.

"Don't let the bears eat you," Rafe teased as she hurried out the door.

"From now on I'm going to appreciate the convenience of indoor plumbing," she muttered as she trudged up the path.

The cold wind cut through her jacket and she rushed to get back to the warmth of the cabin. When she opened the door and stepped inside, her breath caught in her throat. The dark and gloomy interior had been illuminated by candles and lanterns scattered all around the room, the light dancing against the rough walls of the cabin and creating a cozy, romantic atmosphere.

Rafe reappeared from his bedroom carrying a boom box. "We can still have music as long as the batteries last," he said.

"It's beautiful," she said.

He nodded. "I kind of like it this way. Simple. Kind of rustic. I thought we'd eat in front of the fire. And we'll have to sleep in front of the fire. Why don't you bring in dinner and I'll get things set up?"

By the time Keely brought the first course in, Rafe had tossed pillows and down comforters on the floor. He popped the bottle of champagne that had been cooling in a snowbank, then filled two wineglasses. Keely took one from his hand and raised it to her lips, but he stopped her.

"It's New Year's Eve," Rafe said. "We should have a toast."

"All right. What should we toast to?"

"To the fates that brought us together," Rafe offered.

And to the fates that would tear them apart, Keely mused. She touched her glass to his. But before she could take a sip, Rafe bent forward and caught her mouth in a long and lingering kiss. "I've always spent New Year's Eve alone," he murmured. "It just never seemed very important to celebrate. But now I kind of understand what it's all about."

"Old acquaintance and auld lang syne?" Keely asked, gazing into his eyes.

"I think it's about looking at the past, at all our mistakes and problems, and starting off with a fresh slate. It's about hope." He reached up and skimmed his fingers down her cheek.

"And do you have any New Year's resolutions?" Keely asked.

"Not that I've thought of. How about you?"

She stepped away from him, setting her glass down on the coffee table and walking over to the fire. "Well, first, I'm going to try to be less impulsive. But then that's been my New Year's resolution for most of my adult life."

"I like your impulsiveness," Rafe said. "I wouldn't change that if I were you."

"All right. Then I'm going to lose ten pounds."

Rafe shook his head and slowly walked toward her. "No, I don't think that's a good idea. You've got a great body. I like it just the way it is."

Keely sent him a grateful smile. "Well, I'm definitely going to take Spanish lessons."

Rafe didn't have a reply for that. Instead, her pulled her into his arms and kissed her once more. Keely knew that they were playing a dangerous game. They'd put their differences aside for now, but as soon as they left the isolation of the cabin, everything would bubble up around them again.

"We shouldn't do this," she murmured. "It will just make things more difficult."

"It's New Year's Eve." He smoothed his fingers

along her jawline. "Let's just pretend that this is a beginning instead of an end."

Keely nodded and Rafe spanned her waist with his hands. As he kissed her, his tongue warm on her lips, she felt her knees go weak and her resolve falter. There was no way to refuse; she just didn't have it in her. From the time she'd met him, she'd been drawn to him in a way that defied logic and determination. He ruled her body, his command a simple touch.

Rafe's mouth drifted along her throat, then lower as he knelt in front of her. He lifted her sweater and pressed his mouth into her belly, then gently pulled her down to kneel in front of him. It felt like ages since they'd been intimate but it had only been last night when he'd left her shuddering with pleasure.

His hands skimmed over her body, dipping beneath her clothes, teasing her and then retreating as if he wanted to bring her along slowly. But Keely wasn't content to relinquish control this time. She wanted to prove to him how powerful she could be. She wanted to make him ache with need, then explode inside her.

She brushed his hands off her body, then pinned them behind his back. "It's my turn now," she said. "You do what I say."

Rafe smiled, ready and willing to comply. "All right," he murmured. "Seduce me, Keely."

She sat back on her heels. "Take off your clothes. I want you naked."

He stood, and as he removed his sweater, Keely watched the light from the fire dance across his muscled torso and flat belly. After tossing the sweater aside, Rafe started on his jeans.

"Slower," Keely ordered. "Much slower."

He kicked off his socks, one at a time. "How's this?"

"Slower."

He unbuttoned his jeans and dragged the zipper down inch by inch to reveal silk boxers. His hard shaft pressed against the fabric, then sprung free as he skimmed the jeans over his hips. He was already fully aroused and Keely's fingers clenched, fighting the temptation to reach out and stroke him until he came in her hand. To be in control of his pleasure, she'd have to control her own.

When he was completely naked, she stared up at him. "Put your hands on your head," she said.

Rafe laughed. "What?"

"You heard me. Put your hands on your head. Those are the rules. If you touch me, it's over."

He grudgingly did as he was told, watching her all the time, his gaze wary. Keely pushed up on her knees then leaned into him, her mouth just inches from his arousal. When he pressed closer, she moved back, showing him another rule he'd have to follow. She was allowed to move. He wasn't.

This time, when she rocked forward, he remained still. God, he was beautiful, his narrow waist and broad chest, his muscled legs and slender hips, his thick shaft brushing the hair beneath his navel. Keely slowly drew her tongue from the base to the tip of his penis and he sucked in a sharp breath.

When she retraced her path, Rafe moaned, the sound slipping from his throat in a low rumble. His belly quivered as he held his breath, anticipating her next move. But Keely was determined to tease him into submission, to make him beg for release. She pressed her mouth to the hollow beneath his hip bone, his hard-on brushing her cheek, then traced a path to his belly and back again. And when she was certain he'd had enough, she took him into her mouth more deeply, in the ultimate caress.

She didn't linger there long. He was too close and she had so much more in store for him to let it end so quickly. Instead, she worked her way around his body, higher and higher, to the small of his back, to the soft dusting of hair on his chest, then to the nape of his neck, all the while letting her fingers brush along his arousal. He clutched his hands over his head, his eyes closed, breathing harsh, his erection unflagging.

Her bold behavior was shocking, even to herself. Keely had always felt a bit inhibited when it came to sex, but when she was with Rafe, she seemed to lose herself in the pursuit of pleasure. Nothing was out of bounds or beyond imagination, as long as it felt good. And she knew if they could spend a lifetime together, intimacy would always be an adventure.

But they didn't have a lifetime. They had this one night. One more ascent to ecstasy and that would be all.

When she came back around to face him, Rafe looked down into her eyes. "Can I touch you now?"

She shook her head and, while he watched, Keely slowly undressed in front of him. His gaze drifted over her body as she gradually revealed more and more. But he was mistaken if he thought her naked-ness was an invitation to touch. Instead, her goal was to torment him further by doing to herself what his hands couldn't.

She'd always been taught it was a sin to touch her-self in such a way, but there were no rules and no regrets when it came to this game they played. And the next time he remembered this night, she wanted him to grow hard with the thought of what she'd done to him. She imagined him lying in bed alone, pleas-uring himself with images of her swimming in his mind.

Keely met his gaze and she went still. "You've had enough? Or do you want more?"

He cursed softly. "If you keep that up, I'm going to come without you ever touching me."

"I didn't think that was possible," she teased.

"I didn't think so either. But believe me, it is."

"Then I think you'd better lie down and relax."

Rafe sank down into the blankets and pillows he'd spread in front of the fireplace. Keely stepped over his hips then slowly lowered herself until she strad-dled him. He reached up to touch her, but she grabbed his hands and put them above his head. "You're do-ing so well," she whispered. "Don't break the rules now."

She rubbed herself up against him, his shaft nestled between her legs. He arched, the movement clearly more instinct than a deliberate attempt to break her rules. A shiver raced through her body in anticipation of the moment when he would slip inside her, when he would fill her to the hilt.

She leaned forward and braced her hands on either side of his head, then whispered into his ear. She told him everything she wanted to do to him in great detail. And when she was finished, she teased at his ear with her tongue. "Have you had enough?" she asked. "Do you give up now?"

"No," Rafe murmured.

As she rose, she hovered over him, offering him a view of her breasts, the claddagh grazing his chest. Then she slowly brushed her nipple over his lips, daring him, taunting him to take a taste. "What about now?" she asked.

"Maybe," Rafe replied in a low voice.

She shifted above him, allowing him to penetrate her just slightly, then drawing away.

"How about now?"

"Yes," Rafe said. "I give up. You win. Are you happy now?"

Keely smiled, a soft sigh slipping from her lips. She caught his shaft between her legs and slowly sank down, taking him all in, burying him deep within her warmth. "Yes," she said. She pressed her palms to his chest and tipped her head back, then slowly began to move. "Yes, I'm very happy."

Rafe reached up and twisted his fingers around the necklace, then gently tugged her closer, until her lips were just inches from his. She opened her eyes to find him staring at her, his gaze clear. "I love you, Keely."

Her breath caught in her throat. She saw the truth of his words in his eyes and a wave of emotion washed over her. "And I love you, Rafe."

THE LAST of the flames flickered out and the fire turned to glowing embers and cold ash. Curled in the curve of Rafe's body, Keely listened to the deep, even rhythm of his breathing. She was almost afraid to acknowledge the dawn that brightened the cabin windows. Today, she'd return to Boston. She'd finally confront her family and begin an entirely new phase of her life.

But, after last night, she wondered if she'd be ready to make the choice. They'd made love once, then paused long enough for dinner, before they made love again. They rang in the New Year somewhere between her second and third orgasm, then fell asleep in front of the fire, wrapped in each other's arms.

In truth, she couldn't bear to think of going back to Boston. She wanted to stay with Rafe in this cabin forever, shutting out reality. It was so easy to need him—and now to love him. She'd never wanted to fall in love. She'd done everything in her power to avoid it. But she could no more stop herself from loving Rafe than she could stop breathing. It came as naturally as the rise and fall of his chest against her back.

A rumble sounded outside and Keely watched as headlights gleamed through the windows and reflected on the rough log walls of the cabin. The plow. Now there would be nothing to keep them here. Rafe would wake and they'd be faced with the uneasy realization that it was over—that they would return to the real world and go their separate ways.

Keely had tried to think of a way to make it work. Even though her brothers knew Rafe had been the cause of Seamus's troubles, they'd never met him. And she wasn't obligated to tell them that she was sleeping with the enemy. She and Rafe could go on as they had, as lovers, sharing stolen nights now and then. And they'd make a pact never to speak of her family or their differences, putting all that aside.

But, sooner or later, they'd be forced to stop living in limbo. Seamus would either be found guilty or innocent of a crime. If he was guilty, Keely wasn't sure she could ever forgive Rafe for the part he played. And if he was found innocent, Rafe would always wonder if Seamus had somehow eluded justice. The truth, whatever it was, would always stand between them.

Keely slowly rolled over and faced him, taking in the tiny details of his face, his boyish vulnerability and masculine beauty. She smoothed a strand of hair from his forehead. "You'll be hard to forget, Rafe Kendrick," she murmured. She touched her lips to his and he stirred, then opened his eyes.

At first he looked at her as if he wasn't sure who she was. Then he smiled sleepily. "Is it morning?" he asked.

"Not yet."

"Then why are you awake?"

"Outhouse," Keely replied. "I'm just working up the courage to go out in the cold."

He nuzzled her neck. "First thing today I'm going to call a plumber and have a real bathroom installed. I promise."

"Go back to sleep," Keely murmured, kissing him again. "I'll be right back."

She crawled out from beneath the down comforter. The cold air hit her warm skin, sending a shiver coursing over her naked body. Her clothes were scattered over the floor and she quickly tugged them on, her teeth chattering as she moved. But even completely dressed, she was still freezing, her breath clouding in front of her face. Keely tiptoed over to the fire and tossed a pair of logs onto the embers. They sparked and sputtered and then flamed.

She glanced down at Rafe once more, then slowly backed away. It would be so easy to forget all she'd worked for and become a part of his life. But she was a Quinn and she needed to find out what that meant. She grabbed her coat from the hook and pulled it on, then slipped into the oversize boots. Wincing, she tiptoed into the kitchen and found the keys where Rafe had left them, in the cupboard.

This was the best way. She knew if they waited to say goodbye she'd lose her nerve. She'd make the easy choice. She'd choose Rafe, the man she loved, instead of the family she'd never known. And she'd never find the courage to stand up for who she really was. She was a Quinn. Everything she'd become since that moment in Ireland proved it. Keely Mc-Clain was gone and Keely Quinn had taken her place.

Clutching the car keys in her hand, she walked back into the living room. She stood behind the sofa for a long time, staring at Rafe, her gaze skimming his face and imagining his body naked beneath the comforter. There would never be another man like him and, for that, she was sad. But she couldn't regret what they'd shared. Their affair had shown her who she really was—a strong, passionate woman, a woman capable of love, a woman who took chances in life.

Keely drew a ragged breath, then turned for the door, willing herself to walk out without looking back. When she got outside, the sun was just coming up, the low rays glittering on fresh snow. The driveway was clear and Rafe's car had been cleaned off.

She walked toward it, each step more determined than the last. The car door was frozen shut and she tugged on the handle, tears welling up in her eyes. Maybe she wasn't supposed to leave. Maybe this was a sign. She gave it one more tug and it came open. Keely quickly crawled inside and slipped the key in the ignition. The engine roared to life, but she clutched the steering wheel for a long moment before she put the car in gear.

As she steered up the driveway, she wondered why fate had thrown them together that night in front of the pub. If she believed in things like destiny and karma and kismet, then she was meant to meet Rafe.

But maybe it hadn't been to love him. Maybe it was to show her how strong the bonds of family could be.

Whatever was going to happen in Boston, Keely was ready for it. She'd go back and tell her brothers what she knew. And then she'd introduce herself and get to know her family. And someday, when everything was back to normal, then maybe she would call Rafe…and they could have dinner…and talk.

But what the future might hold with Rafe would have to wait. Right now, there were things in her life more important than passion.

HE HAD KNOWN she was gone the moment he opened his eyes. The fire had crackled brightly beside him, but the cabin had been silent. He'd dressed, then used his cell phone to call for a car, finding a limo service that operated between Boston and the ski resorts at nearby Stowe.

All the way back home, Rafe had tried not to think about her, but memories of their night together filled his mind. He'd never wanted a woman as much as he wanted Keely. But it wasn't just about passion and release. He needed her in his life to give him balance and perspective. Keely had shown him what happiness was all about.

When he'd arrived at his apartment, his doorman had handed him the keys to his Mercedes, informing him that Keely had delivered his car safely to the parking garage just hours before. Rafe hadn't even bothered to go upstairs. Instead, he'd hopped in his car and driven directly to his office.

Rafe stared at the mess on his desk. He'd come to the office to get his mind off of Keely. But he'd picked up one project after another, then been distracted by lapses into fantasies. He had to admit, even his fantasies weren't as good as the reality of making love to Keely.

He cursed softly. "Focus, focus."

Digging through the papers, he picked up a prospectus for an office complex Kencor was planning in Portland, Maine. But as he stared at the columns of figures, he lost his concentration once again. Learning what had really happened to his father had consumed his thoughts before he met Keely. And now he wasn't even sure he cared anymore. His father was dead and nothing he found out was going to bring him back. But Keely was alive, she was part of the present, and he'd let her go.

"What the hell—oh. Hello. What are you doing here?" Rafe looked up from his report to find Sylvie standing at the door.

"Nice catch. That will be five dollars. Half a curse."

She shook her head. "It's New Year's Day. Shouldn't you be home watching football and thinking about how you're going to treat me better this year?"

"You know I don't celebrate the holidays."

"Then what were you doing up at the cabin with a woman on New Year's Eve?" Sylvie asked.

"Are we related? Because we should be, considering the amount of time you spend meddling in my life.''

Sylvie walked into his office and flopped into one of Rafe's wing chairs. ''I came to work because my children were driving me crazy and my husband is wallpapering the bathroom. If I didn't leave, I'd be forced to give him advice and then he'd get mad and we'd end up bickering for the rest of the day.''

''So, is that what marriage is like?''

''Why, are you thinking of giving it a try?''

Rafe laughed. ''Why would you think that?''

''I don't know. You've been acting a little weird lately. I thought maybe you'd met someone.''

''Maybe I have.''

A silence descended around them. Sylvie tapped her foot against his desk, always impatient. ''Well,'' she finally said, ''is that it?''

''How did you know you wanted to get married? What was it that sealed the deal? I mean, choosing to spend the rest of your life with one person is a big decision.''

''It wasn't a difficult decision,'' Sylvie said. ''I just knew I couldn't imagine my future without him in it. Whenever I thought of events in my life, he was always there in these photos I had in my head. For a while, I forced myself to remove him from the images, but he kept creeping back in. So that was it. Since he was already in the photos, I decided to keep him.''

''It sounds so simple.''

''It is, if you let it be.''

Rafe leaned back in his chair and linked his hands behind his head. "And what about Tom? Did he feel the same way? Were you in his head photos, too?"

"No. Not at first. It took a little convincing. I think men are more leery about commitment than women. They always believe there's someone better waiting just around the bend. But then, sooner or later, you realize that even if the person around the bend is cuter or smarter or richer, that doesn't make a difference."

Rafe closed his eyes and tipped his head back. "It doesn't make a difference," he murmured.

"What doesn't?"

"Keely." He paused. "Her name is Keely Quinn. And I know I'll never find someone like her. Never."

Sylvie broke into a wide grin. "Then what's stopping you?"

"Problems. Big problems. Her family."

"If you love her, you can overcome anything."

"Didn't I read that on a greeting card somewhere?" Rafe straightened the papers on his desk and then stood up. "I'm going home. I'm not going to get anything done today. Maybe I'll watch a little football and do some wallpapering."

Sylvie laughed. "Seriously, if you need any advice, you can always come to me. Especially when it comes to fine jewelry, chocolates and flowers."

"I'll remember that." Rafe paused before he walked out of his office. "Go home, Sylvie. And count your lucky stars that you have what you have."

As Rafe rode the elevator down to the parking garage, he thought about his conversation with Sylvie.

Besides his mother, she was about the closest thing he had to family. He valued her opinion. But he still couldn't believe that falling in love was simple. In truth, it was the most difficult, confusing, unbalancing thing he'd ever experienced.

"Give it up," Rafe murmured. "Walk away before Keely Quinn cuts the legs out from under you and you can't walk at all."

But he couldn't walk away from his memories, the images that flashed in his head every time he thought about Keely. No matter where he was, no matter what he was doing, she'd be with him. For how long? Months? Years? The rest of his life?

The elevator doors opened and Rafe strolled toward his car in the otherwise empty parking lot. He slipped inside and put the key in the ignition, then turned to back the car out of his parking spot. But as he did, he noticed a pair of gloves sitting on the front passenger seat. He stopped the car, then reached out and picked them up. They were Keely's.

Rafe brought them up to his nose. He could still smell her perfume in the cashmere lining. He closed his eyes and let the scent drift through his head. She probably missed these, especially in this cold weather. Rafe reached into his pocket and pulled out his cell phone, ready to punch in the number for the bed-and-breakfast where she was staying.

But after entering only half the number, he snapped the phone closed. "Damn it," he muttered. He was looking for an excuse to see her again. It wasn't as if she couldn't afford a new pair of gloves. For now, he'd let her go. She could solve her problems with her family and stand behind her father.

Rafe flipped open his phone again and punched in a number on speed dial. The owner of one of Kencor's preferred contracting companies picked up after two rings. "Rafe Kendrick here. I need a favor. I want you to find me an asbestos contractor that can do a small job very quickly. Within the next week. And I want to make some special arrangements for payment. I want them to reduce their rate and I'll pick up the difference. Call me back with a name."

Rafe closed the phone and smiled. So maybe he could repair a few of the bridges that he had burned. And perhaps, someday, he and Keely could meet in the middle.

CHAPTER NINE

KEELY SAT at the table near the front window of the bakery, her gaze fixed on the three sketches she'd laid out on the table. The bride and her mother had been discussing the merits of each design for nearly a half hour and she was starting to get a bit annoyed.

The last place she wanted to be right now was back in New York. But when she'd returned from Rafe's cabin, there had been a stack of messages waiting for her at the bed-and-breakfast. Her mother had been desperately trying to contact her. When she called home, Keely was stunned to learn that both Janelle and Kim had made a New Year's resolution—to open their own cake-decorating business. To that end, they'd both handed in their resignations before the clock struck midnight, leaving Keely with only one assistant, and a rookie at that.

So she'd rushed back home and over the past few days had been elbow deep in buttercream, working day and night to finish the jobs they'd been contracted for, and to meet with customers who had been waiting for over a month to discuss their ideas.

Keely sighed softly and glanced between the bride and her mother. What was so difficult about choosing? If it were her wedding, she'd know precisely what she wanted. She'd wear a simple silk shantung gown with an Irish lace overlay on the bodice and a fingertip-length veil. And her bridesmaids would wear deep blue if the wedding was in winter and pale peach if it were in summer. Her wedding cake would be alive with color, maybe a detailed basket-weave pattern with fresh berries cascading over the edges of the tiers, or gum paste roses with iridescent color. A small combo that played romantic dance standards would entertain at the reception and guests would dine on beef filet with a rich demiglace sauce and sautéed fingerling potatoes.

As for her groom, Rafe would be dressed in— Keely stopped herself. After all that had happened between them, how could she possibly believe that she and Rafe would ever walk down the aisle together? That was just a fantasy now, and it would probably remain a fantasy. She sighed inwardly. But he would have made a handsome groom, dressed in a morning coat and ascot with a single white rose in his lapel.

She could have been planning her wedding right now if she hadn't chosen her family over Rafe. If she had given him a chance, he might have asked her to marry him. She bit her bottom lip. What if *she'd* given up her only chance at true happiness? What if Rafe Kendrick was the last man who would ever tell her he loved her?

"What if I grow old alone, turn into a wretched

old hag and everyone calls me the 'cake lady'?"
Keely murmured.

"Miss McClain?"

Keely shook herself out of her daydream. "Yes?
I'm sorry, what were you saying?"

The bride pointed to the tulip cake. "This is the
one. It's perfect for our spring wedding. But I was
wondering if we might change the color of the tulips
to go with my colors."

"Of course," Keely said. "That would be no problem. Why don't you send me a small swatch of the
color and I'll match it exactly? Then you'll also need
to give me your final guest count so I can size the
tiers accordingly." Keely smiled, then stood. She
took the cake design and rolled it up, then handed it
to the bride. "You can take this with you to show
your bridesmaids."

The bride held out her hand and Keely took it.
"Thank you so much for agreeing to do our cake.
The first time I saw one of your designs, I knew I'd
have to have you for my wedding."

"A Keely McClain cake is the best," the bride's
mother said. "And our Lisa Ann deserves the best."

Keely watched as the bride and her mother walked
out the front door of the bakery. "Keely Quinn," she
murmured. "A Keely *Quinn* cake is the best."

She gathered up the rejected designs, then wandered back into the workroom. Fiona was there, piping a border around the top edge of another Keely
Quinn design, this one for a wedding in the style of

Louis XIV. "That's supposed to be fleur de lis," Keely said. "Not rope. Rope is too simple."

"If you don't like it, you can bloody well do it yourself," Fiona said, arching her eyebrow.

Keely sighed. She had only been back home for a few days and already she and her mother were on the edge of an argument. Fiona still couldn't accept her decision to go to Boston and find her father and brothers, and had never stopped trying to convince her to stop her "foolish" quest. Yet she also seemed desperate for any news Keely might provide about her sons. Add to that her worry over the bakery and the business and she snapped at everything Keely said.

Keely picked up a pastry bag filled with icing and began to pipe the fleur de lis onto the cake. "There's something I need to tell you, Ma."

Fiona looked up. "The only thing I want to hear is that you're home to stay."

"This is serious," Keely said softly.

"What is it?" Worry suffused Fiona's expression. "Is it one of the boys?"

"No, they're fine. At least they were the last time I saw them. It's Seamus. He's in trouble."

Her mother laughed harshly and shook her head. "Well, that's not news now, is it? He always had a fondness for pushing his limits with the law."

The border her mother was piping suddenly became uneven. Keely reached over and grabbed her arm, then slowly lowered the pastry bag to the table. "This is different, Ma. He's in real trouble. He's been accused of murder."

Fiona gasped and the bag slipped from her fingers. "Murder?"

"Do you remember anything about a crew member on my father's boat who died during a fishing run? His name was Sam Kendrick."

Keely saw the subtle shift in her mother's expression, as if she were surprised to hear the name after so many years. "No," she said. "I can't recall the name."

"You must know something. Ma, a man died on Seamus's boat. Surely he must have spoken of it."

"He might have mentioned it, but that was a long time ago." Fiona picked up the pastry bag. "I don't recall the particulars. Are you going to help me with this or are you going to stand there and chatter?"

"Try to remember. It's important."

"I hope you're not planning to go back to Boston anytime soon," Fiona said, changing the subject. "Your absence has put a terrible strain on the business. We haven't booked any new clients since you left and if you don't come back soon we won't have any business next spring. The clients want to meet with you. You're the one with the reputation, not me, and they won't book with us unless they get to talk to you about their weddings."

"This is my business," Keely muttered. "And if I choose to run it into the ground, that's also my business." She paused, realizing how harsh her words sounded. "I'm not going to run it into the ground. But maybe it would be better if we slowed things down a little bit."

"I'm beginning to think you prefer Boston to New York. Maybe we should just think about picking up and moving the business there."

Keely knew her mother was simply being sarcastic. But the idea wasn't a bad one. Boston was only three hours away with decent traffic. She'd have to buy a refrigerated truck and they'd have to make arrangements to deliver the cakes on Friday night rather than Saturday morning, and she would have to travel back into the city once or—

She drew her thoughts to a halt. This was crazy! She promised herself she wouldn't fall into this trap, of fantasizing about a life with a man she could never have. If she lived in Boston, in all practicality her business in New York would be seriously affected. She'd have to build a whole new clientele in a whole new town, where people might not be inclined to spend thousands of dollars on a silly cake.

"When are you planning to tell them?"

Keely grabbed a damp towel and wiped a bit of icing from her hand. "With everything that's going on with Seamus, it didn't seem to be the right time. Just more confusion on top of what they already have. I just wish there was something I could do to help. It would make telling them so much easier."

"Lee Franklin," Fiona murmured as she continued piping.

"What?"

"Lee Franklin. He was a crew member on that run. He saw the whole thing. His wife and I were good friends and she told me what he said about the incident. Your father wasn't responsible for that man's death, Keely.''

"Where is this Franklin guy?"

"I have no idea. I don't know if he's alive still." She stopped what she was doing and grabbed a pad and pencil from the table. After she'd scribbled something on the paper, she ripped the sheet off and handed it to Keely. "That's his social security number. I suppose you could track him through that."

"How could you possibly know his social security number?"

"I used to do the books for the *Mighty Quinn*," Fiona explained. "I made up little tricks to remember the numbers of the crewmen so I wouldn't have to look them up all the time. Lee Franklin's began with Conor's birthday and ended with our house number. His was the easiest to remember."

Keely couldn't believe what she'd been given. She jumped off the stool and threw her arms around her mother's neck, giving her a fierce hug. "Thank you, Ma. You don't know what this means to me."

"But I know what it means to me. You're going back to Boston now and you don't know when you'll be back."

"I'm going to give this to my brothers," Keely said, "and then I'm going to tell them who I am." She rushed out of the workroom then turned around and hurried back in to give her mother a kiss on each cheek. "I'll be home in a few days."

As she grabbed her jacket and tugged it on, Keely couldn't contain her excitement. With this proof, she could make a real contribution to Seamus's defense. If she helped to clear her father of a murder charge, her family would have to accept her. They'd probably welcome her with open arms.

But as she walked to her car, another thought occurred to her. If the truth was known, then Rafe would be forced to give up his vendetta against her father. And once he accepted the truth, then there would be nothing standing in their way. She could love him and he could love her.

Keely glanced down at the paper clutched in her hand, then said a silent prayer that Lee Franklin was still alive and well and living somewhere easy to find. Though she had more than a few issues riding on this, she'd deal with them one at a time. And Seamus Quinn was first up.

"I'M SURE YOU CAN see that this will be the most efficient use of this property and it will provide badly needed office space in this section of Boston. We expect that by the time it's built, we'll have eighty-five percent of the space rented and one-hundred percent occupancy within the year." Rafe pointed to the architectural drawings that were set up around the conference room on easels. "We have most of our financing in place, but we're looking for a few people willing to invest capital with an excellent return on that investment."

The conference room door slowly opened and Sylvie Arnold stepped inside. She nodded to Rafe in unspoken communication and Rafe quickly wrapped up his presentation. As the investors chatted among themselves, Rafe joined Sylvie at the door.

"It's her," Sylvie whispered.

"Who's her?"

"Her. At least I think it's her. It has to be."

"Who?"

"She says her name is Keely McClain."

Rafe tried to hide his surprise, but he knew it was evident on his face by the satisfied smile on Sylvie's.

"I knew it," she said. "I knew it had to be her. Well, I just have to say that she seems very nice."

"You know nothing," Rafe said coolly. He'd wondered if this moment would come. He also wondered how he'd react. Over the past few days, he'd resigned himself to the fact that, though he and Keely had shared an incredibly intense and passionate affair, it was now over. She'd made her choice and it hadn't been him. "Tell her that I'll have to call her back."

"I can't. She's not on the phone. She's waiting in your office. And she looks a little nervous."

"You put her in my office?"

"She said she needed to see you. And you didn't put her on the list. If you don't want to talk to or see one of your women, you're supposed to put her on the list."

"Goddamn it, Sylvie, I—"

"Ten dollars," she said, holding out her hand.

Rafe hauled out his wallet and slapped a fifty into her hand. "Keep the change. I'll need the credit for the little talk you and I are going to have later."

He walked out of the conference room and strode

down the hall, straightening his tie as he walked. In truth, he really didn't want to see her. After what he'd said to her that night in front of the fire, he felt like a fool. He'd risked his heart and his pride by telling her he loved her. And now she was here to remind him of the mistake he'd made.

He couldn't put all the blame on Keely. He had never considered himself capable of love so he had hardened his heart to any emotion long ago. But in the days that he knew Keely, she'd gradually made him see that those emotions weren't gone for good, they were simply asleep. Well, after their time at the cabin, he'd decided to put them away for good. Rafe Kendrick wasn't made for love.

When he reached his office, he grabbed the doorknob, then paused. He ought to have Sylvie say that he was too busy to see her. That would be the easiest way to handle the situation. But Rafe knew how stubborn his assistant could be, especially when it meant involving herself in his personal life. She always claimed to know what was best for him and he had a sneaking suspicion that Sylvie thought Keely fell into that category. Drawing a deep breath, he pushed the doors open.

Keely stood as soon as he stepped inside. Their gazes met across his office and held, and for a moment, he forgot to breathe. Why was he always taken aback by her beauty? There was something about her that drew his eyes to her face, something that he found irresistible. ''Keely.''

''Hi, Rafe.''

Though it had only been a few days since they'd seen each other, Rafe was stunned by his physical reaction. All the old desire came rushing back and he fought the urge to cross the office, pull her into his arms and kiss her senseless. His mind flashed images of their last night together, so vivid that he could barely think. "Please, sit down." Rafe walked past her and took a spot behind his desk, standing with his hands resting on the back of his leather chair. "How have you been?"

"Good. Busy. But good." She hadn't taken a seat. "I told your secretary my name was McClain. I thought it might be better than…well, I wasn't sure how much she knows." She stood next to the chair, shifting uneasily from foot to foot.

"What have you been up to?"

"I went back to New York for a few days to deal with some business at the bakery. Running a business from out of town has been difficult."

Rafe had almost forgotten that, under normal circumstances, Keely Quinn lived in New York and he lived in Boston. That barrier hadn't even come up in conversation, but now that he'd thought of it, it was simply one more reason why he and Keely never would have made it.

"I'm really anxious to tell my family so that my life can get back to normal," she continued.

"You haven't told them yet?"

"No," she replied with a defensive edge. "That's why I've come back. I'm going to tell them tonight."

"Everything's getting back to normal for me, too," Rafe said, changing the subject to soothe her mood.

"Good. You got back to Boston all right, I see."

"I had a cell phone in my coat pocket. I called for a car."

Keely blinked in surprise, her mouth falling open. At first, he was sure she'd react angrily. After all, the lack of a phone had been the major reason they'd spent an extra night at the cabin. But if she was upset over his deception, she didn't show it. "Good. I'm glad. And you found your car?"

"My doorman gave me the keys." Jeez, this small talk was driving him crazy. It was as if they'd just met, fumbling to think of something to say to each other. No one would have guessed that, just a few days ago, they'd been on very intimate terms, whispering wicked things to each other in the midst of passion. "Is that all you came for? To find out if I got back all right?"

"No. I wanted to give you this." She held a small piece of paper out over his desk.

Rafe took it from her, his hand brushing hers, causing a current to race up his arm. "What's this?"

"It's the name and social security number for one of the men on the crew of my father's fishing boat. His name is Lee Franklin. According to my mother, he was there when your father died. And my mother says that he knows everything that happened. She also says that my father didn't have anything to do with your father's death." Keely shrugged. "That's all I came for. I'm going to give the information to Conor so he can give it to the authorities, but I thought you should know that there's going to be someone backing up Seamus's story. You said you wanted the truth and I hope that we'll find Lee Franklin and he'll tell us what really happened.'' She paused. ''And you'll be satisfied.''

''Thank you,'' Rafe said.

''Well, that's all I came for.'' She turned and started for the door.

''Keely, I've missed you.''

She froze. ''And I've missed you,'' Keely admitted, her back still to him.

''Can I take you to lunch?''

Keely slowly turned back to him. ''It's nearly four.''

''Then dinner?''

A smile curled the corners of her mouth. ''Maybe we should just leave things the way they are, at least until everything is resolved with my family.''

''Yeah, you're probably right.''

Her smile wavered. ''And maybe I'm not.'' She drew a deep breath, as if gathering her determination. ''I have to go. I'll…see you.''

A moment later she was gone. Rafe raked his fingers through his hair. This was not what he wanted— Keely breezing in and out of his life with no thought to when they'd see each other again, if ever. He'd always been happy—and even relieved—when the women in his life walked away. But, with Keely, an emptiness had settled in and he found himself missing her a few seconds after she'd gone.

"Damn it," he muttered. He hated this feeling of living in limbo. Either he'd have to do everything in his power to keep her in his life or he'd have to walk away. He couldn't stand this indecision. "So what will it be?"

He glanced down at the paper he still had in his hand. If Lee Franklin could prove Seamus's innocence then he'd have to do his best to find the guy and bring him to Boston to tell his story. He strode over to his desk and pushed his intercom button. But rather than answer, Sylvie came running through his office door.

"Yes?"

"I want you to call Stan Marks in security and have him come up here right away. I've got a job I need him to do."

"And…?" Sylvie asked, a sly grin quirking her lips.

"And what?"

"How did it go? She seems very nice. And pretty. Not your usual type."

"And what's my usual type?"

"Bitchy rich women," Sylvie said. "And that's not a curse word. That was an adjective. This one seems nice. The kind of woman you'd marry."

"Yeah," Rafe murmured.

"Yeah?" A grin broke across Sylvie's face. "You are smitten. I've never seen you smitten before. It looks good on you."

With that, she turned and walked out of the office, leaving Rafe to ponder the true meaning of *smitten.*

At one time he would have considered Sylvie's comment an insult, but now he took it as a forgone conclusion. Somehow he'd managed to fall in love with the one woman in the world that he shouldn't have.

KEELY STARED UP at the facade of the District Four Police Station. She'd called nearly every station house in Boston until she'd located Conor's, then managed to find out when his shift ended. If she just hung around the front door, Keely was certain she'd see him as he left. She glanced at her watch. His shift was over at six and it was nearly six-thirty. Maybe she'd missed him. Maybe he'd parked in the back. Maybe he'd—

"Keely?"

She spun around to find Conor standing on the sidewalk just a few feet away. He always seemed so serious and intimidating. Keely swallowed hard. This was it. This was the moment she had been waiting for. "Hi. How are you?"

Conor frowned. "I'm fine. What are you doing here? Are you in some kind of trouble?"

"No trouble. I'm fine." She shook her head. "I—I have something for you. Actually, for Seamus. Liam told me what was going on my last night at the pub. I know the police are investigating Seamus for a murder and I know he's innocent. And I thought you might be able to use this to prove it."

"I don't understand."

"Lee Franklin was one of the crew members on the boat. That's Lee Franklin's social security number. From what I understand, you can trace a person's whereabouts by their social security number, right?''

Conor stared at her in disbelief and snatched the paper from her fingers. ''How do you know about Lee Franklin?''

She forced a smile. ''I know a lot of things.''

''How did you get this?''

Keely took a deep breath and tried to stop her heart from hammering. It was time. She'd waited so long but now it was finally time. ''My mother.''

''All right, how does your mother know?''

''She used to do the bookkeeping for your father's fishing boat.'' Keely bit her bottom lip. *Just say it!* He was ready to hear it—she just had to get it out. ''And—and she was also married to your father.'' Keely waited for the impact of her claim to sink in.

Conor shook his head. ''My father was only ever married to my mother.''

''Yes, I know,'' Keely said. ''Your father is my father. And my mother is your mother. My name is Keely Quinn and I was born six months after Fiona Quinn walked out of your life.'' That last came out in an unbroken string of words. But once it was out there, Keely wished that she could take it back. That she could have said it with more patience.

For a long moment, he simply stared at her, his expression filled with astonishment. Then he turned and walked five or six steps down the sidewalk. Keely held her breath and waited for him to stop, to say something—anything—that would give her a clue to his real feelings.

Conor spun around. "This is crazy. It can't be. My mother is dead and I don't have a sister."

Keely reached for the claddagh pendant, pulling it out from beneath her sweater. The emerald sparkled in the light from the streetlamps. "My mother gave me this. She said Seamus would recognize it. Do you recognize it?"

Conor gasped, then hurried back to her. He reached out and held the pendant between his fingers, rubbing the emerald with his thumb. "I do. My mother used to have a necklace just like this. She never took it off." He let the pendant drop. "He told us she was dead. We didn't want to believe it, but after a while it made sense. She never tried to contact us."

"She's not dead," Keely said. "She's living in New York City. She moved there after she left your— I mean, my...*our* father. That's where I was born."

"She's alive?" Conor asked, his voice filled with amazement. "My mother is alive?"

Keely felt tears press at the corners of her eyes. She knew what Conor was going through right now— to be told he had a sibling and then to be told that the parent he thought was dead wasn't. "I took the job at the bar so I could get to know you all. I didn't mean to deceive you, but I wasn't sure how you would react to the news. At first, I was going to tell you as a group, but then I got scared. Besides, now that the bar is closed, I wasn't sure when you'd all get together again."

Conor grabbed her arm. "You have to come with me," he said, pulling her along the sidewalk.

"Where are we going?"

"I'm supposed to meet my brothers at the pub. The contractors are starting work in a few days and we've got to clear everything out. Sean and Liam are probably already there. I want you to tell them what you told me."

Keely dug in her heels, pulling him to a stop. "I'm not sure that would be the best—"

"What are you talking about?" He laughed. "You're our sister. And it's sure as hell time everyone knew."

She shook her head. "Why don't I meet you there?" Keely countered. "I have my car and I need a little time alone to work up my courage." She drew a deep breath. "I have to say, this went pretty well but who knows how they'll react?"

Conor smiled. Then his smile faded slightly as he stared at her. "My God. I remember that first time we met on the sidewalk outside the pub. There was something about you that looked so familiar. It was your eyes." He hooked his finger beneath her chin and turned her face up to the streetlights.

"They're the same color as yours," Keely said.

"That shows you what a great detective I am. I didn't even notice." He stared at her for a long moment. "I just can't believe you're real. And that you're here after all these years."

"I can't either." She laughed softly. "If you only knew the time it took me to work up the courage to tell you this."

"Well, I can assure you that the rest of my brothers are going to be happy to hear what you have to say."

Keely winced. "Maybe you should break the news to them."

He took her hand in his and gave it an encouraging squeeze. "No. I think it's better coming from you. My car is parked just down the street. I'll meet you at the pub and we'll tell them together. How's that?"

She never could have imagined that it would go so well. Telling Conor had seemed so easy—too easy. Perhaps there was trouble yet to come. But if there was, she'd have to face it. "That would be good. I'll meet you at the pub."

Keely was almost reluctant to leave him, but she needed time to herself, time to regroup and gather her courage again. At least she had Conor behind her. From what she could tell, he seemed to be the unofficial head of the family, the brother whom the others turned to when a disagreement needed to be settled. If he wanted her in the family, then he'd find a way to convince the others she belonged.

Keely hurried to her car and climbed inside, then clutched the steering wheel. So many emotions whirled inside her. She wasn't sure whether she wanted to laugh or cry. "Hello, I'm Keely Quinn." For the first time, she could actually say the words and have them mean something. It was no longer a dream. She *was* Keely Quinn. As she started the car, she drew a deep breath. By the end of the night, she'd have a family.

The drive to the pub passed in a blur, her mind

occupied with thoughts of what was to come. She felt a little dizzy and light-headed and wondered if she should have accepted Conor's offer of a ride. But then Keely opened a window and let the cold air rush inside, clearing her head. Once she met her brothers, she'd have to call her mother. And then she'd call—

Keely stopped herself. She couldn't call Rafe. Though she longed to hear his voice, he wasn't a part of this. Drawing him back into her life for her own selfish motives wouldn't be fair. Once she straightened out her family life *and* Seamus's legal problems, then maybe she could turn her attention back to her love life.

When she pulled up to the pub, the street was nearly empty. She saw Conor sitting on the steps, his shoulders hunched against the cold. He really was a nice guy, so solid and dependable. It was good to have him on her side. Keely regretted that she hadn't had the chance to grow up knowing him. She imagined she could have learned a lot from her oldest brother.

But then maybe she'd always had a part of him with her. She'd been a Quinn since the moment she was born. No matter how hard she tried to be her mother's daughter, Keely suspected that she'd been her brothers' sister first—emotional and impulsive, stubborn and determined, a Quinn to the bone. For the first time in her life, she felt as if she fit somewhere.

She stepped out of the car and slowly approached Conor. He stood and smiled. "Are you all set?"

Keely nodded. "I guess now is as good a time as any."

Conor took the front steps two at a time, then pulled open the front door. Keely stepped inside the brightly lit pub, a tight smile pasted on her face. The jukebox blared a raucous Irish tune and no one noticed her arrival. But when Conor shouted, they all turned.

"You want to shut that thing off?" he yelled.

Liam reached for the volume control behind the bar and turned the music down. "Hey, Keely! What are you doing back here? I figured by now you'd have a job at another joint."

Keely smiled. "Not quite yet. The market's pretty tight for really bad waitresses."

"Keely came here to tell you something," Conor said. "Go ahead, tell them."

"I can't just blurt it out," she murmured, her face warming in embarrassment.

"All right," Conor said. He took Keely's hand and dragged her over to the bar. Then, grabbing her around the waist, he lifted her up and set her on the edge. The brothers gathered around, curious at his behavior. "Tell them your name," Conor ordered.

"We know her name," Brian said.

Keely shook her head. "No, you don't. Not my real name. It's Quinn. Keely Quinn."

Five brothers reacted the exact same way—with mild shock. "Are you a relative?" Dylan asked.

"Definitely," Conor said. "Look at her eyes."

They all stepped forward, staring at her as if she

were a bug in a jar. Keely smiled weakly. One by one, realization dawned and their expressions turned from curiosity to disbelief.

"Holy shit," Liam murmured.

"What the hell?" Sean said.

Conor cleared his throat. "Keely, tell them who your mother is."

"Fiona McClain."

"And your father?"

She swallowed hard. "Seamus Quinn."

Conor nodded, a wide grin splitting his face. He turned to his brothers. "Keely is our sister."

His announcement was met with dead silence. "We don't have a sister," Brendan finally said. "How the hell could we have a sister and not know about it?"

"Show them the necklace, Keely."

With trembling fingers, she reached beneath her sweater and pulled the claddagh out. Dylan stepped closer. "I remember this. She always wore it. And when she'd tuck us in at night, it would hang from her neck and I'd twist my fingers around it and hold her there until she kissed me again."

"I have a picture of her wearing that necklace," Sean said.

They all turned to look at him. "You have a picture of our mother?" Conor asked.

He frowned. "Yeah. I took it before Da threw everything out. I wasn't about to tell you guys. You would have pinched it first chance you got." He reached into his back pocket and pulled out his wallet, then withdrew the tattered photo. Keely's brothers passed it around the circle, staring at it long and hard.

"I have a picture, too," Keely said. She reached into her purse and withdrew the photo Maeve Quinn had given her in Ireland. The brothers passed it around. "That was taken right before you left Ireland. Liam, you weren't born yet. And, you can see, my mother is wearing the necklace."

"I remember this day," Conor said.

"She was so beautiful," Brendan murmured.

Keely nodded. "She still is. She's alive and she's living in New York."

Suddenly, five pairs of eyes were riveted on her face. "Say that again," Dylan demanded.

"I know it's probably hard to believe. Conor told me you thought she was dead. And I'm not sure I can explain my mother's motives for walking out on you all. You'll have to ask her that yourself. But she is alive and I think she'd like to see you, if you're willing to see her. I don't think you've ever been out of her thoughts, not for one single day."

"She left us with a drunk," Dylan said, a trace of bitterness in his words. "Do you have any idea what it was like growing up in that house? She never called, never even bothered to check on us."

Conor held up his hand. "That's not Keely's fault. She had no control over our childhood. So maybe we should take up those issues with our mother and not her."

They all nodded and Keely relaxed, grateful they weren't going to punish her for her mother's mistakes.

"I'm sorry I waited so long, but I wasn't sure how to tell you."

Brendan stepped up first and drew Keely into his arms, giving her a gentle hug. "Welcome to the family, little sister." He laughed. "Imagine that. The Quinn brothers with a little sister. I suppose we're going to have to start watching our language when you're around."

"Keely brought some other news," Conor explained. "She gave me a lead on one of the crew members who was on the *Mighty Quinn* when Sam Kendrick died. A lead that her mother gave her."

Keely nodded. "My—our mother remembered that there was a Lee Franklin on the boat and she told me that he knew what had happened. If we can find him, he can tell his story and clear Seamus of Kendrick's murder."

"Speaking of Kendrick…" Sean said. Reaching over to the bar, he grabbed a file folder. "I've been doing a little investigating." He held up a photo he took from the folder. "This is Kendrick's son. Recognize him?"

Liam snatched the photo from Sean. "Sonofabitch," he muttered. "He's been to the bar. The past few months, he's been hanging out here right under our noses."

Keely's eyes went wide as the photo was shoved at her.

"Have you ever seen him?" Sean asked. "Did you ever wait on him? Did he say anything to you?"

"I think he has been in the bar a few times," she

murmured, hoping that none of them remembered the
night she threw sparkling water in Rafe's face.

"This is the guy," Sean said. "He's the one causing all our problems. He's some multimillionaire. He
made his money in real estate. I figure he's out for
some kind of revenge. But why spread these lies
about Seamus?"

"Maybe he believes they're the truth," Keely said.
Her brothers turned to her and she felt a blush warm
her cheeks. "Not that I believe Seamus did anything
wrong. But maybe that's what this Kendrick guy was
led to believe. Just like you believed your mother was
dead."

"If that guy ever sets foot in this bar again," Dylan
muttered, "I'll punch his teeth so far down his throat
he'll have to talk out of his ass."

"I think we should find this guy and beat some
sense into him," Sean added.

As her brothers debated how to handle Rafe Kendrick, Keely picked up the photo and stared at the
image of the man who had been her lover. She ran
her fingers over each feature of his face, recalling how
he really felt, the strong line of his lower lip still
damp from her kiss, the rough surface of his beard
when he needed a shave, the intensity of his gaze as
she watched her come.

Keely drew a ragged breath. "Is it all right if I keep
this photo? I might remember something later."

If she couldn't have the real thing, a photo would
have to do. But it wouldn't do for much longer. Keely
needed to see Rafe and she needed to see him soon.

CHAPTER TEN

A BANNER HUNG above the front door of Quinn's, proclaiming the grand reopening of "Southie's Favorite Irish Pub" the day after next. Free Irish stew and corned beef sandwiches should draw all the regulars back after just a few weeks of being closed, Keely mused.

Though progress with the bar had been amazingly swift, her father's problems with the law hadn't followed suit. Liam had called her in New York to give her the news. Though Conor and Sean had tried, they hadn't been able to locate Lee Franklin. Seamus's case would go before the grand jury in two days and they'd decide whether to indict or not, based on the testimony of Ken Yaeger. Though Seamus had professed his innocence, according to Liam the prosecutor wasn't interested in his story. That would be left for a jury to decide, if the matter actually went to trial.

Keely wondered why they'd chosen to reopen the pub on the very same day as the grand jury. She suspected it was wishful thinking, an attempt to will a positive outcome when all looked bleak. But she'd come back to Boston with one final bit of hope for her brothers and father. She glanced back at her car parked in front of the pub. She wasn't sure that what she planned to do now was the right thing, but it felt right…in her heart.

When she stepped inside, she found the interior of Quinn's in chaos. The tables were scattered haphazardly around the bar and boxes of bottles littered the floor. Brendan looked up and called her name, a smile breaking across his face. Liam and Sean stood behind the bar, arranging bottles on the shelves. And Conor and Dylan appeared a few moments later from the door that led to the kitchen. When Brian walked in behind her, Keely was satisfied that all her brothers were present and accounted for.

"Hey there, little sister," Brian said, dragging her along to the bar. "Come to help us fix this mess?"

Keely smiled. "You look like you could use my help."

"Since the pub bears your name, it's a family obligation. Grab a rag and get to work."

Glancing around the bar, she searched for one member of the family who was missing. "Where's Seamus?" she asked.

"He's in the kitchen," Dylan said. "He hasn't come out since we told him you'd be coming today. I hope you're prepared to stay a few days. He might not come out for a while."

"Then he knows about me?"

Conor nodded. "We told him last night. I think he's afraid to talk to you, Keely." He turned and shouted, "Da, come out here. There's someone here you need to meet."

They all waited for Seamus to emerge from behind the swinging door to the kitchen. When he did, he was wearing a dirty apron that he quickly removed and tossed aside. He smoothed his hair with his palms, then approached Keely. She was surprised at how hesitant he appeared, wringing his hands together in front of him. She was accustomed to a brash and confident Seamus Quinn, a man who liked to stand up to people in an argument, the man who teased her and called her "lassie."

"I hear you're my daughter then," he said, his gaze taking in her face.

"I am," Keely replied, nodding her head and straightening to her full height. "Is that all right with you?"

He stared at her for a long moment, a crooked smile twitching at his lips. "I never knew I had a daughter. Might have done things a bit differently if I had." Seamus shrugged. "At least you'll never have any complaints about me bein' a bad father, will ya now?"

"I guess not."

He didn't appear to want a hug, so, instead, Keely stepped forward and gave him a quick kiss on the cheek. Seamus patted her shoulder, his face reddening with embarrassment. "Welcome to the family, lass. If you can stand it."

"Quite a welcome there, Da," Conor teased. "After that, she may decide to go back to New York and never claim us as her own.''

Seamus shook his finger at Conor. "Don't get me started, boyo. I've had enough with surprises lately and I don't want—'' He stopped suddenly, his gaze fixed beyond Keely and the boys, his eyes widening. They all slowly turned to see what had brought an end to his merriment. Keely's breath caught in her throat as she watched her mother step inside the pub. She glanced back at her brothers to see the same look of amazement on their faces that suffused Seamus's. She had told her mother to wait until she came out to get her, but Fiona had obviously grown impatient in the car.

Keely motioned to her to come in, but Fiona stayed glued to the spot just inside the door. "I asked my— I mean, *our* mother to come to Boston with me," she explained. "She has information about the accident on the *Mighty Quinn* and she's willing to speak to the prosecutors on behalf of Seamus. And she thinks she might know where to find Lee Franklin.''

For the moment, her brothers didn't seem to care about Franklin. All they could do was stare at Fiona as if they'd seen a ghost. After a long silence, Conor was the first to speak. "Hi, Ma.'' He slowly approached her. "Do you remember me?'' He slowly drew her toward the bar.

Tears swam in Fiona Quinn's eyes and her lower lip quivered. But joy also lit her face and Keely knew she'd done the right thing bringing her to Boston. "Of course I do, Conor.'' She looked from one son to the next. "I'd be able to pick each of you out of crowd. You haven't changed a bit. At least not to my eyes. Though you have grown taller than I ever would have expected."

"And you haven't changed a bit, either," Conor said.

When Fiona reached up and pressed her palm to Conor's cheek, a tear slipped away. She laughed softly as she brushed it from her face. "You're a good boy, Conor. You always were. And you've become a fine man. I understand you're married now."

He nodded. "I am. And Olivia, my wife, is going to have a baby. And both Dylan and Brendan are due to get married. Dylan in June and Brendan after that, when he and Amy get back from assignment in Turkey."

One by one, Fiona met her sons again after so many years apart. The anger that Keely expected from her brothers didn't surface and she wondered how they could so easily accept her mother's reappearance after her desertion so many years before. Then she remembered that they'd been told Fiona was dead.

By the time Fiona reached Liam, her tears were flowing freely. She drew him into her arms and hugged him fiercely. "You were the one I worried about the most," she said. "I knew that Conor and Dylan and Brendan were strong. And the twins had each other. But I was afraid for you."

"I survived, Ma. We all did. And we're glad you're back, even though it was a long time coming."

Fiona turned and smiled at them all. "You've

grown up to be such fine boys. Fine men, I should say.'' She sniffled, then slowly turned her attention to the last person in the room. She took a deep breath and met his gaze. "Hello, Seamus."

"Hello, Fi."

She slowly walked up to him. "It's been a long time."

He reached out and took her hand in a gesture so gentle that it startled Keely. She felt tears of her own burn in her eyes, the sight of her father and mother together causing a wave of emotion to wash over her. By the way they looked at each other, it was clear there was still something between them.

"We have a fine family here, wouldn't you say?" Seamus asked.

Fiona laughed softly. Keely had expected distrust or animosity or perhaps sarcasm from her mother. But Fiona looked at her husband as if they'd never been apart, as if they were still the same young couple starting out on their grand adventure to America, Seamus with his dreams and Fiona trusting him to make hers come true.

"You haven't changed a bit," Seamus continued. "You're still the prettiest lass I know."

"We have a lot of things to talk about, Seamus," Fiona said.

"That we do," Seamus murmured. "That we do. Can I show you the pub, Fi? I've made a bit of a success here. We serve food and drink. And there's a pool table in the back. Would you like to see the kitchen?"

"I'd like that."

They both wandered off, leaving their seven children completely speechless. Brian shook his head. "Look at the old man," he said. "You'd never know he was the same guy to tell us all those Mighty Quinn stories. After all this time, he's completely besotted."

"Mighty Quinn stories?" Keely asked.

"Ah," Brendan said. "We'll have to tell Keely a few of the tales, so she'll know the perils of falling in love. According to Da, love will destroy a Quinn if he—or she—surrenders to it. As you can see, Conor is a mess and Dylan and I can barely function. And there are evil women lying in wait for Sean and Brian and Liam. You're not in love, are you, Keely?"

She shook her head. "No. Of course not." Though it was a bald-faced lie, Keely really didn't have the guts to explain that she was in love—with a man they all hated. She'd have to deal with that little revelation later, when and if it was necessary.

Conor clapped his hands together. "Well, I suppose we should talk to Seamus's lawyer and let him know about our new witness. And you say our mother might know where we can find Franklin?"

Keely nodded. "She mentioned that his wife had talked about a brother who lived down in the Florida Keys and ran a charter business. If you find him, he might know where Lee Franklin is."

Conor reached out and slipped his arm around Keely's shoulder. "In all those Mighty Quinn tales, our ancestors always used to ride to the rescue of a damsel in distress. There are no damsels here, but you definitely rode to our rescue. I guess you now qualify as a Mighty Quinn.''

"I'm glad I could help,'' Keely said.

But would it be enough to wipe away her other sin—the sin of loving their sworn enemy? Would they look on her help as an even trade for accepting Rafe as part of her life? Or would the grudges run deep, too deep to be erased by a good deed? Keely wasn't going to know until she told them about Rafe. But, as Seamus had said, there had been enough surprises for the day.

This was one confession that would have to be revealed at exactly the right time—if she decided to reveal it at all.

THE GRAND REOPENING of Quinn's Pub was in full swing when Rafe walked in the door. He slowly approached the bar and took a spot near the end. After a quick scan of the crowd, he found Keely. She stood near the pool table talking to two women who were playing darts, women he recognized as Dylan's fiancée and Conor's wife. She wasn't wearing an apron, so Rafe assumed she wasn't working. If he could only get her alone, then maybe they'd have a chance to sort things out.

He'd heard about the grand jury. They had refused to bring charges against Seamus. At first, Rafe was sure the fix was in, that Conor had somehow managed to get his father off. But then he learned that Lee Franklin had been found in Key West. The man had sworn in an affidavit that the fight on the *Mighty*

Quinn had actually been between a drunken Ken Yaeger and Rafe's father. Seamus had tried to break up the fight and Sam Kendrick had been caught by the pitch of the boat in the storm. Talk of Yaeger's behavior had spread through the swordfishing fleet, propelled by Seamus's outrage. After the incident, Yaeger had been unable to get another spot on a boat for years.

Rafe didn't have to guess at Yaeger's motives for implicating Seamus. It all made sense and had Rafe not been so quick to jump to conclusions, he might never have brought these problems down on Seamus Quinn—or into his relationship with Seamus's daughter.

His father's death had been an accident. Rafe had always thought that he couldn't begin a real life until he knew for sure. But now that he did, he still felt adrift…empty…as if he were still searching for something. Or someone. Until now, he'd been too scared to risk it all—to risk his heart. But there was no need to dwell on the past anymore. He could have a future with Keely and he was going to make it happen.

He watched her as she moved to the dartboard. She wore a pair of jeans that hugged her backside and a top that was cut low enough to reveal the spot he'd often kissed between her breasts. She laughed, and though the sound of her laughter was swallowed up by the crowd, Rafe found himself smiling.

"Can I get you a drink?"

Rafe glanced up. He watched the friendly expression on Liam Quinn's face slowly change.

"Christ, it's you," Liam muttered. "You have a helluva lot of nerve showing your face after what you've done to our family."

"I just wanted the truth," Rafe said. "How was I supposed to know Yaeger was lying?"

"Hey, Sean," Liam shouted. "Look who dropped by. It's our old friend, Rafe Kendrick. Come to pay his respects."

The chatter that had filled the bar slowly died down as each of the Quinn brothers made their way to the end of the bar. Rafe stood, prepared to fight them all if required. The hell if he'd back down. Six against one weren't the best odds, but he wasn't about to run away from a fight, or from Keely. They were all about equally matched in height and weight. His only problem would come if they all decided to rush him at once. Then the fight would be over before it began.

"I'm not here to cause trouble," Rafe explained. "I just want to talk to Keely."

"Keely? What do you want with our sister?" Conor asked.

"I came here to tell her something."

Dylan strode up to him and gave him a shove toward the door. Rafe fought the urge to swing around and plant his fist in Dylan's jaw. He wasn't going to be the one to throw the first punch.

"Get the hell out of here, Kendrick," Dylan ordered. "Nobody here wants to talk to you, especially not Keely."

"Don't you think you ought to let her decide?"

Dylan reached out and grabbed Rafe's jacket, but

Rafe brushed his hand away. The move only served to increase the level of Quinn hostility. Sean jumped over the bar and grabbed Rafe's arms from behind. And Dylan drew his fist back and hit Rafe squarely in the stomach. Another punch caught Rafe in the jaw.

"Stop it! What are you doing?" Keely pushed Dylan aside and gave Sean a look that was strong enough to make him loosen his hold.

"Do you know this guy?" Conor asked.

"Yes, I do. And I'd appreciate it if you'd quit hitting him. What are you, a bunch of bullies?"

"Keely, this is Rafe Kendrick," Conor explained. "He's the one who caused all this trouble for Seamus. He's the one who sent Yaeger to the cops."

"He just wanted to know the truth," Keely said, pressing her palm against Conor's chest and pushing him away from Rafe.

"You don't have to defend me, Keely. I'm perfectly capable of defending myself."

Keely hitched her hands on her hips and turned to each one of her brothers, sending them a look that could peel paint. "You shouldn't have to defend yourself. It should be enough that I ask them to leave you alone. Isn't it enough?"

"You two know each other?" Conor asked.

"They do," Liam said, realization dawning on his face. "I remember now. You were here together at the bar one night. Keely, you threw a drink in his face."

"I do know him," Keely admitted.

Sean reluctantly released Rafe's arms and gave him a slight shove. "You said you came here to talk to Keely. Say what you came to say, then get out."

"I don't think you want to hear what I have to say," Rafe muttered, rubbing his jaw and testing the soundness of his teeth.

Keely screamed in frustration. "Just stop it. If the testosterone gets any thicker in here, we're going to have to open a bloody window. You're not going to fight each other and that's it. Conor, you're a cop. If you let them fight, then you're not doing your duty." She turned to Rafe. "Say what you came to say," she murmured.

"Keely, I really think it would be better if we talked in private."

"I've got nothing to hide from my brothers."

"All right. If that's the way you want it." Rafe cleared his throat. "Keely Quinn, I love you. I've known it for a while but I guess I couldn't admit it until that night at the cabin after you seduced me. After you left, I thought I could put it all aside. But I can't." He reached out and took her hand, then drew it to his lips. "Marry me."

Keely gasped, her eyes wide. "Marry you?"

"You spent the night with this bastard?" Brian asked.

"Yes," Keely admitted. "But I didn't—"

Sean jumped in next. "And you seduced him?"

Keely sighed impatiently. "Well, it wasn't the first time. He seduced me the night before. And then the night before that it was kind of a mutual thing." She glanced around at her brothers. "Don't look at me like that. I never said I was a virgin. And you six shouldn't talk. How many women have you seduced?"

Dylan's fiancée stepped into the fray, strolling over from her spot near the dartboard. "Yeah," she said, sending Keely an encouraging smile. "I'd like to hear the answer to that."

"So would I," Conor's wife added.

Another woman joined the group, slipping her arm around Brendan's. "Actually, I'd rather not hear anything about that," she said.

"How did this get turned around on us?" Dylan asked. "I still think we should beat the crap out of Kendrick."

"Enough!" Seamus stepped up, baseball bat clutched in his hand. He slapped it against his palm. "There'll be no fightin' in my pub." He nodded to Rafe. "Your father was a good man and he would have been welcome in my pub anytime. But I'd rather you don't show your face around here again." He turned to Keely. "And you're goin' to have to make a choice, lass. It's him or us. I won't be havin' a daughter of mine keepin' company with the likes of him."

"But I—"

"You listen to your da," Seamus warned.

Rafe gave her hand a squeeze. "I don't care how your family feels, Keely," he said. "I love you and if I have to fight each one of them, I will." He glanced around, from her glaring brothers back to

Keely's stunned expression. Maybe Seamus was right. There was nothing more to be said. Keely knew how he felt and she knew how her family felt. The choice was up to her.

He slowly stepped away from her, then let go of her hand. Keely's gaze remained fixed on his as he moved to the door. It took every ounce of strength to walk away from her. But he had to believe that what he'd said made a difference. If she really loved him, then she'd make a choice and she'd choose him.

But when he reached the street, alone, Rafe drew a deep breath and raked his hands through his hair. "So much for love," he murmured. "I guess it doesn't conquer all." He started toward his car, but then the door of the pub flew open and Keely came running out.

With a soft cry, she threw herself into his arms. "I'm sorry, I'm sorry. I should have left with you, but I just didn't know what to do."

He furrowed his fingers through her silken hair, then brought his mouth down on hers. He'd forgotten how wonderful she tasted, how much he loved kissing her. "I missed you, Keely. I didn't realize how much until now."

His hands skimmed over her body, finding the curves beneath her clothes. She shivered and he realized that she'd come outside without a jacket. He grabbed the lapels of his coat and wrapped them around her, trapping her against his warm body. "I have something for you," he murmured, his lips against hers.

"What is it?"

He hugged her more tightly, then reached into his pocket and pulled out the small velvet box.

"What's this?" she asked as he held it in front of her.

"If you don't like it, we can pick out something else."

She slowly stepped out of his embrace and opened the box. Her eyes went wide and she gasped again. "Is this an engagement ring?"

"What else would it be?" He smiled warmly. "I asked you to marry me. A ring usually goes with the proposal."

"I—I just thought you were saying that to make my brothers angry."

Rafe laughed and shook his head. "Jeez, Keely. I'm not the kind of guy who tosses marriage proposals around lightly. I meant what I said. I love you and I want to marry you."

Keely stared down at the ring. "But we barely know each other. Even though we met in October, we've only really been together a month."

"Do you love me?"

"I do," Keely murmured.

"And do you want to marry me?"

"I do," she said. "But there are so many things—"

"Then you keep this," Rafe said. "You don't have to put it on now. When you're ready—when your family is ready—then I'll slip that on your finger and we'll make it official." Rafe leaned forward and kissed her on the forehead. "I want you to go back inside now. They're going to wonder where you went."

"But I want to stay here with you."

"Sweetheart, we're going to spend the rest of our lives together. For now, I think it's best if you smooth things out with your family. You dropped a pretty big bombshell in there. Next time, I don't think you need to provide the details of our love life."

Keely stared up at him and smiled. "I don't know why I said that. Sometimes even I can't believe what comes out of my mouth. It probably wasn't the smartest thing to say with my brothers standing there ready to kill you."

"Can I believe that you're going to marry me?"

She pushed up on her toes and kissed him. "Yes, Rafe Kendrick. I will marry you."

Rafe captured her mouth once more and kissed her long and deep, a kiss that he knew would have to hold them until they saw each other again. But now that he had the answers he wanted, he didn't care if it took a day or a week or even a month. Keely Quinn was his and nothing could stand between them.

"Call me tonight," he murmured. "I want to hear your voice before I go to sleep. Better yet, come over and you can spend the night in my bed."

"I can't," Keely said. "I've been staying with Conor and Olivia when I'm in Boston. They'll know something is up if I don't come home."

"You already admitted to them that you weren't a virgin. Do you think they'll be surprised?"

"I just don't want to stir up trouble," Keely said. "Give them all a chance to cool down and then I'll tell them how I feel. Everything is still so new between me and my family."

"And between us, too."

"But I know you love me, Rafe. That's something I can count on. I can count on that, can't I?"

Rafe pulled her into his embrace and pressed his lips into her fragrant hair. "Forever," he murmured.

RAFE GLANCED DOWN at the address he'd scrawled on a scrap of paper. "This is it—210 East Beltran." Pulling the car to the curb, he parked a few doors down the street from McClain's Bakery in Brooklyn. After switching off the ignition, Rafe stepped out of the car and drew his overcoat more tightly around him against the January cold.

The old building was impeccably maintained on a quiet street that had a mix of old brick town houses with quaint storefronts at each corner. As he walked to the door, he stared through the wide plate-glass windows to a display filled with cakes of all shapes and sizes. Rafe paused. When Keely had told him she made cakes, he'd had something a little more ordinary in mind. But the samples in the windows were works of art, sculptures made of cake and frosting and a wild imagination. Keely's imagination.

He straightened his tie, then reached out to grab the front door. He hadn't bothered to call to let Keely know he was coming. Over the past week, they hadn't had a chance to see each other, though they had managed a nightly phone call and some pretty amazing phone sex. Rafe smiled to himself. Though having sex over the phone had been exciting at first, it really didn't compare to having Keely in his arms, to looking at her and kissing her and touching her at will. So he'd decided on a surprise.

He'd had Sylvie call for him under the guise of a bride wanting to discuss her wedding cake. Then he'd rented a suite at the Plaza as part of his plan to spirit Keely away from work for lunch, an afternoon of shopping and an evening of real passion, without a phone line between them.

A bell above the door rang as he stepped inside. The front part of the bakery served as a showroom, with narrow mouldings on each wall holding photo after photo of increasingly elaborate cakes. He studied a photo of a brightly colored cake that resembled a Hawaiian shirt. The next photo showed a cake decorated with tiny little fruits cascading over each tier.

"That's one of our marzipan designs."

Rafe turned to find an older woman standing a few feet away. "It's beautiful," he said. "But where do you find fruit that small?"

"It's not real fruit," she said. "It's marzipan, modeled and colored to look like real fruit."

"Marzipan?"

"Almond paste. Everything on that cake is edible and very delicious." She held out her hand. "I'm Fiona McClain. How can I help you?"

Keely's mother, Rafe mused as he shook her hand. He'd known that Keely resembled her brothers, but there was a fair amount of Fiona McClain in her as well, in the delicate nose and the warm smile. He hadn't thought he'd get a chance to meet Fiona on this trip, but now that he had, he was going to take advantage of it. "I want to order a cake."

"And what kind of cake would you like to order?"

"A wedding cake?"

Fiona laughed. "You speak as if you're not sure. Perhaps your bride should be here to help make choices?"

"I'm afraid that won't be possible. At least not on this trip. Maybe you can show me a few things?"

"Well, my daughter, Keely, designs all of our cakes and every cake is a one-of-a-kind creation. She likes to meet the customers and discuss their ideas."

"Is she around?"

Fiona shook her head. "She just stepped out for a few minutes, but she should be back soon. Maybe I could get some information from you first? It would help to know what you have in mind for the wedding."

"How much does a cake like this cost?" Rafe asked, pointing to a multitiered confection that seemed to be draped in layers of lace.

"We do cakes for all budgets." She pulled out a photo album and flipped through it. "That cake was ten thousand dollars. And this one was eight thousand."

Rafe gasped. "For a cake?"

"It all depends on the size and complexity. You must think of the wedding cake much like the wedding gown," she explained. "The gown is the focal point of the ceremony and the cake is the centerpiece of the reception. There will only be one gown and one cake for that one special day. So it must be the best. We often suggest to the bride that she spend as much on her cake as she spends on her gown. Now, when is the wedding?"

"Well, we don't exactly have a date yet," Rafe said.

Fiona frowned. "We can't put you on the schedule unless we have a date. And we do get booked very quickly. Right now we're booking clients for at least a year from now."

"Really?"

"Are you sure you're ready to choose a cake?"

"Actually, you're right. I didn't come here to pick out a cake. I just wanted to meet you."

Fiona blinked in surprise. "Me?"

"My name is Rafe Kendrick and I'm in love with your daughter and I plan to marry her. So I guess you'll have to ask her about the date."

Keely's mother frowned. "I—I don't understand. Do you even know my daughter?"

"Don't worry—I'm not a stalker," Rafe assured her. "We met in Boston. I'm Sam Kendrick's son. I think you may have known him, or perhaps my mother, Lila. Sam worked on Seamus Quinn's boat once."

Fiona frowned. "Seamus was just questioned by the authorities about your father's death and now you show up—"

"It's a very long and complicated story that Keely and I are just sorting out ourselves. We met before she knew who I was and I knew who she was. Needless to say, her father and brothers aren't too keen on me marrying her. I was hoping I might have your support. Keely and I haven't known each other for long, but I do love her. And I know she loves me."

"And you want my permission to marry my daughter?" She shook her head, stunned by his revelations. "I'm not sure I can give that to you, Mr. Kendrick. I don't know you. My daughter has never even mentioned you. And I don't think I can give you my blessing under those circumstances."

"I'm a good catch," Rafe said. "I own my own company. I don't mean to brag, but I'm wealthy. I can give Keely anything she wants, a nice house, a good life. I can make her happy."

"Mr. Kendrick—"

"Rafe," he insisted.

"Rafe," she repeated. "I understand you caused a lot of trouble for Seamus. I know him. He doesn't forgive easily. I think you'd be better off convincing him of your suitability as a husband than me. Besides, Keely would never listen to me once she has her heart set on something."

"Then maybe you should tell her you don't approve."

"I don't," Fiona said. "You two have only known each other for…what? A month?"

"Actually, more like four," Rafe admitted. "But sometimes four months is enough."

"And sometimes five years isn't. My daughter has a life here and a successful business. She can't go running off to Boston."

"I know there are a lot of things standing between us, but I'm determined to marry her."

The bell above the door rang again and they both turned to watch Keely walk in. When she saw Rafe, she smiled, then ran up to him and threw her arms around his neck. "What are you doing here? Why didn't you tell me you were coming?"

"I came to take you to lunch. I had my secretary call and make an appointment, so there's no turning me down. I've got reservations at five different restaurants, so you get to choose." He turned to Fiona. "Would you care to join us for lunch?"

Just then, Keely noticed her mother standing there. She slipped from Rafe's embrace with an embarrassed smile. "I—I suppose I should introduce you two."

"We've already met," Fiona said.

"Rafe and I have been seeing each other," Keely explained. "We met in Boston the first night I went there, last October."

"Is that so?"

"Ma, I know I should have told you, but there was so much going on. Rafe has asked me to marry him and I've said yes."

"You've only known each other a very short time, Keely."

"I know. But it's not like we're getting married tomorrow. You and I have a wedding to plan and so many decisions to make. And we can't set a date until we've designed a cake. A very special cake.''

"Keely, I can't approve of this. And I don't think your father would either, even if he didn't happen to detest your fiancé.''

Keely shook her head. "I'm not going to listen to this. Rafe and I are going to be together and nothing you or Seamus says is going to keep us apart. Now, are you coming to lunch with us or not?''

"I'm not," Fiona said. "And you'd do best to stay here and help me finish this cake.''

Keely slipped her arm through Rafe's. "I'll finish it later. Tomorrow. I'll have plenty of time tomorrow. Right now, I have to go to lunch with my fiancé.''

As they walked to the door, Rafe slipped his arm around her shoulders and gave her a hug. But when they got outside, Keely's bravado dissolved and a worried expression replaced her smile. "What are we going to do?'' she asked.

"Well, first we're going to have lunch. And then I thought we could shop for some things we'll need after the wedding and then I have a suite at the—''

"No! What are we going to do about my parents and my brothers? They all hate you.''

"They'll get over that, Keely. If you and I are together, they'll be forced to accept me.''

"How can you be sure of that? What if they don't? Conflict like that can tear a marriage apart.''

"Keely, we won't know until we try. You just have to stand up for us the same way you stand up for yourself.''

"And that's not the only thing we have to worry about. I have a business here. People depend on me. I can't just pick up and move to Boston, any more than you can pick up and move here. Besides my parents standing between us and six brothers, there's also three hundred miles of interstate—very congested interstate."

"And don't forget the measly three or four months that we've known each other. That should count for something, too." Rafe couldn't keep the sarcasm from his voice. He drew a deep breath, then pulled her back into his arms. "Let's just forget about them for today. We have a whole afternoon and evening to spend together in New York. And we're going to make the most of it." He stepped back and looked down into her eyes. "Do you love me?"

"I do, but—"

Rafe pressed his finger to her lips. "No buts. For now, that's enough. And we'll figure out the rest later."

CHAPTER ELEVEN

A WINTER STORM raged outside, the snow blowing so hard that it hissed against the windows of Rafe's apartment. Keely snuggled farther down beneath the comforter, pressing up against the warm, naked body beside her. On the mornings after the nights they spent together, Rafe never bothered with an alarm clock. Instead, he waited for her to wake him up. They'd make love once more before they shared a relaxed breakfast. And then she'd either jump in her car or hop a train back to New York. Or rush over to Conor and Olivia's apartment for a short stay with the family.

It had almost become second nature, sneaking around. And, at first, it had been exciting. But Keely knew all the subterfuge was wearing on Rafe. They'd share a stolen night or afternoon once or twice a week, then go on with their lives as if they barely knew each other. And every time they said goodbye, she'd see the impatience in his gaze, feel it in his kiss, and wonder how much longer he'd pretend to understand.

Keely had hoped that once she felt more comfortable with her newfound family, she'd be able to broach the subject of her continuing relationship with Rafe. But if she'd learned one thing over the past month, it was that the gene for holding a grudge ran deep in the Quinn family. Her brothers still spoke of Rafe with such disdain that she wondered if their hatred would ever fade. So she'd stalled and made excuses and tried to pacify Rafe, all the while hoping for some miraculous attitude adjustment from Seamus and his boys.

Rafe moved beside her, pulling her more tightly into his embrace and kissing her shoulder. "What time is it?" he murmured, his voice ragged with sleep.

"It's early. Seven, maybe. It's still snowing. It's going to take me forever to get back to the city."

He groaned. "Then don't go back. Spend the day with me. We can hole up here and watch old movies and make soup and take naps."

"I can't. I've got meetings scheduled this afternoon with three brides. And I still have to put together some sketches. And you have to go to work."

"When is this going to stop?" he asked, his voice edged with frustration.

"What? This is life, Rafe. We both have jobs. We both have responsibilities."

"This is limbo," he said, "not life. We're just waiting. I want to begin *our* life together."

Keely pushed up on her elbow and looked at him. Reaching out, she smoothed a strand of hair off his forehead. "All right. Maybe I should stay the day."

"Answer me, Keely. How long is this going to go on?"

"I admit that we do spend an awful lot of time in bed," she teased, trying to lighten his mood.

He sat up. "Don't try to placate me. I asked you to marry me and you said you would. So, let's make some plans. When are we getting married? Where are we getting married? Who are we inviting to the wedding?"

"I can't just decide these things all at once," Keely said. "A wedding takes a lot of thought and planning."

"Have you decided anything? Have you given a minute's thought to any of it?"

Now, he was angry. She scolded herself for not accepting his invitation to stay the moment it was offered, thus avoiding the same old discussion. "How many times have we talked about this in the past month?" she asked, turning the question back on him. "Remember when you told me that it didn't matter how long it took to work things out with my family? Did you really mean it or were you just overestimating your capacity for patience?"

"I just don't understand why this is taking so long. I feel like a kid, sneaking around as if we're both doing something sinful. We're adults and we should be allowed to see each other whenever we want. I should be able to call you five times a day and stop by to see you on a whim. We should be able to take a vacation together and spend holidays with your family."

"Oh, that would be fun," she said sarcastically. "You and the Quinn brothers at Thanksgiving. Hide the carving knife."

"What am I supposed to do? I want you in my life, permanently. Not just when it's convenient for you. Or Seamus. Or your mother. Or your damn brothers."

She sighed. "Can't you at least understand how they feel? What you did caused a lot of trouble for the family."

"They feel that way because you haven't given them a good reason to feel differently. I did what I had to do and I'm not going to make any apologies. We learned the truth and life goes on. I've accepted it—why can't they? Tell them you love me and you want to marry me and then tell them if they don't like it, they can all go to hell."

Keely pushed aside the covers and crawled out of bed. She grabbed the silk robe he'd bought her and wrapped it around her naked body, shivering against the chill in the apartment. "I don't want to talk about this anymore."

"And I do. We're going to solve this problem now or—"

"Or what? It's over between us?"

"Yes," Rafe said, a stubborn set to his jaw. He crossed his arms over his chest. "Maybe it is."

Keely's breath caught in her throat. "You don't mean that."

"I do."

"Are you giving me an ultimatum?"

"I guess you could say that." Rafe shrugged.

"Yeah, I am giving you an ultimatum. It's me or your family. You're a big girl, Keely. Make a decision. I'm going to take a shower. I'll expect your answer when I get out."

Rafe tossed aside the comforter and walked naked to the bathroom. Keely heard the water go on, but she wasn't ready to end their discussion there. She stalked to the bathroom and stood outside the shower.

"My mother used to give me ultimatums and they never worked. When someone tells me I have to do something, I usually do the opposite."

"That's what your mother told me," Rafe shouted over the running water. "She said if she opposed our marriage that you'd probably go ahead with a wedding."

"Now you're conspiring with my mother?"

He stuck his head out of the shower, his hair dripping wet. "I'll take any ally in your family I can get. If you had a dog, I'd probably try to make friends."

"This is between you and me," Keely said.

"Exactly my point." He stepped back into the shower, then turned up his shower radio until the morning news echoed through the marble-tiled bathroom, ending all conversation between them.

Keely turned and stalked out of the bathroom, then began to gather her clothes and toss them in her overnight bag. Yes, they'd talked about these same things over and over again since Rafe made his marriage proposal. And no, she hadn't made an effort to change the status quo, even though she had accepted his proposal. But that didn't mean she deserved a bloody ultimatum!

She threw her clothes on the bed and walked back to the bathroom, then stepped inside the shower, still wrapped in her silk robe. Reaching over, she shut off the morning business report and turned to him. "If you really loved me, you'd give me more time."

"And if you really loved me, you wouldn't need any more time."

"I'm not going to argue with you anymore," Keely said. "You're being unreasonable." She started out of the shower, but Rafe grabbed her arm and pulled her back beneath the water. He pressed her up against the marble tile, pinning his hips against hers. The silk robe clung to her skin, heightening the sensations of the warm water and his determined touch.

"I can kiss you and peel that wet robe off your naked body and make love to you right here and now. But it's not going to change anything. You won't love me any more than you do at this very moment. So you have to decide. Is that enough?"

"I don't know," Keely said stubbornly.

"I guess I have my answer then," he said.

"That's not what I meant."

His mouth came down on hers in a desperate, almost punishing kiss and his fingers fumbled with her robe. The water poured over them both, washing away the heat of his mouth the moment he moved on to a new spot—her neck, her breast, her belly.

Keely tipped her head back and closed her eyes. She did love him, more than she could have ever imagined. And she was crazy if she thought she'd be able to walk away from this and not regret it for the rest of her life. But her family's objections would weigh heavily on their marriage and Keely wondered if someday the resentments might bubble to the surface. What if her family never accepted him?

He grabbed her legs and drew them up around his waist, then slowly entered her. Weaving her fingers through his wet hair, Keely arched her back as he moved inside her. "Tell me you can't live without me," she murmured.

"I won't live without you," Rafe said, his voice ragged.

Satisfied that she'd proved her point, Keely surrendered herself to her desire. The water continued to rush over them, filling the shower with steam, creating a world where passion was all that mattered. And when he finally exploded inside her, Keely sighed softly, secure in the fact that Rafe was the only man she'd ever truly love.

"Let's go back to bed," she whispered, teasing at his earlobe with her teeth.

Rafe drew away, gently lowering her legs to the floor of the shower. Then he pressed his forehead against hers, his eyes closed, his jaw tight. "Go home, Keely. And don't come back here until you've made a decision." He pushed her out of the shower, then turned up the radio again.

Keely opened her mouth, ready to start the argument anew. But then she shook her head and slowly walked back to the bedroom. They'd just go round and round for another hour and still not solve anything. She wanted more time, and he wasn't willing to give it to her.

Why the hell did she even bother? With Rafe, there was never any compromise. He was completely close-minded when it came to her father and brothers. There were times when she felt as if she were caught in a tug-of-war between them, each side demanding her loyalty and tearing her apart in the process.

"He's had enough?" she muttered as she shoved her clothes in the bag, her temper rising. "*I've* had enough. I'll marry him when I'm damn well ready to marry him and not a minute sooner."

She tugged her jeans on over damp skin, then pulled a sweater over her wet hair. Her watch and engagement ring were sitting on the bedside table. She picked up the watch, but left the ring where it was. She never should have accepted it, at least not until everything had been solved with her family. She wouldn't put it on again until Rafe agreed to be more reasonable.

Keely left the ring where it was, then finished dressing. She grabbed her overnight bag and headed to the door, snatching up her coat and purse on the way out. But before she opened the door, she glanced down at her hand. Wearing the ring had made her feel secure, as if nothing could shake what they shared.

But a ring didn't make their relationship strong. They did—together. Unfortunately, her feelings weren't nearly as black-and-white as Rafe's. It wasn't an all-or-nothing choice for her. Just a few months

ago, all she'd had in life was her mother. And now
she had a father and six brothers and a fiancé who
loved her, each one wanting her to be a part of their
lives. She shouldn't have to choose.

Keely yanked open the door then headed toward
the elevator. When she reached the lobby of Rafe's
building, the doorman greeted her. "Morning, Miss
Quinn."

"Morning," Keely replied, forcing a bright smile.

"Can I get you a cab?"

"Yes, thank you. I'll be going to South Station to
catch the Amtrak."

The doorman punched in a number on his phone
and ordered a cab and Keely sat down on a pretty
sofa near the door, peering out into the blizzard to
watch for her ride. She fought the temptation to go
back up to the apartment and retrieve the ring. In the
end, she walked out into the blizzard and hopped into
a cab, determined not to give in to her own fears—
or Rafe's ultimatum.

As the cab skidded through the snowy streets of
downtown Boston, Keely stared out the window at
the dismal weather. She always lived her life by impulse, but now that she had something too precious
to lose, she was going to take her time. If Rafe loved
her, then he would wait. And if he didn't love her,
then it was better to find that out now than after a
wedding.

KEELY ARRIVED at the trendy Manhattan restaurant
ten minutes late. The hostess showed her to the table

where Olivia, Amy and Meggie waited. She'd been surprised by the invitation, wondering if the trio had traveled all the way to New York just to have lunch with her or if their invitation had been an afterthought. Olivia insisted they had planned a day of shopping, so Keely had immediately accepted, then suggested a good spot for lunch.

"I'm sorry I'm late," Keely said as she sat down. She grabbed the linen napkin from her plate and spread it on her lap. "It took me forever to get a cab. I should have just taken the subway. Have you ordered already?"

"We've just ordered our first bottle of wine," Olivia said. "Our lunches tend to go on until the late afternoon. And since we've decided to spend the night in New York, this one might go on well after dark."

"Have you been doing this for long?" Keely asked, curious about the camaraderie that had formed between the women in her brothers' lives.

Meggie took a sip of her wine. "It started with Olivia and me. And then when Amy and Brendan got together, we added her to the group. And now that you're a Quinn, we figured you might want to join us, too."

"What are we celebrating?" Keely asked as Olivia poured her a glass of white wine from a bottle that was nearly empty.

"It's a goodbye lunch for Amy. She and Brendan are leaving for Turkey next week. He's writing a book about something...exciting or important or—"

"An archaeological dig," Amy said.

"And she's going with him," Olivia continued. "They're going to live in a hut in the middle of winter in Turkey. I think she's crazy, she thinks it's romantic, Meggie's just worried whether they'll be able to get good coffee."

"It won't be so bad," Amy said. "And we're only going to be living at the site for a month in May. Before that, we're going to be with the research team in Ankara."

"How long will you be gone?" Keely asked.

"Three months. We'll be back right before Meggie's wedding in June."

"That's the real reason we wanted you to join us," Meggie said. "My wedding."

"Of course I'll make the cake," Keely said, not waiting for the obvious question. "I'd be happy to."

"That's not what I was going to ask," Meggie said. "I wanted to know if you'd be a bridesmaid. Olivia and Amy have already agreed and my wedding wouldn't be complete if I didn't have Dylan's only sister in the wedding party."

Keely was stunned by the invitation. "I—I don't know what to say."

Meggie laughed. "Say yes?"

At first, Keely wasn't sure she should. What if she wasn't around in June? But then, she realized that she was now a permanent part of the Quinn family. They'd accepted her as one of their own—for the rest of her life, she'd be a Quinn. "Yes. I'd love to be a bridesmaid. And I'll also make your cake if you'd like me to. It will be the most special wedding cake I've ever made.''

"Take the offer on the cake," Amy said. "You should see what she does with frosting. Her cakes are like art. I wanted her for my first wedding but she wouldn't do any jobs outside New York City."

"I didn't know you were married before," Keely said.

"I wasn't. I ran away from home about a month before the wedding, but it had already been all planned. My mother saw your cakes in *Town and Country*. She had the pictures in her little wedding file and she was determined that you do my cake."

"When you marry Brendan, I'll do your cake, too. No charge for either of you since you're family now."

"So," Olivia said, "now that we have that business taken care of, we can get down to the reason we really invited you to lunch."

"I thought you came here to go shopping."

"We can shop in Boston," Olivia said. "We want to know about *your* wedding. To Rafe Kendrick. Ever since that night of the grand opening at the pub, we've all been a little curious."

Keely glanced back and forth between them, taking in their inquisitive expressions. Of all the conversation topics to choose from, Rafe Kendrick would have been her last choice. Since she'd walked out on him a week ago, they hadn't spoken. It was as if they were playing a game with each other, each of them unwilling to concede their point. "I'm not sure I'm going to marry Rafe Kendrick.'' Keely took a sip of her wine. "In fact, I might not ever see him again.''

Olivia frowned. "What happened?''

"It's a long story.''

Meggie reached out and grabbed Keely's hand. "You're family. You can tell us anything. And we do have a ladies' agreement here. Nothing that's said between us gets back to the men in the family. If you haven't noticed, the Quinn boys have a tendency to overreact.''

Keely had never had a sister, but always dreamed that this was what it was like—secret conversations, unbreakable promises, an understanding ear. She'd been aching to talk to someone about her problems and now that she'd been given the chance, she wanted to tell them every detail.

"The last time I was in Boston we had a huge argument. He's been pressuring me to straighten things out with my family. You know how Seamus and my brothers feel. And my mother doesn't approve of him, either. So we've been sneaking around like a couple of teenagers, seeing each other whenever we can. It was kind of exciting at first, but Rafe is getting impatient and he gave me an ultimatum. Either I tell my parents and brothers that we're together and we're getting married, or we're finished.''

"He's right,'' Amy said. "I mean, family *is* family. But love is love. My parents weren't pleased I wanted to marry Brendan. But I didn't care. I loved him. And my grandmother thought he was hot. So I wasn't going to let them stand in my way.''

"At least you had someone behind you," Keely said. "No one wants me to marry Rafe."

"I do," Olivia said. "The way he proposed to you that night in the bar was so romantic."

"So do I," Meggie added. "It's obvious that he adores you. And he looked like he would have taken on all six of the brothers to prove his point."

Amy nodded. "And you have my vote, too."

Amazed by their unconditional support, Keely's spirits brightened. "I don't know. Marriage is difficult enough already. And my brothers could make our lives pretty miserable if they continue on with this grudge."

"Don't be such a coward," Meggie said. "You and Rafe are lucky to have found each other. If the family is the only thing standing in your way, then you're crazy to turn him away."

"And don't worry about the boys," Olivia said. "They'll come around once they see how happy Rafe makes you. And if they don't, we'll just have to apply a little pressure, won't we, ladies?"

"The Mighty Quinns aren't so mighty after all?" Keely asked.

Amy ordered another bottle of wine from the waiter, then grabbed a piece of bread and buttered it neatly. "Not when faced by the mighty women in their lives," she joked.

Keely took another sip of her wine, before Olivia filled her glass again. "It's not just my brothers. I have my business in New York. I have responsibilities. It would be hard to pick up and leave. I'd have to reestablish myself there. And I'm not sure Boston is ready for me and my cakes.''

''Work *is* work,'' Olivia said. ''And love is love. Besides, who says you'll have to move here? Maybe Rafe will move to New York.''

''Maybe,'' Keely said. ''I guess we never talked about it. I can bake cakes anywhere. And I do love him. And maybe I've been too obsessed with my family's reaction. They're not going to kick me out of the family, just because I marry Rafe.''

''We won't let them,'' Meggie said.

Keely pulled her napkin off her lap and tossed it on the table. ''I—I need to go.''

''But we haven't had lunch yet,'' Olivia protested.

''I can't stay. I have a cake to make.''

''Your customer can wait,'' Meggie said.

Keely shook her head. ''Nope, not this customer. I have to make a wedding cake for me. I'm going to marry Rafe Kendrick.''

''When?'' they all asked.

''I don't know. Maybe tomorrow, maybe the next day. But soon.''

Keely gave each of them a quick kiss goodbye, then hurried out to the lobby. She found her coat at the coat check and quickly slipped into it. If she grabbed the subway out to Brooklyn, she could start working on the cake right away. By tomorrow morning, it would be done and on its way to Boston. After all, she couldn't possibly get married without a proper cake. It would be bad luck.

''I'm going to marry Rafe Kendrick,'' Keely murmured to herself. "I'm going to marry Rafe Kendrick and to hell with what my family thinks."

RAFE SAT at his desk, his feet kicked up on the edge, the *Wall Street Journal* open in front of him. He tried to concentrate on the article he was reading, but he'd started and stopped so many times he was ready to give up completely. Interest rates on municipal bonds would have to wait. With a soft curse, he swung his feet off his desk and refolded the paper.

He'd been working so hard lately, throwing himself into projects simply to occupy his mind with something other than Keely. He blamed himself for their fight and their broken engagement—even though they never really were engaged, not officially. She had warned him against his ultimatum, yet he'd refused to back down. And when he'd emerged from the shower, she'd been gone, her engagement ring left behind on the bedside table. The message was clear. As far as she was concerned, it was over.

So where did he go from here? Rafe had done everything he could to convince her that they belonged together, short of standing out on Boston Common in his boxer shorts and shouting his devotion to the world. They'd just fallen in love at the wrong time. Until she worked out her worries about her family, he'd always come in second.

If he didn't have an ego, then maybe he could put himself second. Maybe he could go on as they had, carrying on an affair outside her family's knowledge, never really committing themselves fully to a relationship. But if he was willing to put Keely first in his life, he expected the same from her.

Rafe pulled his desk drawer open and withdrew the small velvet box. He wasn't sure why he'd kept the ring. Maybe he still held out hope that Keely would wear it one day. He did have a money-back guarantee with the jeweler so he wouldn't have to worry about the ring turning into a constant reminder of Keely. When he was ready, he'd simply return it and that would be the end of that. Maybe he'd take a nice vacation with the money. Somewhere warm with the maximum number of beautiful women in the minimum amount of clothes.

A knock sounded on the door and Rafe tossed the ring back into the drawer along with the box. A few seconds later, Sylvie entered carrying a large package. "This was just delivered for you."

"What is it?"

"I don't know. It's marked personal and confidential." She set it on his desk. "Should I open it?"

"Why not? Isn't that what 'personal and confidential' means? 'Sylvie may open this package.'"

Sylvie rolled her eyes then ripped the top off the box. She peered inside, then frowned.

"What is it?" Rafe asked.

"I'm not sure." She reached down then pulled her hand back and stuck her finger in her mouth. "I think it's a cake. Only it looks like a pair of shoes and a shoe box. Loafers, I think."

Rafe stood up and looked into the box. Then he

stepped back and laughed. "Italian loafers. Made in Milan. Keely sent this."

"She sent you a cake that looks like shoes."

"The night we met, she threw up on my shoes. Ruined a very expensive pair of loafers. She promised to get me a new pair."

"Oh, that's so sweet," Sylvie said.

"Yeah," Rafe murmured. "It is." The ball had been in her court and she just hit it back, Rafe mused. So things weren't completely over between them. He raked his hand through his hair and shook his head. "That woman could drive a man seriously insane."

"The frosting is absolutely sinful," Sylvie said. "Can we eat it now or is it just to look at?"

"It's supposed to be enjoyed," said a soft voice. They both turned. Keely stood at the door, a sly smile on her face.

She was dressed for the cold in a long wool coat, a slouchy hat and a wildly patterned scarf. "It's a banana cake with a ganache filling." She met Rafe's gaze. "I told you I'd get you a new pair of shoes. They're not Italian, but they taste a lot better."

Rafe stared at her for a long moment. Though he'd tried not to think about her over the past week, he'd never been able to get her completely out of his head. And now he knew why. She was the most beautiful woman he'd ever known and the only woman he'd ever love.

He slowly walked over to her and tugged off her hat, then pulled the scarf from around her shoulders.

Sylvie looked between them both. "I think I'll go

see if I can find a knife and some plates." She hurried out of the office, closing the door behind her.

"It's a nice cake," Rafe murmured. "You're very talented."

"It's an original design," Keely said. "One of my specialty wedding cakes."

Rafe's eyebrow rose. "A wedding cake? For whom?"

"For us. I figure if we go get the license today we can get married on Thursday."

He stared at her for a long moment. "You mean it?"

"I do," Keely said. "I don't want to wait until my mother and father and brothers approve. I want to get married now, Rafe. I want to prove to them that you're in my life for good and there's nothing they can say that's going to change that. I love you and that's all that matters."

"But don't you want a big church wedding?"

"It doesn't make any difference. I never thought I'd say that, but it really doesn't. What matters is that we'll be married and we'll be able to start our life together. So, will you marry me, Rafe?"

"I will, Keely."

She wrapped her arms around his neck. Rafe couldn't believe that it was really going to happen, that Keely would finally be his. He hugged her tightly, then kissed her slowly and thoroughly, until he'd finally convinced himself that he wasn't imagining the whole thing.

Keely tipped her head back and looked into his

eyes. "I want my ring back," she said. "You better not have returned it to the jeweller."

"It's in my desk."

Keely slipped out of his embrace, then began to search through desk drawers. Rafe bent over and pulled the middle drawer open, then fished the ring out of his pile of paper clips. "You're going to leave it on this time, aren't you?"

"Just try to get it off me." Keely held out her hand and Rafe slipped the ring on her finger. Then she pressed her palm to her heart and smiled. "So, what should we do first?"

"Have you told your parents?"

Keely shook her head. "Nope. And I'm not going to. You and I are going to get married and if they don't like it, then they can…go to hell."

Rafe reached out and took her hand. "Maybe you should think about this, Keely. They're going to be pretty angry if you just run off and marry me. They're going to think I talked you into it."

"Well, you did," she said. A frown wrinkled her brow. "Are you backing out now? I thought this was what you wanted."

"Of course it is. But is this the way to go about it?"

"This is the way I want it," Keely said. "I used to think I wanted a huge wedding, the more elaborate the better. But I've realized that it's not the wedding that's important. It's the marriage. I want to be married to you, Rafe. For now, till death do us part and happily ever after. So let's just do it."

"All right," Rafe said with a smile. He cupped her face in his palms and gave her a quick kiss. "Where?"

"Here in Boston, at the courthouse. I called about a license. There's a three-day waiting period, so if we go down today and apply, we can get married in three days."

"All right. But if we have three days, then I think we should at least make it special."

"All right," Keely agreed. "I'll buy a dress."

"And I'll get you flowers. And what about a honeymoon?"

"I don't know," she said. "We might have to put it off for a while."

"I'll take care of the honeymoon."

Keely smiled. "Then that about does it. We've managed to plan our wedding in what—ten seconds? That's got to be some kind of record."

"We'll need a witness, too," Rafe said. He reached over and pushed the button for his intercom. "Sylvie, can you come back in here?"

A few seconds later, she appeared at the door. "Do you want a piece of cake?"

"Put the cake in the refrigerator. Then cancel all my appointments for the next two weeks. And clear your calendar for Thursday. Keely and I are getting married and we'll need you to serve as a witness."

Sylvie's eyes went wide and she gasped. "Married? You're getting married?"

"And give Judge Williams a call and see if he'll do the ceremony for us. I worked with him on that charity dinner last year for the mayor. And I'm going to need some plane tickets, too.''

"I'm invited to the wedding?" Sylvie asked. "Would you like me to call the other guests as well?"

"You're the only guest," Keely said. "We decided to keep our wedding very simple."

"All right then. I guess I better get to work." She rushed out of the office, pulling the door shut behind her.

Rafe grabbed Keely up and swung her around, giving her a fierce hug. He was almost afraid to let go, afraid that she might change her mind. Though this was exactly what he'd wanted, Rafe couldn't help but feel a little hesitant. They really hadn't solved the problem with her family. They'd just taken a detour around it. Sooner or later, Keely would have to tell them they were married and face the consequences.

If he were a sensible guy, he'd put the brakes on. After all, Keely did have a history of impulsive behavior and this was a prime example. But Rafe wanted Keely more than he wanted to do the sensible thing. If she was determined to get married in three days, who was he to argue?

CHAPTER TWELVE

KEELY STOOD outside the judge's chambers, clutching the small bouquet of white roses and trying to calm herself. She hadn't expected to be so nervous. The decision to marry Rafe had been easy to make. She just hadn't realized the impact of that decision until this very moment. In less than an hour, she was going to be Mrs. Rafe Kendrick. Her stomach lurched and a wave of nausea washed over her. "Oh, God," she murmured.

"What's wrong?" Rafe asked. He sat calmly on a wooden bench, watching her pace back and forth in front of him.

"Nothing," Keely said.

"You look a little pale."

"I'm fine," she insisted.

He reached for her hand. "Sweetheart, why don't you sit down and relax? It's going to be a little while."

"Relax?" Keely asked, trying to keep the hysterical edge from her voice. "It's my wedding day. How can I relax?" She stared at him shrewdly. "And why aren't you nervous? You're the groom. Aren't you supposed to be having second thoughts right about now? *You* should be throwing up on *my* shoes!''

Rafe pulled her down to sit next to him on the bench. "No, I'm not nervous. I'm marrying the woman I love today. Why would I have second thoughts?"

"Because that's what grooms do!" Keely said. Another surge of nausea overwhelmed her and she pressed her fingertips to her lips. "Oh, God."

Rafe cursed softly, then slipped his hand over her nape and gently pushed her head down. "Breathe," he said. He chuckled softly.

"What's so funny?" Keely asked.

"Isn't this where we started? It has a perfect kind of symmetry, doesn't it?" Keely groaned and Rafe gently rubbed her back. "If you don't want to go through with this today, we can always come back another time. The license is good for three months."

Maybe they had rushed into this a little too impulsively. Keely had always struggled with her impetuous nature, that dominant gene that she now knew came from the Quinn side of the family. How many tales had she heard in the past few weeks about all the dangerous and reckless things her brothers had done? And here she was, following suit.

But this was marriage, the biggest decision of her life. Maybe she should have taken a little more time in planning a real wedding, given herself a chance to get used to the idea of happily ever after. "Do *you* want to get married today?"

Rafe tipped her chin up until her gaze met his. "I want whatever you want, Keely. I get the feeling I may have pushed you a little too hard for this. Maybe we should wait until you've told your parents. They really should be here."

"Well, now is a fine time to start backtracking," she muttered, plucking at the pearl-encrusted jacket that covered her sheath dress. "I bought this new dress, you've got a surprise honeymoon planned, I—"

"You'll save the dress and we'll freeze the cake and take a vacation instead of a honeymoon. But that's not going to change my feelings for you. I love you and I'm willing to wait if that's what you decide."

"No," she said, sitting up. She drew a deep breath. "I'm ready. There's no reason to wait."

"You don't want your mother to attend the ceremony and your father to walk you down the aisle?"

She had always dreamed of the fairy-tale wedding—the beautiful white gown and the flower-bedecked church, her friends and family all gathered around and the bridal march swelling from the organ as she walked down the aisle. "They've made that impossible," she said. "And I've accepted that."

The door to the judge's chambers opened and his clerk stepped out. "Kendrick-Quinn marriage. You're next."

Keely quickly stood up and smoothed her skirt, fighting back her nerves. Rafe rose, then took her hand and tucked it in the crook of his arm. Then he looked up and down the hall. "I guess this is it," he said.

They stepped inside and found Judge Williams waiting for them. He shook Rafe's hand, then introduced himself to Keely. "Well, here we are. Why don't we step into my office? Do you have witnesses?"

Rafe glanced at Keely. "We did. She should be here any minute. I don't know what's keeping Sylvie."

"Your clerk can be a witness, can't she?" Keely asked. "Or we could just go out into the hall and find someone?"

"We can do that if you like," the judge replied. "Or we can wait for a few more minutes. I'm not due back in court for another fifteen minutes. The ceremony only takes three or four."

Keely swallowed hard. The most important event in her life reduced to three or four minutes. Somehow she'd expected it to be so much more...grandiose, more dignified. She drew in a sharp breath. But this was what it was! And now that she'd decided to marry Rafe, she wasn't going to let anything stand in her way. Not even an absent witness. "No, I'd rather proceed."

Judge Williams nodded to his clerk and she returned a few moments later with an elderly couple. She introduced them as the Swansons, married fifty-two years. The couple took their place at the rear of the judge's office and waited. The judge opened a small book. "Dearly beloved, we are gathered here in the presence of these witnesses to join this man and this woman in matrimony."

Keely tried to listen to the words of the ceremony, but everything seemed to be happening so fast. She wanted to ask the judge to slow down, or even to stop, to give her time to absorb the whole experience. Was this what all brides went through, this odd surreal feeling, as if the wedding was happening to someone else?

"Is there anyone here who can show just cause why these two people should not be married?" The judge smiled, then looked over to the Swansons. They shook their heads. "I didn't think so."

Suddenly, the door to the judge's chambers burst open and Conor Quinn strode inside. "I object to this wedding," he said. "Am I too late?" Dylan followed him through the door, dressed in his BFD uniform, followed by the twins, then Liam and finally Brendan.

The judge's assistant rushed in behind them all, flustered. "I'm sorry, Judge Williams. I couldn't stop them."

"We object to this wedding," Brendan shouted. He turned to Conor. "Or did you already object?"

Judge Williams frowned, then turned his attention back to Keely and Rafe. "They're objecting."

"Go on," Keely whispered. "Don't listen to them. They're just my brothers. We knew they'd object, that's why we didn't invite them to the wedding."

"I'm afraid I'm compelled to listen to them," the judge said. He cleared his throat. "Under what grounds do you object?"

"Under the grounds that I don't think my sister should get married today," Conor said.

"I agree." Keely's brothers turned around, then slowly stepped aside as Fiona walked into the office. "I don't think this is a good idea, Keely."

Seamus followed her inside and added his two cents. "I agree."

Keely cursed softly. "What are you all doing here? How did you know where to find us?"

"I called your mother last night," Rafe admitted. "And I had Sylvie call Seamus and your brothers about an hour ago and extend an invitation."

Keely gasped, staring at him in shock. "Why would you do something like that?" She hit him with her bouquet, sending flower petals showering to the floor. "Why would you purposely try to ruin our wedding?"

"Because they're your family, Keely, and they should be here, objections or not."

"But they don't want us to get married," Keely cried. "Not today. Not ever."

Rafe shrugged. "I think they deserve to know that we've decided to get married. I don't want to get married in secret, Keely. We've been living like that ever since I proposed. We're going to start living our lives out in the open now so we should do it right from the start."

She stared up into his gaze for a long moment. He had a point. This was no way to start a marriage, sneaking off without letting anyone know. She was happy to be marrying Rafe and she wanted everyone to know. Keely drew a ragged breath, then turned to her family. "Thank you all for coming. I can understand why you've tried to stop our wedding, but it's not going to do any good. I'm going to marry Rafe. I love him and I want to spend the rest of my life with him. Now, either you can accept that and accept him, or you'll be seeing a lot less of me. It's your decision." Keely grabbed Rafe's hand and gave it a squeeze. "If you support our decision, you're welcome to stay for the rest of the ceremony. If you don't, you're welcome to leave."

They all stood silently, like repentant school children. Keely waited for all of them to march out. But then Conor stepped forward. "If Kendrick is the man you really love, then I guess we'll learn to—"

"Tolerate him," Dylan interrupted.

"Maybe even like him," added Liam.

"We're never going to love him, so you can forget that," Sean finished.

Conor stepped closer and took her hand. "But you should have a real wedding, Keely," he said. "At a church with a priest and with all your friends and all the trimmings. You deserve that. You're our only sister."

Keely turned her attention to her mother. "What do you have to say about this?"

"I would be happier if you had the wedding you've always dreamed of—even if it is to a man you barely know. You are my only daughter and I want you to do it right. In a church, with a priest." She turned to Judge Williams. "Not that you're not a fine judge and I'm sure quite competent at putting criminals in jail. But this is my daughter we're talking about here."

Seamus cleared his throat. "And I'd like the chance to walk you down the aisle," he added.

The door burst open again, and Olivia, Meggie and Amy stumbled into the office, followed by the judge's clerk. She gave the judge a frustrated look, then backed out of the office and closed the door.

"I understand there's a wedding happening here today," Olivia said. "You'd think a good husband would at least invite his wife to accompany him."

Keely smiled at the three women. Besides Rafe, they were the only people in the room who really supported her choice. And now that they were here, she felt even more resolved to marry Rafe.

"I appreciate all your input and understand your feelings," Keely said to Conor. "But my wedding is my wedding. And though it isn't the most perfect of ceremonies, now that you're all here, it's a lot closer to what I'd hoped for. I am going to marry Rafe today. Right here and right now."

Conor stepped forward and held out his hand to Rafe. Rafe smiled and grabbed his hand, giving it a firm shake. In turn, each of the brothers did the same.

Olivia, Meggie and Amy then stepped up and kissed Keely's cheek.

Then, to Keely's amazement, her mother moved to stand at her side. "I think we've taken care of all our objections," Fiona said. "Please, proceed."

The judge cleared his throat. "Once again, can anyone show just cause why these two should not be married?" He glanced around the room, looking at each of her brothers individually, then turning his gaze to her parents. They both shook their heads. He opened his mouth to continue, but then Rafe's voice interrupted him.

"I have just cause," he said softly. "I don't think we should get married today."

Keely gasped, then turned to stare at him. "What?"

Rafe grabbed her hand and pulled her along to the door. "Excuse us for a minute. We'll be right back."

When they reached the outer office, Rafe closed the door behind them. Then he drew Keely over to a leather sofa and gently pushed her down. He sat beside her and grabbed her hands in his. "I don't think we should get married today."

"You don't want to marry me?" Keely asked, tears threatening.

"Of course I do. Just not today. Sweetheart, your mother said it. This isn't the wedding you've always dreamed about. And you said it—it's not perfect. You deserve that perfect wedding, in a church, with a priest and a long, white veil. And I want to give that to you.''

"But a wedding like that takes time to plan.''

"Not necessarily. And now that we have your family's support, maybe we should take a few more days and make it just right. The flowers, the dress, maybe a tux for me, and some bridesmaids for you. My mother might even be able to see it.''

The idea appealed to Keely. Maybe that's what was missing from this ceremony—all of her dreams. "I guess we could do that. It would be a little more expensive to plan things so quickly, but now that my family is behind us, why not?'' Keely giggled, then wrapped her arms around his neck and gave him a fierce hug. "So when should we get married? In June? A June wedding would be nice.''

"How does a week from Saturday sound? We can delay the honeymoon for a week. Can you get everything together that quickly? Money is no object.''

Keely nodded, her excitement growing. They wouldn't have to wait! "I can. We'll have to buy the dresses off the rack, but that's no problem. I'll even have time to make a really great cake. I have the perfect design. And maybe we can have the reception at the pub. With the proper decorations, it could look so perfect.''

Rafe drew back and gave her a soft kiss. "Then it's settled. I guess we should probably go tell your family.''

"We could leave them in there, wondering what's going on," she said devilishly.

He stood, then pulled her up beside him. "That's a bit impulsive, don't you think?"

"But it would serve them right for everything they put us through." She glanced over at the clerk who was busy trying to appear as if she were working rather than eavesdropping. "Excuse me, but can you tell the people in Judge Williams chambers that we're not going to get married today?"

"You're not?" she said.

Keely shook her head. "Nope. And once they settle down from that little bit of news, ask them to keep a week from Saturday open on their schedules."

With that, Keely wrapped her hand around Rafe's arm and walked to the door. "Let's go," she said. "We have a wedding to plan."

THEY STOOD in the center of the stone circle, holding hands and staring up at the fluffy white clouds racing across the sky. "It's a magical place," Keely said. "I felt it the first time I came here." She looked at her husband, then pushed up on her toes and gave him a quick kiss. "And a perfect place for a honeymoon."

In truth, everything had been perfect, from the moment she walked down the aisle of the chapel with her father, to this moment, standing on the cliff high above the sea, the same spot she'd stood on months ago.

She'd had Amy, Meggie, Olivia and Sylvie Arnold as her bridesmaids and Rafe had chosen Conor as his best man. The chapel had been filled with flowers, the air heavy with the sent of roses and beeswax candles. They'd married at seven in the evening, and after the ceremony, had enjoyed a catered reception at Quinn's Pub. There had been dancing and champagne toasts, all enjoyed by the patrons who just happened to stop in. Seamus had laughed and joked and had even pulled her mother out onto the dance floor for a lusty Irish jig. And the cake had been a masterpiece of Irish lace and tiny shamrocks. It had all been perfect.

"What are you thinking about?" Rafe murmured.

Keely sighed softly. "Our wedding. How wonderful it all was."

"It was great," he said, drawing her into his arms and hugging her. "I just wish the honeymoon was better."

Keely looked up at him. "What do you mean? You're not having fun?"

"You don't think it's too cold? I should have checked the weather before I decided to surprise you with Ireland."

Though they were bundled up against the near-freezing temperatures, Keely didn't mind at all. "Rafe, we've been here four days and this is the first time we've left the room." He had rented them the most exquisite suite at Waterford Castle and they'd spent most of their days curled up on the sofa in front of the fireplace and their nights making love in the huge carved bed. "There isn't any other place I'd rather be."

"Then you're deliriously happy?" Rafe asked.

"Absolutely. I had the wedding I've always dreamed about, I'm married to the man I love, my family has been reunited. What more could I want?"

"I can think of a few more things," Rafe said.

"What?"

"Children might be nice."

Keely smiled. "Really? We never talked much about children. I guess I just assumed we'd wait."

"Do you want to wait?"

"Not necessarily. I'd like to have a big family. I grew up an only child and so did you. I've always wanted to have three or four...or five."

"Well, I think you'd make a wonderful mother. And I know I'd make a terrific father. So all we really need now is the baby."

Keely laughed and have him a hug. "Your money was able to buy a quickie wedding, Rafe, but no matter how determined you are for instant gratification, a baby takes nine months."

"Then maybe we should get started." Rafe reached for the zipper of Keely's jacket and slowly pulled it down.

"What? Right here?"

Rafe glanced around. "Why not? We made love in the bathroom of the plane on the way over. Your idea, not mine, may I remind you. This place is much more secluded. A few very cold cows and some seagulls. Not much of an audience. You aren't losing your reckless streak now that you're a married woman, are you?''

Keely grabbed the front of his jacket and yanked him toward her. Then she gave him a very pagan kiss, filled with wild promise and unfettered passion. What better place to start a family, she mused, than here in such a magical spot? "Is that a dare, Mr. Kendrick?''

''I think it might be, Mrs. Kendrick.''

''Well, if you want me, then you're going to have to catch me.'' With that, she gave him a gentle shove, then raced across the slippery ground, weaving in and out of the tall stones.

When she'd left Ireland the first time, Keely had wondered if her life would ever be the same again, if she'd ever really know who she was. But there was no confusion anymore. She was the woman who loved Rafe Kendrick and would spend the rest of her life loving him. She was the daughter and the sister who had brought her family back together again after so many years apart. And someday soon, she'd be a mother.

But, most of all, she was a Quinn, descended from a long line of clever and courageous Mighty Quinns who had inhabited this special land. Over time, Keely knew that she'd come back to Ireland again and again, to soak in the magic of a land she'd grown to love.

Yes, she was a Quinn. And here, in this spot, at this moment, Keely felt like the mightiest Quinn of them all.

*   *   *   *   *

Don't miss the upcoming romantic misadventures of the last three Quinn brothers. Look for them next summer in Harlequin Temptation.

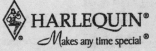

This is the family reunion you've been waiting for!

TRUEBLOOD
Christmas

JASMINE
CRESSWELL
TARA TAYLOR QUINN
& KATE HOFFMANN

deliver three brand new Trueblood, Texas stories.

After many years, Major Brad Henderson is released from prison, exonerated after almost thirty years for a crime he didn't commit. His mission: to be reunited with his three daughters. How to find them? Contact Dylan Garrett of the Finders Keepers Detective Agency!

Look for it in November 2002.

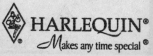

HARLEQUIN®

Makes any time special ®

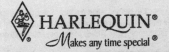

This special volume about the joy of wishing, giving and loving is just the thing to get you into the holiday spirit!

CHRISTMAS *Wishes,*
CHRISTMAS *Gifts*

Two full-length novels
at one remarkably low price!

USA Today bestselling author

TARA TAYLOR QUINN
DAY LECLAIRE

The perfect gift for all the romance readers on your
Christmas list (including yourself!)

On sale November 2002 at your favorite retail outlet.

HARLEQUIN®
Makes any time special ®